DESERT UNDERWORLD

ALSO BY FRED G. BAKER

FICTION

The Black Freighter

ZONA: The Forbidden Land
Einstein's Raven

The Detective Sanchez/Father Montero Mysteries:
An Imperfect Crime
Desert Sanctuary

The Modern Pirate Series:
Seizing the Tiger
Prowling Tiger
Restless Tiger
Raging Tiger
Hong Kong Takedown
The Good Deed/Chen

NON-FICTION

Growing Up Wisconsin:

The Life and Times of Con James Baker

The Ancestors of Con James Baker of
Des Moines, Iowa, and Chicago, Illinois,
Volumes 1–3

The Descendants of John Baker (ca. 1640–1704) of Hartford,
Connecticut, Through Thirteen Generations,
Volumes 1–2

Light from a Thousand Campfires,
with Hannah Pavlik

Desert Underworld

A Detective Sanchez/Father Montero Mystery

Fred G. Baker

Other Voices Press
Golden, Colorado

Published by Other Voices Press, Golden, Colorado

ISBN 978-1-949336-18-4 paperback
ISBN 978-1-949336-19-1 eBook

Cover Design by Nick Zelinger, NZ Graphics.com
All Rights Reserved by Fred G. Baker.

Printed in the United States.

Acknowledgments

I would like to thank the following people for their aid and support in the writing and production of this book, Dr. Hannah Pavlik, for her support and encouragement; my beta readers who provided helpful comments and ideas; Donna Zimmerman for word processing and interior design; Hidden Gems Books for proofreading, and Nick Zelinger for cover design.

Acknowledgments

Chapter 1

Sunday night, March 31, 2019

Phoenix, Arizona

Nick Carter watched the young woman balance delicately on the competition beam, her back arched in proper form, her arms thrust over her head with her wrists cocked for effect, her chalked feet clinging to the suede surface of the wooden apparatus. She looked confident as she stepped forward with precision, making a little hop to transfer weight from one foot to the other. She arched her back again and waved her arms at her sides like a magician about to perform a trick. Then she sprang up and pivoted 180 degrees to land in the reverse direction as both feet gripped the beam.

She did a switch leap that was one of her best moves, appearing to float in the air in a split position for a second while landing on her opposite foot. She had to do it again to get in position for her close, pausing to once more arch and spring, this time doing a 360 with an imperfect landing, one foot slightly off the beam, saved by a last-minute big-toe hook. She balanced again, stepped forward two paces, and spun 180 degrees on the ball of her foot, stopping perfectly on her mark.

She smiled because she loved this dismount and was good at it. Without a pause, she ran down the sixteen-foot length of the beam, performing a forward handspring and then a back handspring before leaping off the end of the beam in a whirl of motion. She landed on the mat exactly as planned except for the little hop she made at the very end, arms thrown up in a stylish finish. Her smile was radiant as she looked at Carter for his approval.

He clapped his hands and shouted, "Lo, you looked absolutely perfect, except for the first correction! But the dismount was right on." He smiled at her as he pushed his long brown hair out of his eyes. He held out a white towel to her as she beamed with pride.

"You think so, Nicky?" She grinned as she took the towel and wiped sweat from her face and chest. "I wasn't sure I could hold the backspring in check." She quickly ran the towel over her leotard to pat off the moisture before handing the towel back to him.

"Now let's get this smelly thing off you." He pulled on one of her long sleeves as she backed her arm out of it.

"Hey, don't be in such a hurry," she said as she stepped back from him and pulled her other arm free. Then she drew the top down and stripped the fabric right down to her ankles. She kicked it off onto the mat and took the towel back from him to wipe down her bare skin.

"Wow!" he said as he ran his hand down her tight, rippling abs and stepped up to her side.

"Hey," she said playfully. "Give me a minute, will ya? I've got to shower first." She tossed the towel at him and retreated toward the locker room in the nude, giggling about her successful routine. It was nice to be in the gym after hours with absolute privacy.

"Hey, not so fast," he said as he reached around her waist and pulled her over to him for a wet kiss, running his hands over her back and muscular bottom. Then he lifted her up, and she wrapped her legs around his waist. He carried her to the vault table and laid her on her back.

"So this is what you had in mind, you dirty bastard." She smiled as wickedly as she could. "We haven't made it on this rig for a while." She lay back and arched her spine as if taunting him as he pulled off his basketball shorts.

"Come on, big boy. Let's see what you got."

Chapter 2

Early Monday morning, April 1, 2019
Phoenix, Arizona

Detective Lori Sanchez was stretched out in the sunshine on an air mattress in a huge swimming pool at a large tropical resort. She floated comfortably on her back as small ripples pleasantly rocked her in the warmth of the day. She had her eyes closed behind her large Ray-Ban sun shades and smelled the rich odor of the Banana Boat tanning cream she had coated her body with earlier. It was very pleasant here, and she would have to return again to find this level of enjoyment on her next vacation.

But there was something under her back that had started to annoy her. Something hard that was vibrating silently but persistently. Had she lain on an insect when she got on the mattress? It was destroying her mood with its persistence. How would she get back to this level of peace again here at . . . *Say, where am I, anyway? Beaches?* she thought.

She reached under herself to sweep the insect away but hit the hard object that was vibrating violently. *What the . . .?*

It was her cell phone.

She woke up. No warm sun, no gentle waves on a pool. Just her lying in a pool of sweat on her mattress with the phone vibrating like crazy and the air-conditioning still on the fritz.

"Who the hell is calling at . . .?" she mumbled as she struggled up on an elbow to look at the bedside clock. *"Two in the morning?"* she said in a loud, surprised voice. "Who the hell is this, anyway?" she wondered angrily as she gaped at the phone.

Her phone listed Clara Alvera as the caller.

Oh shit, she thought. *Now what?*

She had to hit the Callback symbol because she had taken so long to figure out the difference between her pleasant dream and her present reality. She crawled out of bed and sat at its side as she waited for the call to go through. She wondered what her good friend Assistant District Attorney Clara Alvera wanted at this late hour.

"Lori! Thank God you're there!" Alvera sounded frantic. "Oh Lori, I need help right away. There's been an accident . . ."

Sanchez snapped out of her sleepy wakefulness and sat up straight. "An accident? Are you OK?"

Alvera hesitated a moment, and her voice sounded shaky. "Oh—not that kind of accident . . . It's really . . . well, a murder, I think."

Now Sanchez stood up, surprised. "Murder? What do you mean, a murder?"

"Look, Lori . . . I can't explain over the phone. I just need you here right away. I don't know what to do."

"What do you mean?" Sanchez already was shedding her sleeping gear and heading for the bathroom. "Did you call the police? What's going on?"

"No. I didn't call the police. It's a delicate situation . . ." Alvera dropped her voice. "I can't explain until you get here, OK? I just can't."

Sanchez stood there looking at herself in the mirror—not her best look at this time of day. "Where the hell are you, Clara? What's happened?"

"Look, I need you to drop everything and come here. Do

you have a pen? I'll give you an address."

Sanchez didn't like the sound of this. Something was terribly wrong if the assistant DA hadn't called the cops. She looked around the sink and realized she didn't have anything to write with in the bathroom. She turned and walked quickly through the bathroom door and the darkened apartment toward the kitchen, stubbing her toe on a chair on the way. She swore and hobbled into the kitchen where she kept a notepad and pen for her grocery list.

"OK, where are you?"

"I'm at the Maraxx Pharma gym out near South 16th and Elwood Street. I'll text you the address. Come down right away. And don't tell anyone—I may be in trouble." Alvera hung up.

"Clara? Clara?" Sanchez stood there in shock for a second. Then a text message came in with an address.

She set her phone down and ran into the bathroom to wash her face and comb her long brown hair. She didn't have time to do anything with it, so she pulled it back into a ponytail. She rubbed her wide brown eyes and had a fleeting thought of how much better she would look and feel if she could have finished that dream and had a couple more hours of sleep. It would have been nice. Then she snapped out of her reverie and rushed into the bedroom to dress in her usual black slacks, a short-sleeve blue shirt, and black tactical boots.

On the way out the door, she checked to be sure she had all she would need: utility belt with all her gear on it, badge, and her trusty Glock .45. She rushed out the door and along the sidewalk of her apartment building to her unmarked Ford Interceptor.

***

Sanchez drove recklessly fast on the nearly empty Phoenix

streets and had no trouble finding the address. This part of town was where many of the newer businesses and corporate headquarters were located. Maraxx Pharmaceuticals was one of the huge drug companies that had relocated their offices here from California a few years before. They had a compact, four-building campus consisting of three small office towers and a conference/recreational facility. The corporate gym was located on the side of the conference building, providing easy access for company employees. It was apparently one of the perks for those in company management.

She pulled into the parking lot and stashed the Interceptor in one of the visitor slots. Then she jogged around the corner of the building and found the gym where Alvera said it would be.

Sanchez found Alvera huddled outside the glass door. She looked like a wreck. Sanchez saw the look of fear and panic on her friend's face and immediately gave the woman a hug while they talked.

"Hey, Clara. What's up? Are you OK?"

"No," Alvera said quietly. "Thanks for coming so quick." She wiped back a tear. "I just didn't know what to do." She looked miserable and shaken, clenching a tissue and hanging on to Sanchez more than she usually did during a greeting.

Sanchez pulled away and scanned her friend's features. Alvera was dressed in her usual immaculate business suit with her blond hair in disarray—not her regular look. Her face was a mess of smeared makeup. She had been crying, and that surprised Sanchez.

"What happened?" Sanchez decided she needed to take charge of the scene. She looked past Alvera at the gym's door, which was closed.

"I came here to meet a friend. She said she had information

about a story she was working on."

"What? Why meet here—and at this time of night?"

"Well, she's a reporter, and she's been working this story. She said she found out something really sinister and had to tell me right away. She said it was a legal issue."

"Wait," Sanchez said impatiently. "Who was this reporter, and why did she need to tell you in the middle of the night?"

"Her name is Josie Vale. You met her at my place a month ago." Alvera raised her eyes to look into her friend's. "She confided in me about the story. Anyway, she was scared. She thought someone was following her. She came here because she was afraid to go home. I was working late on a case at the office and hurried over after her call."

"So you met her here?" Sanchez noticed that Alvera was ready to break down into tears again. She suspected there was much more to the story. She had known Alvera for a few years now and considered her one of her best friends but knew that she played portions of her private life very close to her chest. There was something going on here that had Alvera emotionally torqued.

"So where is she? Where's Josie?" Sanchez looked at the gym door, and Alvera turned to follow her gaze.

"She's in there." Alvera pointed at the door and finally broke down. "She's dead!"

Chapter 3

Early Monday morning, April 1, 2019

Phoenix, Arizona

Sanchez bolted through the door of the gymnasium with Alvera right behind her.

"Wait here, Clara," she said tersely. Then she stopped and asked, "Where is she?"

Alvera pointed to the far side of the darkened gym, where floodlights illuminated a portion of the area. "She's on one of those vault pieces." She looked like she would cry some more.

Sanchez realized that Alvera was barefoot. "Where are your shoes, Clara?"

"I saw her and ran over to check on her, but—there was blood. I took them off."

Sanchez pulled out her weapon and her Maglite. "So you just came in and looked for her? Was anyone else here?"

"I don't know. I looked and found her, then ran out."

"OK, stay here by the door. Don't touch anything. It's all a crime scene now."

Sanchez proceeded to clear the room and determine if anyone else was present. She held her pistol in her right hand and had it crossed over her left that held the flashlight. She proceeded cautiously, making sure she scanned any place where an intruder might be hiding.

She reached the far side of the gym where women's

gymnastics equipment was clustered and came upon the body of Josie Vale. She was obviously dead, lying facedown and tied to a broad bench-like table with a white cord and blood surrounding her body. Sanchez stepped close to her head while avoiding the pool of blood on the floor and felt for a pulse in her neck. Absolutely nothing. The body was cooling fast, so she had been dead for a while.

She checked out the rest of the area and got as far as the locker rooms, one for men and one for women. She entered and did a quick scan of the rooms and showers. Nothing. Whoever did this was long gone. A hallway led back into the building, but a large locked wooden door ended her search. She decided she had better get back to Alvera.

Alvera had calmed down somewhat and looked truly distraught sitting on a bench by the door. Sanchez felt sorry for her but had a job to do.

"There's no one else here. I've got to call this in. Your friend's dead and it's clearly a homicide, so we need the full deal—crime scene investigators, coroner; the works." She stopped to let it all sink in. "I'm calling Jeff Bordou first so he can come down here and take charge of the scene. That way we can keep a lid on whatever it is you're afraid to tell me about."

Alvera looked up at her and nodded slightly. "I'll tell you. Just not here like this. Part of it's personal, and part is about a gang."

That got Sanchez's attention. She made the calls.

Within minutes, a squad car pulled up to the building with lights flashing but no siren. Sanchez got the officer to put up crime scene tape around the perimeter in case there was evidence outside the building.

Detective Jeff Bordou, her partner, showed up next. She

asked him to take charge of the scene and direct the work when the crime scene investigators showed up. Meanwhile, the patrolman located the number for the gym's manager so they could enter the locked area and find any closed-circuit cameras they had. The on-site night watchman would be right over.

Sanchez called Bordou aside to talk.

"Look, Jeff," she said. "This seems to be sensitive for the DA's office for some reason. Clara is the one who found the DB, and the woman was a friend of hers, a reporter working on some gang-related story."

"Is Clara OK? She looks pretty shook up." Bordou knew Alvera pretty well since she was a friend of Sanchez and they had worked cases before. "What's going on? Is she afraid some info about a case will leak, or is she protecting someone—a witness?"

"I don't know yet, but she just told me she doesn't want her name to get out related to the victim or the case. She said she would tell me more, just not now." Sanchez looked over at her partner and knew he could keep things discreet. "She found Vale dead, apparently killed an hour or so before she arrived. The vic called her to meet here about a story, so I'm guessing she had info about a crime. We've got to keep a lid on this and Clara's involvement until we have more to go on, OK? So just keep that in mind."

Bordou stood up straight and ran his hand over his blond hair, which was cut short but not exactly a crew cut since he still combed a part in it. His blue eyes shined from Nordic features, giving him a clean-cut, alert, Ivy League look, even at this hour of the morning.

"Well, we can do our work and say that we have no statement at this time to any reporters that show up—the usual story," he said as he scanned the parking lot. He saw a man in a security uniform walk up to the door. "Hey, you better get her out of here while I talk to the night watchman." With that, he walked toward the door.

Sanchez walked over to Alvera, who seemed out of it. She took her arm and led her out the door.

"Can you get home OK? I need you out of here if you want to keep your name out of this mess." She guided her toward her car in the lot.

"Yeah, I'd better go. I'll go home and wait for you. I need a drink about now." She gave Sanchez a grateful look. "Thanks for helping me. I'll explain later, OK?"

"Yeah, get out of here and see if you can get some rest. You look like you could use it." She thought, *I could use a drink and some sleep too. It's going to be a long night.*

Sanchez waited as Alvera backed her silver Volvo S90 out of the parking space and headed home. Then she marched back inside the gym and slipped on a pair of plastic gloves.

Bordou was standing in the hallway, talking to the security guard about opening the hallway door and video cameras. Sanchez walked up to them just as the door swung open and a short, blonde, muscular teenager stood inside the doorway. The look of surprise on her face as she stood there wearing only an oversize T-shirt was classic.

"Oh shit!" she cried. "Who are all you people?"

"Who are you?" Sanchez asked. "Where did you come from?"

"I was asleep in back," the blonde said. "Where's Nick?"

"Who's Nick?" Bordou asked cautiously. "Who are you?"

"Tell me what's going on first," the blonde demanded as she crossed her arms. "What are you doing here? Who are you?"

Bordou held out his badge and ID wallet. "We're police, and

this is a crime scene. You'd better explain what you're doing here in the middle of the night." He stared at her T-shirt.

"Hey, don't stare at me like that. I was just sleeping in back in Nick's place." She looked at Sanchez, perhaps hoping for some feminine support as she realized she had a lot of skin showing. She pulled the shirt down lower and said, "Ask Nick. He'll tell you I'm his girlfriend."

Sanchez sized her up and decided she was no threat. "Look, how about you and I go back there and you get some clothes on? You can show me your ID then." She looked at Bordou. "Why don't you look around the back area here and see if this should be part of the crime scene or if anyone else is here?"

The blonde turned around and led Sanchez down the hall while Bordou and the guard explored the remainder of the building.

"My name is Lolita Thompson. My dad's Eric Thompson. He's a vice president here at Maraxx." She stopped just short of a doorway to an office. "Hey, where is Nick, anyway? Is he in trouble or something?"

"I don't know any Nick. Who is he?" Sanchez asked as they entered an oversize office that had a double bed and a microwave oven. She scanned the place and saw a lot of men's clothes on hangers hooked on a pipe that was balanced between two filing cabinets. A suitcase and other miscellaneous household items were stacked randomly around the room on cabinets and a desk. "What the hell? Do you live here?"

"Nick does. He's the gym manager. He lets me stay over sometimes."

Lolita dug in a purse and handed over an Arizona driver's license. Then she pulled the T-shirt over her head and pulled on panties that lay on the chair near the bed. Sanchez couldn't help but notice Lolita's perfect abs and muscular legs. She looked at the license and verified Lolita's name and age. "You just got this license. Says you're sixteen. Is that right?"

Lolita pulled on a pair of shorts and a tank top, and turned to Sanchez. "Yeah, I just passed the test." She looked at Sanchez, who passed her badge and ID to Lolita to verify who she was.

Lolita passed the ID back and said, "You can just call me Lo. That's what most people do instead of my whole name. I went for years not knowing that the name Lolita had so much dross attached to it."

"Yeah, I guess that's a loaded handle," Sanchez sympathized. "Anyway, keeping it official, I'm Detective Lori Sanchez with the Phoenix PD. We got a call that there was trouble here tonight, so we came out to investigate." She eased back on calling it a murder, afraid she might tip off or upset the girl. Although from the look of the room, this was not some immature teenager. "We've been here nearly a half hour, and you were back here all that time? Didn't you hear us out front?" She nearly answered her own question by listening to the activity in the gym. She could only hear muffled voices from this location.

"I was asleep . . . well, until after about midnight or so, when Nicky went out to meet with one of his clients in the gym, that is." She looked like she had said something she shouldn't have. "I mean, someone came for a meeting, and he went out front. I walked down the hall to see who it was because he said it was a lady. So I wanted to see what she looked like—this blonde . . . you know."

"So what? You work out here and stay with this Nick guy?" Sanchez asked cautiously. "You were worried about possible competition? You went to see what she looked like?"

Lolita strongly blushed. "Well—yeah. I guess." She turned

away to hide her feelings. "Anyway, she was some older blonde chick, and they didn't seem—you know. So I came back and crawled into bed to wait for him." She turned back to Sanchez with an annoyed look on her face. "Where the hell is he?"

Sanchez thought she was reading the situation right: this guy was popular, and he hadn't come back to bed. Lolita was afraid he was out somewhere doing something that would piss her off. There must be some history there.

"You've been in here the whole time? You didn't go out front until just now?" Sanchez was surprised. "So you don't know what happened in the gym?"

"No. What?" Lolita looked worried. "Is Nick OK? He isn't hurt, is he?" Concern flooded her features as she stared at Sanchez. "What happened?"

"Look, Lo, I haven't seen anyone named Nick tonight. He's not here. But we have a situation here. A woman . . ." She hesitated. "A woman has been killed in the gym. It's a crime scene. I can't let you go back out there. But I can assure you that Nick isn't in the gym."

"What? Killed?" Lolita went into a panic. Her face now seemed pale, and her eyes flashed back and forth the way someone did when they were about to lose it and cry or shout or become emotional. "I've got to find Nick. He could be hurt."

Sanchez wondered why she would be worried that he was hurt. As she studied Lolita's face, she had an idea. She had better find out who Nick was and why he was meeting someone late at night here at the gym. She looked around the room and saw a wallet and a set of keys lying on the desktop. She stepped over to look at them. Then she picked up the wallet and opened it to see the driver's license inside.

"Nick Carter—that's your boyfriend's name? Born

December twelfth, 1985, in Denver?" She rifled through the wallet and found cash, credit cards, a Costco card, and a condom. There were also a few business cards: *Nick Carter, Personal Trainer, Health Consultant, (480) 957-1669.* She thought the guy was a real operator to be thirty-four and have an underage girl in his bed. "Is he your trainer?" Sanchez looked at Lolita, who now seemed to be younger than she had at first thought. "Are you a gymnast or something? Do you train here?"

Lolita was nervous. "Yeah, he's my trainer." She seemed about to do something like run for it, so Sanchez moved to block the door.

"Look, Lolita." Sanchez tried to be as calm as she could be. "I can't let you go out front right now. It's a crime scene, and you don't want to see what happened, believe me." She saw Lolita tense up at first but then seem to accept that she might be there for a while. "I'm going to call up front and see if we have a female officer who can come back here and take your statement. I'm concerned that your friend Nick has not come back after meeting the woman in the gym. So I have to check on some things, OK? Then I'll be back to talk to you some more." She waited to see if Lolita understood, and her head bobbed up and down a couple of times.

Sanchez called Bordou over the radio and found out that Officer Debbie O'Neil had responded to his call for backup. She was headed back to take over babysitting the witness, because that was what Lolita was—a witness.

Sanchez introduced the two and then hustled to the gym. When she arrived, the medical examiner was inspecting the body and explaining his preliminary results to Bordou. She stepped up next to them and donned a pair of plastic booties that Bordou held out to her, listening intently.

"As I was just telling Jeff here," the ME said as he pointed to elements of the immediate scene, "this woman was apparently knocked on the head to subdue her. Further examination will establish the sequence of events, but I think someone hit her on the head here." He pointed to the back of her head, where a small amount of blood could be seen amid her long blonde hair. "There are some defensive wounds, here and here, on her arms, and she may have been hit in the face a few times during the altercation, but this wound on the head probably would have been the final blow. We'll know more when we get her cleaned up at the shop."

"Why is she on the table, then—rape?" Bordou asked as he looked at the bruised lower body.

"Rape for certain, and maybe torture," the ME said as he pulled back a sheet that covered part of Vale's lower body. "Look here at these burn marks, like from a cigar or other hot item. See the burns here?" He pointed. "And they were apparently applied once she was on the table because they are only on her back and buttocks, along with this bruising in the same areas where she had been repeatedly beaten. She was savagely beaten by more than one person from the looks of it, but to me, it seems like it was meted out like they were trying to get her to talk. I've seen this before in gangland-style torture."

Sanchez poked at the woman's neck. "And so they knocked her out at some point and then tortured her?"

"Yes, but with a blow like this to the head, she may have been unconscious for a while." The ME shook his head. "Once they had her on the table, my guess is they raped her while she was unconscious. When she woke up, they began the torture."

Bordou looked ill and said, "These were some sick puppies to do that."

"We think they did not use condoms because there is plenty of semen—likely from more than one man. We have samples. They made a great mistake there in leaving evidence behind."

"Where'd all the blood come from, Doc?" Sanchez asked. "From the throat wound there?" She pointed to a deep knife slash in Vale's throat.

"Either she told them what they wanted to know and they killed her, or she didn't and they killed her anyway. In either case, she was aware of her last moments when they slit her throat." He pointed again. "See here how she moved her head around, spraying blood over this part of the vault's surface?"

Sanchez walked away. As she did so, she saw an evidence bag containing a pair of expensive black pumps, the kind of shoes that Alvera favored. She saw a few tracks in the blood on the floor where she apparently had stepped in the blood pool before she had realized it was there. Sanchez wanted to take the evidence bag and hold it out from being logged as part of the site evidence—at least until she knew what the hell was going on.

"These are the shoes that made those prints there?" She pointed at the small tracks in the blood.

"Yes, I believe so," was all the ME said.

"Any sign of her purse or phone?"

"No."

"All right, then," she said as she picked up the bag. "Bordou, can we talk a little bit here?" She nodded her head toward the gym door.

Crime scene technicians arrived just then and spread out searching for evidence, dusting for prints, and photographing everything that might be important in solving the case. Bordou followed her to the door, and they both stepped outside.

"Jeff," she said when they were out of earshot of everyone,

"we've got a complicated problem here. The girl in back said she was asleep when all this shit was going down in the gym. I believe her—it's real quiet back there. We couldn't hear what you guys were doing up front while I talked to her."

"OK," Bordou said. "It's not like the vic screamed a lot. They had the woman gagged when they were torturing her, so there may not have been a lot of noise. Why's that important?"

"The girl is Lolita Thompson, daughter of one of the big shots here at Maraxx Pharma. She said she was in bed with a guy named Nick Carter when someone came to the door to the gym about midnight. She saw a blonde woman talking to him and then went back to bed. She slept through the rest."

"So this woman, probably Vale, came here about midnight and this guy Nick met with her. Then what?"

"Well, we don't know yet." Sanchez swatted something on her neck. *Mosquitoes at this time of night?* "And a little later, this woman is killed—maybe at about one or a little before Clara shows up to meet with this chick, the DB." She hesitated. "I'm trying to remember. Clara said I met Josie at her house a month or so ago, but I didn't really talk to her much. I just remember this good-looking blonde that was getting a lot of attention from some of the guys there that night."

"She must have been a looker, all right. Even lying there, her face seems like a model's." He stopped and stared at Sanchez. "God, Lori, she looks a lot like Clara."

Sanchez stopped dead in her tracks. "What? Are you kidding?"

"No, go back in and take a careful look. She could be Clara's sister."

"What the . . .?"

Sanchez marched inside and reached the body just as the ME was bagging it for transport. "Excuse me," she said. She reached inside the bag to turn the face of the victim toward her for a look.

She nearly vomited. The woman looked uncannily like Clara Alvera!

"Holy shit!" she blurted out. Then she put her hand over her mouth and ran outside the building to blow in the potted shrub by the door.

"Is everything all right, Detective?" the ME called after her, unsure what had caused that response.

Chapter 4

Early Monday morning, April 1, 2019

Phoenix, Arizona

It was 4:00 a.m. by the time Sanchez walked down the corridor to talk to Lolita again. Lolita had fallen asleep on the bed, and O'Neil was fighting to stay awake herself.

"Hey, Debbie," Sanchez said as cheerfully as she could with a headache, exhaustion, and the taste of bile in her mouth. "Why don't you go up front for a break? Someone brought in coffee and Krispy Kremes. I need to talk to our witness and see if she has a place to stay tonight."

"Yes, Detective. A break would be nice. Thanks."

Sanchez shuffled over to the bed and shook Lolita's shoulder. She was dead asleep and only came around after the third series of shakes.

"What? Huh?" She rubbed her eyes. "Oh, it's you." She sat up slowly and tried to rearrange her clothing. "What time is it?"

"It's about four in the morning, Lo. How are you doing?"

"I'm fine, but I guess I fell asleep." She looked around. "Hey, where's Nick? I want to know. Do you have him or something?"

"No, Lo." Sanchez shook her weary head. "We have no idea where he is. But he may have had reason to hide when the other shit went down out front. We don't know what happened yet, but it doesn't look like he had anything to do with it."

Lolita lowered her head to stare at her pillow. "Where the hell is he, then? He just disappeared. He doesn't have his wallet or keys, so he can't have gone too far. Did he dump me or something?" Tears appeared in the corners of her eyes. She collapsed on the bed and buried her face in the pillow.

Sanchez walked over and sat on the side of the bed. She felt sorry for the girl. *This must be really shitty for her*, Sanchez thought. She was trying to be tough, but it must have been frightening to have had her lover disappear in the night. She put a hand on Lolita's shoulder as she quietly sobbed away.

Lolita turned to look up at Sanchez and then pulled herself up to sit next to her. She leaned on Sanchez and put her head on her shoulder to cry openly. Sanchez put an arm around her and pulled her over to comfort her. The sobbing continued for five minutes.

"Hey, how about you go home and sleep? We can talk more in the morning."

"I can't. I live here most of the time. Besides, my dad's away on a business trip until the weekend. I'd be alone in that big house. I don't like it there."

"How about your mom?"

"She lives in Denver, not here."

"Where can you go where you have someone to talk to?"

"Nowhere. Just here."

"You can't stay here. It's a crime scene now. Even this room will have to be examined because Nick is apparently missing." Sanchez regretted saying that as soon as she had said it.

"What?" Lolita pulled back and stared at her face with even more tears ready to flow.

"Shit, I'm sorry. I didn't mean it that way." Sanchez hugged the girl to her and said, "Hey look, maybe I can find you a safe place to stay for a night. I'm just worried to leave you alone right now. I need to keep you safe. You're a witness, even if you wouldn't think of it that way."

"A witness?"

"Well, yes. You're the only person to have seen the blonde woman arrive. She's the one who was killed."

"Oh shit. I'm sorry. I wanted her to go away, but not like that . . . I feel bad."

"You had nothing to do with her demise." She saw right away that Lolita had no idea what that meant. "You did nothing to be worried about. But as a witness, it's my duty to keep you safe."

"But where would I go?" Lolita looked hopeful. "Can I stay with you? I trust you."

"I don't think that would be a good idea. I'll be here all night and most of tomorrow working this case. I can't take good care of you."

"I could just hang out until you're done, can't I?" She smiled prettily even with her sad eyes.

Sanchez felt on the spot. She had no idea where she could stash the girl to keep her safe. Maybe Bordou would have an idea. Maybe his house? No, he had enough on his plate, and she already had imposed on him way too many times, both professionally and personally. And at this late hour? Where could she take her? Maybe she could just sleep in the car while Sanchez wrapped things up. Then she suddenly focused. Her place? Her tiny apartment, which seemed too small already for even one person? Her boyfriend Tom Smith's place, even though he was away on a training course in Boston? No way.

"Let me work on it, OK? Why don't you call your parents and see if they have any ideas and if you could stay with me for a day or two if they don't have another option, OK? I still have a number of things to do to wrap up the investigation." She turned to leave as two CSI people came through the door into the office.

"We need to search this room too, Detective Sanchez," one of the men said as they stood there with their instrument boxes. "Can the young lady wait somewhere else while we work?"

"Oh yes," she said. "I guess so." She hadn't considered that she and Lolita would need to move from the office so soon. "Lolita, why don't you come to the gym to wait? It's cleaned up now, I believe." She looked at one of the techs she knew and raised an eyebrow.

"Oh yes, ma'am. The DB has been removed, and the area is tented off."

Sanchez was glad to hear they had brought in a tent to cloak the most gruesome parts of the scene. This was a new innovation the department had implemented lately for crime work. No need to scare the living daylights out of the public just because they needed time to process a crime scene.

As she and Lolita walked down the hallway, Sanchez texted Alvera to see if she had a photo of Vale that she could show the girl for ID purposes. They reached the gym, and Sanchez peeked through the doorway first before letting Lolita observe the scene. As reported, a large tent of about fifteen feet square covered the bloody location of the murder. She walked through to the far side of the room where Bordou and the security guard were screening security recordings.

Bordou was surprised and at first tried to prevent Lolita from seeing the images, but then he smiled at her. He put out his hand to shake hers.

"I'm Detective Jeff Bordou. There is something you could

help us with if you don't mind looking at a few security pictures. We have a camera on the outside of the building that shows two people talking just outside the door of the gym." He showed a single image from a camera mounted on the ceiling near the front entry. "This man and woman who are standing here talking—do you recognize them?"

He ran the video for a minute so she could get a good look at the people as they moved around while they spoke. Both he and Sanchez hoped for something useful.

"Yeah, that's Nicky right there." Lolita pointed to the man. "There's his funny mustache. And that's the woman I saw him talking to." She hesitated and asked, "Is she the one who was killed?"

"Yes," Bordou said quietly, looking up at Sanchez for her reaction. "She's the one."

Bordou closed the video clip and moved to another one showing two men entering the gym door with what looked like a baseball bat. He froze the frame just as they came through the door. "How about these two guys? Lolita, have you ever seen them before?" he asked.

The two men were not clearly visible because one wore a ball cap that covered part of his face. One was a big Latino man with tattoos covering his face and neck, and the other was of mixed race with dreadlocks. Both looked fairly muscular and angry by the way they moved and appeared to be shouting. Bordou waited for Lolita to respond.

"No. I don't know them. I haven't seen them around the gym before." She scrutinized the image. "That was taken at twelve twenty-one, it says. Was Nicky still here then? Maybe they were here to see him."

"I don't know, Lo," Sanchez said. "We still don't know what

happened between midnight and about one forty-five this morning."

Bordou said, "Thanks for your help, Lolita." He turned away to talk to the guard.

Sanchez looked at her watch and saw that it was already 5:30 a.m. She decided she would have to leave Lolita with O'Neil again so she could do her job. She still had to talk to Alvera. She settled Lolita with O'Neil and promised to be back to get her by 8:00 a.m., hopefully with a place for her to stay. She doubled back to tell Bordou that she was leaving the building. She also called Alvera to let her know she was coming soon. "There is one other thing that we found," Bordou said. "It surprised the security guard. They have cameras inside the gym too—liability concerns. But they were all turned off for some reason. So we have no footage of the murder or of anything that happened here this morning." He seemed frustrated. "I'd hoped we would have more to work with, but no luck there."

"OK," she said. "Just keep at it while I talk to Clara, and we'll see how she ties into all this mess. I hope she has a good story."

"Yeah, me too."

***

"Thank God you're here," Alvera said loudly as she hugged Sanchez. "Lori, I'm scared."

She held on to her friend longer than usual for a hello hug. Sanchez realized that she must have been waiting in trepidation all night and not have rested. She pulled back and stared at Alvera to be sure it was really her and not the dead woman. *What a strange idea*, she thought. *My friend looks surprisingly like the dead chick.* Same long, straight blonde hair. Similar bright-blue eyes,

Nordic good looks and high cheekbones, a lovely slim figure, and perfect skin. Well, it might not have been perfect right now because she looked like she had been through hell.

She looked around the immaculate apartment with the walls some interior designer had painted a neutral shade of arctic blue. The carpet was a unique but subtle blend of earth and sky tones. The furniture was of Danish design, and every surface was spotless. It was a two-bedroom unit, but the common areas were spacious and carefully thought out, including a cute but functional kitchen with a breakfast island bar. What a difference from Sanchez's small apartment that she still had kept even though she had moved in with Smith last year. She had hung on to it just in case things didn't work out with Tom. Fear of settling down was one of her less favorable traits. Her place looked older and not as well laid out or maintained. It also lacked a central theme and color scheme, as well as reliable air-conditioning. Sanchez tried not to think about it.

"Let's make some coffee," she murmured as she let Alvera go. "Did you sleep at all?"

"Hell no. How could I?" Alvera said softly. "I can't believe Josie's gone. Just like that and in that horrible way."

"Yeah."

Sanchez bent down to take off her boots that she had been standing in for hours. The kitchen's cool tiles felt pleasant under her bare feet. She set about making coffee in the Braun MultiServe coffee maker that Alvera relied on every morning. She set out a couple of cups and pulled up one of the stools to the breakfast bar as Alvera did the same.

"Do you want to hear the details or just the highlights? We got a few things figured out, but I need your input to build the timeline."

Alvera shook her head. "No details. I've been trying to get the image of her body out of my mind. It was so horrible, and I've seen a lot of crime scene photos before. It just hit me hard."

"It's always different when it's someone you know." Sanchez watched the coffee maker do its job, waiting with anticipation. "Say, you got any donuts or sweets around? I'm starved."

Alvera stood up and walked over to the kitchen counter to retrieve a fruit bowl and placed it in front of Sanchez. She smiled weakly. "Not what you had in mind, is it?"

"I'll live . . . So, tell me the whole thing from start to finish, OK? How do you know Josie?"

"I met Josie last year at one of the DA's fundraisers. She was a journalist with the *Phoenix Tribune* then, but later she became independent. We talked and felt an immediate chemistry, so we stayed in touch. She was quite good looking, don't you think?"

"Yeah, as far as I could tell," Sanchez said, reacting to Alvera's mention of chemistry. "I looked at the photo you sent me tonight. She was quite attractive—just like you. I was surprised by how much you two look alike."

Alvera blushed. "That was one of the things that brought us together—our appearance. It was like looking at my reflection in the mirror in some ways. Of course, we both found it intriguing."

"Did she talk to you about the story she was working on? You implied that when we talked earlier," Sanchez asked.

"Yes, she told me about stories sometimes. But this new story was different. She was very secretive about it until last night." Alvera looked up at Sanchez. "We had a deal to not burden each other with work issues, except for a few light moments. But lately, she had been nervous about her work. She had said she was getting close to something big. That it could make her career."

"And why meet last night?"

"She called and was in a panic—all confused about what to do and whether she was in danger. Things she never had mentioned before. She wanted to talk to me right after she met with a source and get my input on what to do next." Alvera's face changed from being composed to emotional. "She was to talk to someone to verify something and then meet me. She chose the gym at one thirty. She said she would leave the door open for me."

Sanchez tried to remain calm. Why in the world would they meet at the gym, especially if that was where Vale was meeting her source? And why not at a more public place or at home?

"She apparently met with the source at the gym, a guy named Nick Carter. Did she mention that name to you?"

"She mentioned a Nick, but I thought he was just someone she knew, not a source." Alvera looked surprised. "He was the guy she met last night?"

"Yeah, it appears so, right at midnight. We don't know what happened to him after the meet. He seems to have vanished. He apparently lives in the back of the gym with a young girl. She's the one who ID'd Vale as the woman he met at midnight."

"So Josie was there for what? An hour and a half until I got there?" Alvera seemed surprised. "Did she talk to the source the whole time?"

"We don't know. But at twelve twenty-one, two suspicious men showed up and entered the gym. We don't know anything else until you arrived on the scene."

"Two men? Who were they?" Hearing this news, Alvera sat up straight. "Did they talk to Josie? Or the snitch—I mean, source?"

"Again, we don't know. Only the exterior security camera

was working last night. We have no cameras working inside the gym."

"That's not surprising. A lot of gyms dropped indoor cameras after being sued for intrusive surveillance."

"Oh, I never thought of the legal angle." Sanchez wondered if they had other cameras they still ran, like in the women's locker rooms. She always felt creeped out when she visited a new gym because of all the perverts out there.

"Someone is always suing somebody," Alvera said matter-of-factly.

Sanchez didn't comment because she thought there were way too many lawyers out there suing all the time. "So you arrived, and then what happened?"

"Well, I was running a little late because I wrote the address down wrong, but I got there about one thirty-five or so. I saw Josie's car in the parking lot, parked far from the gym. I parked next to it and walked up to find the gym door. Everything looked dark, but I found the door. They have those black glass windows that change with the amount of light outside. I looked in, and the only lights on were over on the far side of the room. I called out Josie's name, but there was no answer."

"The door was open or just unlocked?"

"Well, let's see. It was ajar, I think . . . Yes, ajar. I pulled it open and stepped inside. I knew it was a gym but expected to see a reception desk or something in the front."

"Yeah, I guess it's less formal because it's just for the corporate types at the company. I found that odd—unless that's not the main entrance. I'll check on that."

"Anyway, no one answered and it was very still, so I crept forward to look for her. I went to the lighted area and saw her on the . . ." She couldn't go on.

Sanchez had a few more questions to ask and thought she had better get on with it even though it would upset Alvera. She put an arm around her friend's shoulders.

"Look, this is a hard one," she said. "Josie was tortured before she was killed. Any idea why someone would do that? Did she have information on gangs or drugs? Is that what she was working on?"

Alvera shuddered at the word *tortured*. Then she began crying. "Oh God, I knew it. It's so awful. Poor Josie."

She let out a lot of angst for a few minutes, alternately sobbing and swearing under her breath. Then she stated, "All she said was she had a big story about gangs and drugs. She wouldn't say more, but, you know, we deal with drug gangs all the time in the DA's office. I assumed it was just another story about gangbangers." She looked straight ahead and grimaced. "I should have asked her more questions, been more supportive."

"Why were you meeting at Maraxx Pharma?"

"Oh, she said they were involved somehow. I assumed the informant was dealing drugs down there on their campus. But she never really said so." She looked at Sanchez. "That makes sense, doesn't it?"

"Maybe, but we don't know." Sanchez had one last question, and it was personal. She took her arm from around Alvera's shoulders and turned toward her to make eye contact. "Look, I don't want to pry here, but I haven't seen you so upset since your mother died. How well did you know Josie, anyway?"

Alvera looked up into Sanchez's eyes and said, "Oh." She shrugged her shoulders as she reached out for one of Sanchez's hands. "I guess it's obvious. Josie and I were involved." She stopped to scan her friend for her response, then continued. "We were in love—I guess. We really liked each other and could talk so freely about so many things. It wasn't about sex, at least not at first. We were just starting to experiment with that. I hadn't tried that before." She looked up again. "Have you? I mean, in college or some other time?"

Sanchez shook her head. "Clara, I don't think you should tell me about that." She never had imagined Alvera being into women.

"Well, it was nice, but we were more about the friendship part of it. Do you understand, Lori?"

"Maybe I sort of get it, but I haven't gone there myself," Sanchez replied. She had a million questions for her friend, but right now she had to focus. "Did she live with you here, or were you at her place?"

"Her place, mostly. I was afraid of being seen here by the neighbors. They are really nosy." She became very silent and looked worried.

"What?"

"Oh Lori," Alvera said, "I left stuff at her apartment!" She jumped to her feet. "I have to get it."

"What?" Sanchez stood up with her. "What kind of stuff? Anything from work?"

"Oh my God. Maybe. I don't know for sure." She had a panicked look on her face. "We have to go there now, before the CSIs get there."

"Wait! Wait!" Sanchez said, holding on to her friend's hand.

"I'm missing a file. I may have left it there by mistake. We have to go get it, or it will be logged into evidence. Really, Lori. Please, we have to go," she pleaded with Sanchez.

"Hey, Clara. Stop it. We can't interfere."

"Why not? It isn't a crime scene. At least, I hope not. I hope nothing happened there—and I would just be retrieving my personal property from the premises." She rushed over and dug in her purse for a moment. "I have a key."

Chapter 5

Monday morning, April 1, 2019
Phoenix, Arizona

Sanchez pulled up to the apartment building on West Monroe Street just before 8:00 a.m. The sun was already up, and it looked like it would be a warm spring day with cloudless skies. She parked the Interceptor in one of the handicapped lanes and slammed the door. She should have stopped for coffee on the way; her energy levels were beginning to tank. She checked her watch again. She would need to get back to Bordou soon, and she still had to worry about Lolita and where to place her too. It was going to be a long day.

They entered the ordinary-looking three-story apartment building with a small patio in front with chairs for people to sit and enjoy the day. They stepped into the empty lobby, and Alvera led the way up a staircase one floor and to the left. She rustled through her purse and pulled out her key ring, fingering the right key from the bunch as she walked down the hall.

"It's right here," she said as Sanchez followed her. She stopped right in front of the door to 207. "Hey, it's open."

Sanchez snapped out of her mental checklist of things she still had to do and asked, "What? Let's see."

She slipped around Alvera to view the door that was open a crack. She heard muffled voices inside the apartment and then the sound of something like books being thrown on the floor.

She stepped closer to the door and held her hand out to keep Alvera from coming closer.

"I think someone's inside. Does Josie have a roommate?"

"No. Let's see who it is. Maybe it's a burglar." Alvera tried to push past Sanchez, but her arm held her back.

"You wait here while I check it out."

Sanchez pulled the Glock .45 from her belt and slowly pushed the door open a few more inches so she could see inside the apartment. She couldn't see anyone at first, but noticed that someone had been searching for something and was trashing the place in the process. She pushed the door open farther until it hit an object on the floor.

She stepped inside with her pistol projecting in front of her in a two-handed grip. Someone was making noise down the hall in what was probably a bedroom. It sounded like they were rummaging through papers, making that characteristic sound that can drive you crazy if you are trying to work at the desk nearby.

Then something struck her arms from the left, and she dropped her handgun. A large, darkly dressed man had been hiding behind the door and now slammed into her like a freight train. She couldn't turn fast enough to counter the charge and fell sideways over a chair and onto the floor.

"*Vámonos! Es la policía!*" he shouted. He was a heavyset, muscular man with a weird, almost purple head—too many tattoos for her liking. He held a baseball bat next to his head like he was ready to hit a home run, a wild look in his eye.

A second man with dreadlocks ran out of the room down the hall, carrying a laptop computer in one hand and a handgun in the other. The first man stood by the door as the second one ran up to him and aimed his gun at Sanchez where she lay.

She dove behind the sofa in the direction her gun had slid

just as the man fired a round at her. Luckily, he missed and hit the end table next to her as she recovered her gun. She rose to her knees and swung her Glock around to return fire. By that time, the men had burst out of the apartment and were running full speed down the hallway, knocking Alvera off her feet as they sprinted away.

Sanchez jumped up and ran to Alvera in the hall. She was ready for a fight. "You OK, Clara?" she asked as she helped Alvera up.

"Yeah, I guess," she responded, shaken.

Sanchez ran down the hall to the stairs and took the steps two at a time. She banged into the glass front door, but it was blocked. One of the men had moved a wrought iron chair in front of it. It took nearly a minute for her to push it open far enough to squeeze through. She saw a dark-green sedan roar away down Monroe Street and around the next corner. She could only glimpse the first three letters on the license plate as it vanished: *BCH* maybe, or *BCN*.

She stopped running and walked instead to her unmarked car. She reached inside to radio in a report but hesitated a second. If she called in the incident right away, the nearest squad car would respond within minutes. She wasn't sure she wanted backup that fast—not before they had time to retrieve Alvera's personal items. She hung the radio back in its cradle and jogged back into the apartment house.

She didn't see Alvera in the hallway, so she stepped inside the two-bedroom apartment and turned on the lights in the entryway. It apparently was a cozy little place that received early warm light now that morning had arrived. It had the usual white walls and plain windows that most rental units had, but Vale had decorated it with colorful tablecloths, curtains, and flamboyant paintings and prints. It was moderately crowded with Vale's possessions, giving it a well lived-in look. But now it was half-trashed.

Alvera called from the master bedroom where she was searching for something she had left there. Sanchez was not too pleased with the situation. She stared at the queen-size bed that dominated the room and tried to imagine Alvera and Vale on it. Then she looked away and saw a disarray of clothing thrown across the back of a chair and shoes scattered around the floor. *Josie may look like Clara, but she wasn't the same compulsive organizer she is*, she thought. *Maybe that was the attraction.*

"I'm not sure this is a good idea, Clara. Now we have a burglary to report. I don't want to be accused of evidence tampering." Sanchez felt on the hook to placate her friend's fears and at the same time not break the rules of evidence. She had a handful of evidence bags with her as she caught up to her friend. "Those guys were carrying a laptop. That must have been Josie's word processor too, right? Is that what she typed her story into?"

"Shit!" Alvera said loudly. "They got that? Then they may have everything—drafts of the story, notes, sources. Josie was careful to not keep a lot of papers around."

"Yeah, that could be a problem. If her killers were with the cartel, they may have the names of her other sources too. Now they could be in danger. Anyway, now I have to explain why we were here in the first place."

"Lori, it's OK. I'm just going to get that one file and a few other things and get out of here. I can't leave that file here. But I don't want my name to be involved in a murder investigation either. It could hurt my career."

"Yeah, Clara, I get that, but the CSI team will find evidence that you were here anyway. You must have left hair and prints all over the place." She shook her head as Alvera handed her a thick manila folder. "Oh, you found it? Good." She took the folder and placed it in an evidence bag as Alvera glared at her. "Look, I'll give it back to you once we figure out the protocol. It shouldn't have been here anyway. Right?"

"Let me take these things too," Alvera pleaded nicely. "They're personal items." She handed them to Sanchez.

"What are these? Sex toys? Really, Clara." She held up a small vibrator and smiled. "Well, I guess it *is* a personal item." She laughed as she dropped it in a plastic bag, and Alvera cringed.

"I left her playthings here." Alvera moved into the bathroom, which the burglars had not bothered. "This can all stay." She rushed to the living room and scanned several items to see if they were worth taking. Then she raced into the kitchen. "I think we're done."

"I'm going to have to let Bordou know about this, you know. He'll have to know you were sleeping with the victim in order to do his job."

"I know that, but maybe we can keep my name out of it officially. Make me an informant or something? Can we do that?" She stopped for a minute to think. "I could be a protected witness since I know why Josie came to the gym. Maybe that's an angle to use."

"I don't know, but it sounds iffy to me. You're a witness and therefore should be protected for now, at least. But you know there's a process for this sort of thing."

"Yes, and as ADA, I can grant myself this status. So there." Alvera rushed off to the other bedroom, and Sanchez followed.

"I'm not sure DA Davies would agree with that," Sanchez said. "It may show poor judgment." She entered the bedroom.

"Did she use this as an office or something?"

There were three filing cabinets along the back wall and a big desk in the middle of the room. The intruders had been digging around in the filing cabinets when they were interrupted. Papers were scattered over the floor and desk as if they were looking for something in particular. Maybe for Vale's notes on a story. Or evidence. They hadn't gotten very far in their search but had stolen some files judging by the gap in the drawer's contents.

A framed photo of Alvera was standing in one corner of the desk. *With love* was scrawled across the glossy print. Alvera handed it to her for the bag.

"I feel like I'm your bagman here," Sanchez quipped. "Say, what's this? Her diary?" She saw the book on a small table next to the desk.

"Oh shit! Her diary!" Alvera lurched for it. "She probably wrote about me in there." She picked it up and flipped to the last pages. She read silently for a few moments as Sanchez tried to take it away from her.

"You shouldn't look in there, Clara. There might be stuff she didn't want you to know." She finally tore the diary away from Alvera and closed it. "I know you're personally involved, but you can't do things that may interfere with the investigation." She dropped the diary in another evidence bag.

"But she wrote about me," Alvera said weakly. "She loved me." Her face softened, and her eyes seemed misty.

"I assume that, Clara, but you can't just take everything. I'll take the diary into custody and somehow log it into evidence later. You can't have it. At least, not now."

"All right, Lori," Alvera sniffled. "Maybe I'm getting too emotional, but we should see what she said about the meeting last night. It could be helpful."

"OK. But we're getting out of here right now so I don't have to explain why the assistant DA is interfering with an ongoing homicide investigation." Sanchez gently pushed her friend toward the door. "Come on, we're heading back to your place. We can read it there."

Sanchez looked at her watch. 8:30 a.m. She closed the door and marched to the Interceptor, taking Alvera by the arm. She radioed in the burglary and explained her role in the discovery. She explained that this break-in was likely related to the murder at Maraxx Pharma last night. She and Bordou would be the lead investigators. She left Alvera's name out of it and had her wait in the car in order to stay off the books.

It was quiet in the car as she drove back to Alvera's apartment to drop her off. She thought about what she was going to do with Lolita.

Maybe Montero has an idea, she thought.

***

"We saw it further on in the recording," Bordou said over the radio. "At one seventeen a.m., the two men left the gym with Nick Carter. Carter did not look like he was leaving willingly. He had blood all over his shirt as he was dragged along the sidewalk. Then at one thirty-eight a.m., we saw Clara show up and look for the door. She went inside at one forty-one and ran back outside at one forty-seven. She was screaming, even though we don't have any audio. She looked terrified and ran away. Must have gone to her car to call you."

"Yeah, I guess." Sanchez was catching up with Bordou as she drove back to the gym crime scene. "Say, how is Lolita doing? Debbie still have her in the gym?"

"No, Deb had to leave, so she turned her over to me. The

girl's sleeping on the stack of floor mats behind the weight room. You need to speak with her?"

"No. Let her sleep. I've got to find her a place to stay. She isn't safe on her own, so I guess I'll pick her up when I get there."

"No problem. Out."

So now they had more to go on. Apparently, the two men had kidnapped Carter and then showed up at Vale's apartment to search her belongings. Assuming it was the same two guys. And why so much later than when they were at the gym? It seemed like they had followed Vale to the gym to see whom she was meeting and then captured them both. The fact that they had tortured Vale suggested it was about her story. When they were done with her, they took Carter away. Why? For further interrogation. *What does that tell me?* she thought. *Did they know who Vale was meeting?*

On the other hand, maybe they were watching Carter. They might have watched the gym and just happened to encounter Vale. But that wouldn't explain why they had showed up at her apartment too.

She pulled into a parking space in front of the gym where several police cars were still huddled. She double-checked that her evidence bags were out of sight and walked toward the gym. As she approached the door, Bordou came running out and looked right and left as if he were looking for someone or something. He seemed distraught.

When he saw Sanchez, he stopped. "She's gone! Lolita is gone!" he called out.

"What? I thought you had an eye on her."

"I couldn't watch her every minute. Last I saw, she was asleep." He looked all around the parking lot. "Maybe she went to another building."

Just then, a blue sedan pulled into the handicapped space, and the back door flew open. Out stepped Lolita, dressed in shorts, a halter top, and flip-flops. She waved as she walked up to them carrying a small duffel bag.

"Hi, officers!" she called out. "I'm back."

Sanchez gave Lolita the hard eye. "Where have you been? We were just looking for you."

"Oh," she replied. "I just went home to shower and get some fresh clothes. I wasn't sure how long you were going to be, so I Ubered over and back. It's not too far."

"Well, next time you do something like that, let one of us know, OK?" Bordou seemed a little angry she had given him the slip.

By then, Sanchez was getting tired and needed a break from all the variables rolling around in her head. "Look, guys, I'm beat. I'm not sure I can do any more until I've had a couple of hours' sleep." She looked at Lolita. "I haven't found a good arrangement for you yet, but if it's OK with you, I'll take you to my place to get something to eat and some shut-eye. I'm glad you were able to get a few winks in the gym, but I've been hitting it all night."

"Sure," Lolita said. "I'm pretty tired too. Let's go."

"Jeff, I'll catch up with you later. You should take a break too and get home to that beautiful wife of yours." Sanchez smiled in encouragement.

"I can pass the rest of this off to the CSI boys and come back around one p.m. or so. Thanks." With that, Bordou trudged back inside the gym.

Sanchez and Lolita walked to the car, Sanchez shuffling and Lolita practically skipping. "Would you like some pancakes before we go to my place? I'm thinking IHOP." Sanchez was exhausted but also dying of hunger.

"Sure. Let's do it."

Lolita laughed, and so did Sanchez. The girl's enthusiasm was contagious.

Chapter 6

Monday morning, April 1, 2019
Phoenix, Arizona

The vibrating sound was now persistent and annoying. It came to Sanchez like a chain saw clawing its way through the wall of her bedroom, loud and destructive. She couldn't quite pull herself up to stop the angry noise, but it suddenly ceased.

She was pleased as she rolled to her side and punched her pillow into a better shape before letting go of all her thoughts and worries. It was warm in the apartment; the air conditioner was struggling to keep up with the hot night. Her mind processed that it was not her alarm clock that had made the noise but her phone on her bedside stand. That location always caused some weird resonance that defied physics. *Good, it was the phone. No problem . . . But then, why'd it stop like that?*

Her mind began to drift back to consciousness. She opened one eye and realized it was still daylight. Then she realized she was not alone in the bed. From zero to ninety in one second, she sat up.

"Good afternoon, sleepyhead." It was Lolita, lying a foot away from her on her side, facing Sanchez. "I didn't want to wake you, but your phone had a fit. I shut it off. It was Bordou calling."

"Why are you here and not in the living room on the couch?"

Lolita shrugged. "There was a weird noise coming from that box out there—the one marked *Evidence*. I couldn't get any sleep, so I came in here." She grinned from the pillow. "You were dead to the world, anyway."

"Evidence box?" Sanchez wasn't sure what she was talking about. Then she remembered that she had put the three evidence bags from Vale's apartment in the box for safekeeping in her perfunctory cleanup of her place when she had arrived with Lolita.

"Oh, that box."

She sized the girl up. She had on a simple sleeveless pajama top and presumably the matching short bottoms—Victoria's Secret, no doubt, since Daddy was paying. Sanchez had on her usual summer sleeping gear: an old T-shirt and loose boxer-like briefs, both showing about ten years of wear. Then there was the perkiness that was going to drive her crazy if she didn't have either more sleep or strong java in a few minutes. The kid was hard not to like, though, even if she had invaded Sanchez's sleeping zone.

"OK, better give me the phone in case it's important." She reached out a hand and lay back down when Lolita passed her the mobile. "If you need to shower again, now's the time to go for it." She paused as she looked at the phone. "Did you get enough sleep?"

"Yeah, I got a few hours last night while waiting around too, so I'm good."

"Great. Now let's check out this sound in the box."

Sanchez threw off the covers, stepped out of bed, and walked quickly to the living room to find the offending box. She threw back the lid and saw right away that the bag of sex toys she had taken from Vale's apartment was making a vibrating sound.

Oh great, Sanchez thought, *an out-of-control vibrator*. As she reached for a pack of rubber evidence gloves, Lolita leaned in to see what was making the noise.

"Oh my God. Is that what I think it is?" she asked in a giggling tone.

"I'm afraid so." Once gloved, Sanchez reached into the bag to select the annoying toy and shut it off. She turned to Lolita as she removed the gloves. "Don't ask where it came from."

Lolita began to laugh, and then Sanchez couldn't help but laugh too. "Well, now you know what kept you up last night."

More snickers.

"I'm going to answer this call, shower, and get dressed. You get first shot at the bathroom. I set out towels last night—I mean, this morning."

She walked back to her bedroom, closed the door, and dialed Bordou's number.

"Hey, Lori, how'd you sleep?" he asked when he answered.

"Not enough, but that's another story. What's up, Jeff?"

"We found out that there are extra cameras installed in the gym building. Apparently, our friend Nick made a habit of videoing women he had back in his office. He even had a camera set up in the gym centered on one piece of apparatus. It's the vault thing that Josie Vale's body was tied to. He has three videos of him doing different women there, including our little friend, Lolita."

"What a dirtbag!" she said loudly. She stopped to listen to be sure Lolita hadn't heard her. All she heard was the sound of the shower in the bath nearby. "So the pervert was making videos. Who were the other women besides Lo?"

"We don't know, but I wondered if he's just a voyeur or if he was using the videos for blackmail." Bordou paused. "They are on thumb drives, and there are several of those, so there may be dozens of videos . . . Hold on." Bordou talked to someone else for a few moments. "It looks like there is a video of what happened in the gym last night. We'll check it out and see if it has anything useful for the investigation. Anyway, there may be more going on here than meets the eye."

"OK. Keep me posted." She punched the End button.

***

Sanchez quizzed Lolita as they drove back to the gym crime scene, "So you talked to your dad? That's good. Is he OK if you stay with me so I can keep you out of trouble?"

"Yeah," Lolita replied. "He's real worried and is coming home early to spend time with me this weekend—Thursday afternoon. It will be nice to see him after all this."

"Does he know you were sleeping with Nick?" Sanchez asked bluntly, "I mean, I don't want to pry, but—you know—I wondered."

"Can I call you Lori, since we're getting personal here?" She looked over at Sanchez and received a nod. "I've been pretty independent for a while, and my dad knows that. So I've had a few boyfriends that he knows about and some he doesn't. He doesn't know about Nick, except that he runs the gym where I train."

"OK, just wondered. Most parents would be upset about their daughter dating a guy so much older. That's all."

"He's not that much older, just twenty-five or something. And he's helped me with my training, getting me in after hours to practice."

"Lo, he's thirty-four, not twenty-five. I can show you his driver's license if you want proof."

"No way," Lolita countered. "He can't be that old."

"Are you sure? How much do you know about him, anyway?"

"Well, I've known him for a few months. I met him through the gym. He runs the place pretty much by himself. That's why he's so busy. Someone else does the membership stuff—new members, rentals, and things like that."

"Who's that?"

"Her name is Megan Faux," Lolita sneered. "How's that for a name? She's a real sleazy woman."

"Why sleazy? What's she done to you?"

"She reminds me of a coach we had who was too friendly with some of the girls when I was still doing competition in high school. She was sleazy too—got quietly fired for what she did . . . I'm not supposed to talk about it."

"I didn't know you did competition. How long did you do that?"

"Oh, for three years, I guess. Then I had the injury and never made it all the way back, so I got dropped." She looked miserable for a quiet minute. "Well, I'm better now. My left leg is at like ninety percent now. But I'll never compete again. I just do it because that's what I do."

"I'd like to see you do your routine sometime. You must be pretty good at it," Sanchez said as they turned into the gym parking lot. "So what's the story on Megan Faux?"

"She and Nick were lovers at one time. They compete over clients sometimes. I guess they get some money if they sign up a new member. They both sell extra training services, so I guess that keeps them fighting over people too. I just don't want her around Nick too much, or he might be tempted. You know what I mean." She stopped in her tracks. "Say, where is Nick, anyway?

You saw him leave the gym on a camera, right? Did he ever come back?"

"Not that I know of. I have some things to tell you about that, but let's hear from Bordou first, OK?"

They stepped out of the car and walked to the gym door, where Bordou was waiting. He looked perplexed. It had been a long day for him too.

"I'm going off shift for the night right after we talk. I'm beat," he said.

"Right. I needed a few hours, so thanks for covering for me." Sanchez lightly punched him in the shoulder. "Give us the download, and you can head home to Kathy."

"We're still going through recordings. And we found out he has a padlocked locker in the main men's locker room. I've requested a warrant to open that—probably late tomorrow." He looked at Lolita carefully. "The crime scene is wrapped up—just waiting for lab tests there. We have some recordings that Lolita might be able to help us with. We need to ID some people."

Sanchez put her hand up like a traffic cop. "You aren't going to have her watch the recordings, are you? I should probably screen them first based on what I know."

Her rebuff caught Bordou off guard. "Well, we just have a couple of close-ups of faces. Nothing upsetting, Lori. I wouldn't do that." His face showed the stress he was under.

"I'm sorry, Jeff. You're right. I'm sure you already screened them." Sanchez was sorry she had reacted the way she had. "Yes, let's see if Lo knows who these people are. It could save a lot of time." She exchanged a glance with Lolita to see if she was game. She in turn gave Sanchez a questioning look and raised her eyebrows.

Bordou nodded and led them inside to a laptop computer

that was set up on top of a stack of chairs. He moved the cursor over and clicked on the first still image of a woman with long brown hair, dark eyes, and a wide face.

"Have you seen this woman before, Lo?" he asked, looking back and forth between the screen and Lolita.

"No, but I think I've seen her around here before. She's one of Nick's customers."

They looked at three other photos of people, including one man who looked like he was in pain. Lolita said she thought he might be one of the managers at Maraxx Pharma. He had been to her father's house for drinks once. She couldn't remember his name—maybe Elbert or something like that. Then they came to a photo of a long-haired blonde who had her eyes closed in concentration in an odd close-up shot. She was quite attractive with high cheekbones and a lot of mascara on her dark eyelashes to make them look dramatically long.

Lolita's face tightened up at the sight of the photo. She turned to Sanchez. "See why I don't want Nick around her?" Lolita asked.

"So that's Megan Faux? She's attractive, isn't she?" Sanchez said offhand. Then she realized that this was not what Lolita wanted to hear about her rival.

"At least my boobs are real," Lolita said. She frowned at the picture and set up her face. "She's tall and slender too. She can really turn it on when she wants to. Guys like that." She turned back to Sanchez. "Nick couldn't resist her charms, the bastard."

Bordou quickly closed the window on the computer and looked at Lolita. "Sorry, Lo. I didn't know you two knew each other that way." He hesitated and then said, "But thanks for the help ID'ing people. That will save us some time." He motioned for Sanchez to step away for a word.

Lolita seemed to be in a funk now, so they let her stand on her own and fume. Bordou walked to the side of the CSI tent and waited for Sanchez to join him.

"Wow. She hates that woman. Any idea why?" he asked.

"She's Nick's ex, and I guess he might still be involved with her. A definite source of friction in the gym." She paused to look and make sure Lolita was not close by. "Were all those photos made from the sex recording?"

"All but one. Apparently, Megan Faux is in on the recording scam because she used the same camera for her training sessions. Those are some special pointers she gave."

Sanchez just shook her head. "I guess Lo didn't know anything about these recordings. Poor kid. She fell in with a real shithead." She scanned the few people remaining in the gym. "Looks like things are wrapping up. Any word on Nick and his whereabouts?"

"I have people checking for the license plate number you got off the car at the apartment, but no results yet." He looked at his watch. "Hey, I'd better clock out, or Captain Teller is going to shit bricks about the amount of overtime we're running. I'll call you this afternoon to see how it's going. OK?"

"Yeah, fine. Get some rest," Sanchez said as he shuffled out the door.

She looked across the room to where Lolita was talking to one of the younger officers. She was a genuine person who seemed to get along with everyone. She was quite attractive herself with her long blonde hair, blue eyes, pleasant features, and toned body. She had a presence that radiated from her determination and training for gymnastics. That gave her a measure of self-confidence that quickly drew people close. She seemed to have her shit together for someone so young, except, it appeared, in the area of picking men. But that was a mystery that few figured out over a lifetime. Sanchez knew she herself had made enough mistakes there. Tom Smith, her current boyfriend, was certainly proving to be her soul mate so far. *So far? Now that's cynical!* she thought.

As she looked at the teenager, she thought about how mature she had been at that same age, sixteen. The memories that came back were of a teen looking for identity and fighting for independence from her parents. She had never been a wild child, but she cringed at some of the things she had done without thinking back then. Well, she had grown up fast and had goals early enough to keep her from doing anything irreversibly damaging. She had little good judgment about guys back then, so she hoped that the news about Carter's activities with the recordings wouldn't hit Lolita too hard.

She had to come up with a place to keep Lolita safe now that they knew two armed and dangerous guys were out there, who might not like to hear that there was a possible witness to their crimes last night. Lolita was in potential danger, so she needed protection. Maybe when her father came home, Sanchez could talk to him about getting her a bodyguard. She doubted the city would pay to protect her unless they could make a case against the two killers. Until then, it was Sanchez's duty, but she didn't want to place Lolita in the foster system, even temporarily. It was pretty impersonal and not conducive for people to stick with for long. Then she had an idea.

She dialed the one man who might have a solution and on whom Sanchez could lean when the going got tough: her old drinking buddy, Father Guillermo Montero. She hoped he was in town and not too busy.

"Hello, Lori. How are you? I haven't heard from you in two

weeks. You must be busy," Montero said in his reassuring voice. "Let's see—it's not Friday, so you must not be calling to go for happy hour somewhere. To what do I owe this pleasant surprise?"

"Surprise? What do you mean?" She was supposed to call him the week before but had gotten overwhelmed by cases. "I said I'd call you this week about doing dinner, remember? Maybe Salvador's? We haven't been there in a while."

"Yes, Salvador's would be delightful. Excellent roasted chicken." He paused. "And is there anything else on your mind?"

"What do you mean? Can't I just call you up to say hello?" She had a feeling he knew she was going to ask a favor. He had the uncanny ability to see through her subterfuge so easily.

"And I was just reviewing one of my favorite books—one by Vladimir Nabokov—a truly underrated author."

"OK, you're onto me. Did Bordou call you already?"

"Yep."

"Come on, Guillermo. You'll like this girl. She's very sweet and easygoing," she tried to convince him. "Besides, it's only for tomorrow until I can get her another place to stay while her father is out of town."

"Lori, you've tried this before. You make it sound so easy. Then it gets complicated or it takes much longer than you originally say it will be."

She tried to play to his sense of fairness. "Come on, Guillermo. I don't want to put her into the system. She's a minor, and you know how that can be, especially for a pretty girl."

"And what will I get out of doing you yet another favor? You haven't made good on the last two or three I've done for you." He sounded severe, but Sanchez detected that it was largely put on. He was playing a role now. He had a way of trying to steer her efforts in the right direction. He was sort of fatherly in that regard, a part of their relationship that she both appreciated and resented at the same time. He tried to show her the right path, for all the good it did either of them.

"Why, Guillermo, you know I keep my word. I've just been busy, and you haven't exactly needed anything from me lately." She realized this was not going to get her anywhere. Negotiating had been her downfall with her father too. He would see her minimizing her responsibility. She remembered how she had broken an impasse with her dad long ago. At least it was a show of good faith.

"I'll come over and wash your truck tonight after work. I'll even bring a sixer of Sol beer to make up for interest on my long overdue quo." She knew he would get the drift. The car wash idea had worked with her father.

"Ah," Montero said. She could tell he was trying to keep his voice from breaking. "You mean you will make up for this quid pro quo in advance. That's something new."

"So do we have a deal? I can be there at six o'clock or so." She was hopeful.

Montero broke into a loud bout of laughing. "Lori, you really know how to work me," he said merrily. "Come over about six, and bring your young friend with you for dinner so I can meet her. I can't take her overnight. I'm in enough hot water with the diocese already without rumors of me housing a pretty girl named Lolita, and a minor to boot." He chuckled.

"Sure, you'll like her. She's staying over with me for a couple of days, but I need a safe place for her when I'm working. That's the favor. Are we OK?"

"Yes, certainly. But I may have to come up with a way for

you to work off the other quos you owe me. We can talk tonight." He paused and put her on hold. He must have gotten another call because he soon said, "Hey, I have to go. See you tonight," and hung up.

Chapter 7

Late Monday afternoon, April 1, 2019
Phoenix, Arizona

Sanchez and Montero stood inside the sliding glass door that opened out on to his driveway. They each had a cold bottle of Sol beer in hand and were enjoying the evening weather from inside the house. It was still hot outside after an unseasonably warm day for April in Phoenix. It was ninety-six degrees in the shade, according to Montero's outdoor thermometer. They caught up on small talk while watching Montero's white Toyota pickup being cleaned.

Montero was a tall man with longish dark-brown hair and expressive brown eyes set wide in his face. He had the kind of features that told you on first meeting he was of solid character. The small lines around his eyes indicated he had seen many things and still viewed the world with a sense of humor. He had been a soldier in Iraq, a policeman in El Paso, and was now a secular priest working to counsel prisoners about their lives. He and Sanchez had worked together for three years and shared a penchant for Mexican beers, good food, and lively music, although they disagreed on some of the mariachi tunes that Montero favored.

They stood observing the spectacle of a good old-fashioned car wash. On the driveway outside in the fading late-afternoon sun, Lolita was scrubbing the sides of the truck with a sudsy sponge. She was wearing one of her old leotards that she said could get wet, as she stretched and flexed to get every bit of desert dust and mud off the vehicle. She picked up the hose to rinse a fender and sprayed it on herself to stay cool. When she saw her two spectators laughing at the water show, she sprayed the sliding door with water for good measure. They jumped back, and it was her turn to laugh.

"It was clever to challenge your new friend to wash the truck," Montero said lightly. "But I haven't seen this Tom Sawyer side of you before—getting someone else to do your chores for you."

"She said she was bored just standing around and waiting all day. I offered her a fair trade for her work." She smiled. "She accepted."

"Do I dare ask what this quid pro quo entailed?"

"No. I don't think you really want to know." Sanchez smiled cheerfully at her friend, her partner in more than a few adventures and criminal cases.

He chuckled at her secrecy. "Well, before Lolita comes inside, I wanted to talk to you about a problem that I've uncovered at the local VA hospital. You've no doubt read in the papers about the management troubles here in Phoenix."

"Yes, of course. They seem to be the worst-managed hospital in the world—well, maybe not that bad, but close. I thought the wait times for veterans have improved lately."

"Better, yes. But still not at all reasonable. There seem to be a lot of restrictions on changing personnel and procedures—even simple management methods. They make the best argument for taking away Veterans Affairs' money and giving it to a privately run hospital."

"Well, that's never going to happen," Sanchez said

cynically. "The politics are as entrenched as their archaic procedures and administrators."

"Well—here's the thing: I've been working with a therapist out at the VA who specializes in treating veterans who have PTSD. You know something about that because I cautioned you about it when you were shot two years ago."

"Hey, I remember. You looked out for me like you always do." They clicked bottles, and she frowned at the memory of fighting for her life. She still had flashbacks about her desperate shoot-out in an alley against members of the Sinaloa drug cartel that she kept to herself. "Yeah, so this is what you started last winter, right? Talk to guys who were in tough combat situations that may have messed up their brains?"

"Your description doesn't do the subject justice, but yes, that's what I'm doing." He went on after watching Lolita carefully buff his truck with a chamois cloth. "I talk to the men and find out how their therapy is working out, how they feel, and if they think their stress is receding. You'd be surprised what they tell me about the hospital and the assumptions made there. The hospital still relies heavily on medication to control anxiety but doesn't always deal with the root cause of the fear and psychological trauma. It's discouraging."

"Sounds like really heavy shit, Guillermo. But I can see them opening up and talking to you since you're both a priest and a veteran yourself. You have a different perspective on the subject."

"I'm concerned because some of the men have complained that they're not getting the meds they rely on or that the meds don't work properly any longer. A few of them think that something funny is going on, like the VA is giving them placebos or just reducing their doses way down without telling them.

They're afraid they're seeing cutbacks in their treatment, maybe caused by new budget cuts or just a lack of care."

"That sounds pretty awful. Imagine you have flashbacks and the meds you count on to keep you from freaking out don't work. It would make everything worse."

They watched Lolita dump the bucket of soapy water on the gravel next to the driveway and coil up the garden hose. She walked into the garage to put it away.

"Well, I'd like you to look into a few aspects of it when you can. You know—off the record to see if there's anything to it. Then if there's reason to be concerned, I could bring it up officially—assuming I can find anyone who can do anything to help."

"I can do a few things without it being official. Let's talk about it more tomorrow or the next day. I've got this investigation to handle right now, and it looks like it's getting serious."

"Murder and kidnapping always are," he said gravely.

Then Lolita burst through the door, soaked in sweat and soapy water. "Man, is it hot out." She stood there dripping water on the entryway tiles. "Can I take a shower and change somewhere? I need to cool off."

"You did a great job on my truck. Thank you, Lolita. I think I owe you a shower and a dinner at least," Montero said with a huge smile. "The truck hasn't been that clean in years."

"Here, Lo," Sanchez said. "I'll show you where the bathroom is so you can clean up. I really owe you for actually doing the wash. You made our day."

She led Lolita down the hall as Montero walked out into the heated evening to pull the truck into the garage.

Chapter 8

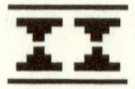

Tuesday morning, April 2, 2019

Phoenix, Arizona

Montero drove his Toyota pickup directly to the visitor parking lot at the Carl T. Hayden Veterans' Administration Medical Center north of downtown Phoenix. He turned off East Indian School Road and pulled into a vast parking lot on the south side of the complex. Numerous buildings were spread over the medical campus, immediately creating an intimidating impression. If there was any doubt before arriving here, this confirmed that you were going to encounter bureaucracy.

"Wow!" Lolita said loudly. "It's huge."

"Yeah, really big and slow moving," Montero said sadly. "I wonder sometimes if the place is designed to serve veterans or to just scare them away."

"Well, hospitals are scary enough as is," Lolita said. "My mom was in a hospital in Denver a year ago, and we lost track of her. For about an hour, the hospital couldn't find her after she came in for an emergency."

"How'd that happen? Most hospitals have very clear procedures for admitting patients. She should have been in their cloud."

"Somehow they listed her under her maiden name, not under her married name. It took a while to figure that out. My dad and I were terrified that something had happened to her and they wouldn't tell us the truth." Lolita looked very distraught. "Anyway, I don't trust big institutions. You don't know what's really going on in them sometimes."

They parked the car and walked into the main lobby. Montero approached a side desk to ask where the PTSD group was meeting today. They got the number of a room in an outlying building and walked out the side door. He knew his way to the other building, so he led Lolita along a convoluted path to that location.

They rode the elevator to the third floor and found the room easily. Montero knew a few of the people who were scattered around sipping coffee or water as they waited for the meeting to begin. Montero and Lolita took seats in the circle of chairs that had been arranged for the discussion.

"Are you comfortable sitting here during the discussion?" Montero asked.

"I'd just as soon sit next to you. That way no one will hit on me."

"Oh, I didn't think about that," he said as he scanned the men and women who were taking seats. "I don't think it will be a problem. These guys are all ex-military, so I think they will have good manners."

A man wearing a tan jacket entered the room and, noticing Montero, came over to greet him. "Guillermo, it's good to see you. I'm glad you could make it to our little gathering again."

Montero and the man shook hands, and then Montero turned to introduce Lolita. "I brought a new friend with me to see how this sort of therapy group works. Lolita, this is Dr. Kurt McMillan; he's the psychologist that runs the group here for the VA. This is Lolita Thompson. We shouldn't use her last name in introductions anyway, and she should keep a low-key profile."

"Nice to meet you, Lolita. We don't use last names here, just so you know." He looked at Montero and back at her again. "If you would like to speak, you could use a nickname, if you prefer."

"I go by Lo most of the time. It's cool," she said quietly. "You know, I had a form of PTSD once too. When I took a fall off the balance beam a few years ago, they said I got it from wrecking my knee. I was knocked out and everything."

"Really? I had no idea, Lo," Montero said sympathetically. "Is it getting better?"

"Oh yes. I seem to have overcome it for now. I've even talked about it to other gymnasts who had similar injuries." She seemed shy about it. "If you want, I could say a few words. I assume everyone here has had it too."

"Maybe," McMillan said. "Let's see how many people want to speak today. It's purely voluntary, and some guys don't want to talk. It can be devastating."

"We'll see," Montero said. "I don't want to put any pressure on you, Lo."

McMillan saw that most of the people had settled into chairs. He said, "It looks like everyone is here and ready to start. Let's go around the circle and give our names and occupation or specialties." He smiled at each person as he scanned the room. "I'm Dr. Kurt McMillan, as most of you know. I am a psychologist here at the VA, specializing in brain trauma and PTSD." He sat down and turned to Montero.

"I'm Guillermo, a secular priest and counselor with an interest in PTSD because I experienced it after serving in Iraq during Operation Enduring Freedom." He finished and turned to Lolita, raising his eyebrows.

"Hi, I'm Lo. I'm in high school and am a gymnast. I had

PTSD from a really gross accident I suffered during a competition." She smiled at the man next to her.

"Hi. I'm Lloyd, and I was a communications specialist in the 'Stan."

All twelve people took their turn introducing themselves. After that formality, McMillan asked for volunteers to talk about their experience with PTSD and what had caused it. Only three people spoke about their troubles. Then the room became quiet.

"Anyone else?" McMillan asked, looking at each person searchingly. He turned to Lloyd sitting next to Lolita and held out his hand palm up. "How about you, Lloyd? You haven't said much lately. You got anything to say—any insights to how you're doing?"

Lloyd shook his head and looked at the floor. "We was drivin' the usual road and bam! We took an IED under the Humvee. Now they're all dead, and I'm left all fucked up." He looked over at Lolita and said, "Sorry, ma'am, for the language." He looked at the floor again, and a tear rolled down his cheek.

Lolita reached up and put a hand on his shoulder to comfort him. She whispered, "It'll get better. It really will. You just have to hang in there and have a little faith that it *will* get better."

He raised his head a little to listen to her. He nodded a couple of times and let her keep her hand on his shoulder while he said, "I hope to Christ you're right, ma'am. I need it to get better. I need to believe it will get better."

"That's good, Lloyd. You did good," McMillan said in a kind way. "It *will* get better."

"I'd like to speak," a young woman with short dark hair said as she waved her hand in the air. "I'm Joyce, and I was hit by an IED while drivin' convoy out of Kandahar three years ago. We were making a run with supplies to outpos' six north of there on the road ta Maranjan. We took it big-time right in the ass by the dualies—the rear wheels—when we'd slowed down next to the river. I was drivin', so I got thrown out the side and inta the ditch. I got some broken bones and knocked out, but lived to tell. My friend Martin was killed when the truck rolled over on him. He was cut up real bad too—from the metal and shit. Probably woulda died anyway." She stopped to look over at Lloyd. "What got to me is that it was so—unexpected. We knew it was goin' ta happen one of these days, but no—not today."

The room was silent as everyone waited for her to continue. "It was the suddenness of it all and that we 'spected it—but not just then." She stared at the floor and wept. "Now if I'm drivin' and there's the slightest sound of a backfire or a bang from a truck bed or a dumpster gets bumped—you know, with that loud clang sound—then wham! I'm right back in the shit. Even though I *know* it's over—it *still isn't*."

Another man put his hand up to speak. "I'm just curious about what happened to the lady over here—Lo. What happened to you, and how'd you get through it?"

Lolita looked like she suddenly had been thrown out on a stage and was expected to perform. She looked startled but then took a few deep breaths and seemed to settle down. She glanced at Montero to see if she should say anything.

"Only if you want to talk, Lo. It's up to you," he said with an encouraging smile.

She smiled at him and then looked at the young man who had asked the question. She took a deep breath and spoke quietly.

"I'm a gymnast, as I said. I specialize in the balance beam apparatus. That long wooden beam raised up on legs about a meter off the floor. When I was fourteen, I was in a competition—a high school regional meet. You've all probably seen balance beam routines on TV or at the Olympics. Well, I had this routine that had some really tough elements to it. The kind of thing that gets you a lot of points from the judges if you can do it perfectly." She looked around the room to see if anyone was interested in her story. Most of the people were listening.

"I'd done this routine hundreds of times in practice and a dozen times in competition. I knew I had it down cold. But there was always the chance I would make a mistake. And that's OK. I mean, gymnasts make mistakes all the time. You just try to minimize them in your routine, right? It's like the lady over there said—you know that one day something is going to happen that's really bad, and you go on doing what you do. But then, bam! It happens."

Lloyd turned to look at her face and asked almost in a whisper, "What happened to you?"

"Well, remember that the beam is only four inches wide, so you must have perfect balance to start with, but if you do a jump or a flip or a back handspring, you have to go upside down as you rotate while you jump and you have to land perfectly on this little four-inch thing. Well, I did a back handspring near the end of my routine, and I missed the landing. My foot came down wrong, and my foot slipped off the beam and I twisted my knee at the same time. Then I hit my head on the edge of the beam and dropped onto the mat."

Nearly everyone in the room had been holding their breath by this time, and a collective gasp filled the silence. They were all staring at this young woman who was telling them her story so honestly.

"Well," she continued with a pale, taut face, "the audience thought I was dead. So did my mom and dad, who ran down from the stands. They hauled me out of there in an ambulance, and I was out for about three hours . . . My head is unusually hard, it seems. At least, that's what my dad says." She looked up and tried to smile, but her eyes were wet. She sniffled. "But my leg was shattered. My knee was so twisted that three tendons had torn loose, and my tibia just broke into splinters. They told me I wouldn't walk again." Now tears began to flow down her cheeks. "I would never do gymnastics again."

She stopped crying after a minute or so while everyone looked on. Lloyd put a hand on her shoulder to let her know it was OK. He smiled at her. "You're doing fine," he said.

"Well, for the first few weeks, I relived that split second as I went upside down and came around for the landing, and I knew I was out of line before my foot ever reached the beam. And I relived the landing and the fall over and over again. I had nightmares about it, even when I was awake. It terrified me. They had me on sedatives for weeks and lots of painkillers. My head healed fine, but my leg was pinned together in one of those steel cages with bolts and screws and stuff. It hurt, and then they decided it wasn't healing right, so they broke part of it again. The pain was . . ." More tears.

"Hey," Montero said quietly, "take a minute." He smiled at her, and she smiled sadly back.

"Three months later, when I was out of the hospital and wearing an air brace, my coach called up and asked me to come to the gym. My dad told him that it would be too traumatic, and my mom forbade it. But my dad talked to my coach a few times, and then one day, he took me down there in the car. I hobbled into the gym on crutches, and the coach said he had the beam that I fell off of. No one at the other school wanted to practice on it now. It was cursed. He asked if I wanted to see it." She paused and looked at the faces in the room.

"My dad said we were leaving, but I wanted to see it. Well, we walked in there, and my coach had me touch it. It was weird because all I ever wanted to do since I can remember was to do gymnastics. And here I was afraid of this beam—this piece of wood. I put a hand on it and remembered what I had wanted all my life. My dad said my face changed right then and there from being completely glum to being hopeful."

She looked around the room at all the friendly faces. She wiped her eyes. "I overheard the coach telling my dad something about getting back on a horse after you fell off. I just stood there and leaned on the beam with my arms around it.

After that, Dad took me down to the gym to spend time with the beam every afternoon. A few days later, I was sitting on the beam, straddling it, and lying down on it. The coach said I was relearning to balance on it. He and my dad encouraged me and kept telling me I was doing better. Each day, my fear became less. The nightmares were fewer and not so bad." She now looked around the room with a ray of hope in her face, and the veterans nodded as they listened to her story.

"My coach had me do exercises to strengthen my ruined leg so I could stand normally. I had favored it ever since the accident. I was finally able to stand on just that bad leg after six months of training. Every day, I did exercises and strength training and spent time sitting on the beam or standing on it with two legs. One day, as my coach and Dad watched, I stood on the beam with only my bad leg and balanced. I stopped having nightmares after that."

The room was completely silent, and then Lloyd reached over and squeezed her shoulder. "You're amazing," he said.

Montero placed a hand on her other shoulder and smiled

benevolently at her. Then someone began to clap his hands, and soon everyone else was clapping too. She looked at them appreciatively. They stood up and continued to applaud.

She stood up and held out her hands, signaling for them to stop. "I just want to say that if I can come back from having my dreams shattered, then you can do the same thing. You just have to stick with it and listen to a coach or someone who loves you."

She stepped out into the middle of the circle of people and waved back at the ones who stepped forward to congratulate her. "And now see what I can do."

She swung her arms forward and back at her sides as she crouched down a little bit and bobbed up and down. Then without warning, she threw her arms up and sprang into the air with her head thrown back. They watched as she launched into a backflip, her feet flying over her head as she spun backward in a tight tuck. Then she pulled her arms forward as her feet touched the floor. A perfectly executed backflip, landed with perfect balance. She finished with her arms held over her head as if landing her routine in competition, a huge smile extending from ear to ear.

Everyone cheered and clapped even louder. Then they pushed in around her and slapped her on the back and told her how great her flip was.

Montero looked at McMillan and said, "I had no idea." He raised his hands in front of him in a shrug. Then he stepped forward to congratulate Lolita.

The PTSD session went on two hours past its scheduled end time. Everyone was excited by the day's conversation, and several veterans who had been suffering from their trauma began to open up and talk about what had happened to them. The unpretentious Lolita had made a difference in their lives.

Chapter 9

Tuesday morning, April 2, 2019

Phoenix, Arizona

Sanchez walked into the cramped reception area of the *Phoenix Tribune* and looked around at an establishment that had obviously seen better days. A battered mahogany counter that blocked any visitor from entering the door behind it led to the inner sanctum of the operation. Newspapers were stacked on one end of it, and the surface was marred by too many wet coffee mugs. The receptionist's desk was built into the rear of the structure where a ringing telephone sat on top of a stack of white pages that were covered with typed text and an equal amount of red ink between the lines of text and around the margins. An ancient keyboard lollygagged in front of a flat-screen monitor that was half-full of text, a cursor blinking expectantly.

No humans were in sight.

She stood there for a minute hoping that someone would appear from the back room, then searched for a bell to ring to get attention. Finally, she knocked on the mahogany barrier and called out, hello, stretching out the last syllable as if calling into a vacant cave to see if an animal would appear.

When no one replied, she stepped around the barricade and knocked on the door. Still no response, so she twisted the doorknob and looked inside. She could see a medium-size workroom with twelve desks lined up in two rows facing the back of the room. All of the desks looked as though they had been used up until a moment ago and then suddenly their occupants had vanished. It was like one of those medieval villages after the plague had swept through, killing most of the villagers and leaving the rest of the town intact. The only real evidence that people worked here was the Mr. Coffee pot on a sideboard, filled with coffee that looked as if it had been burning for some time. There were rumpled papers scattered across each of the desks, and some personal items sat conspicuously on top of the mayhem.

She heard shouting coming from the hallway at the back of the room. It was the shouting of an editor who had a deadline and was addressing several writers who were behind schedule. The sort of violent cajoling needed to energize a lagging staff. Sanchez had heard that sound before at the station where the chief of police would come over to the office to give the troops a word of encouragement when some crime had not yet been solved according to the whim and schedule that suited the mayor.

A door opened in the hallway, and voices filled the air as men and women flooded into the room and occupied their desks, some looking angry, some worried, and a few amused. A few final shouts of assignments rang out, and then a red-faced man stomped into the workspace wearing a wool vest resembling a college don. Nobody in Phoenix wore wool or a vest of any kind after February. It was just not practical.

The man raised his head and stared at her. He checked his watch and then waved for her to join him at the back of the room away from the riffraff—his reporters. She strode through the sea of busy scribblers and stepped into his office as he reached his seat.

"Close the door," he said sternly. "You must be Detective Sanchez. Pleased to meet you. I'm Virgil Dodson, editor of the *Phoenix Tribune*—or at least what's left of it." He waved his hand at a chair and said, "Have a seat and state your business. I have a deadline to meet if these baboons could just write some copy."

Sanchez sat there and waited for him to say more, but he lowered his head and began to edit a story on his desk instead. He had reddish curly hair and a similar full beard, the trendy look, with round brown plastic-rimmed glasses and skin that spoke of a Celtic heritage. Probably born and educated out east somewhere—Boston, maybe, by the accent—and not yet adapted to life in the southwest desert.

"I'm here about Josie Vale. I need to know what she was working on." She was very matter of fact, hoping he would respond to that approach.

"Why don't you ask her?" he said, looking up. "She's just freelance nowadays, so she isn't here, and I don't know where you can find her at this minute. So if that's what you want, just do some detecting and locate her." He seemed pleased with this possible resolution of the meeting. "Is that all?"

"Well, I know exactly where she is, and you apparently don't. She's in the city morgue."

That got his attention. "What? You're joking." He seemed genuinely surprised.

"No. It happened night before last. Word hasn't gotten out yet because of the circumstances." She decided to make him work for information since he had been so abrupt. "I need to know what she was working on because gang members were involved."

"Wait, wait!" he said loudly. "Josie's dead? How can that be? I just talked to her—well, let's see—Monday afternoon. She was really excited about something but wouldn't say what."

"That was the night she died, apparently while meeting a source at Maraxx Pharma. Do you know anything about that?"

"Really? Well, she said she was onto something big—something that would make her name again. I offered to print whatever she came up with. She was a reliable reporter."

"Did she work here? Why was she freelance and not on the payroll?"

"Look around you. We're down to a skeleton crew here. Budget cuts and low advertising revenue, fewer subscriptions—you name it. We're struggling to keep the paper alive."

"So did you pay her as a stringer or just by the word? Do you even care that she's dead?"

His head snapped up, and he looked insulted. "Hey, I treated her fairly. She wrote some good copy, but I can't afford to keep someone with her talent on staff. Costs too much and would hurt her résumé when she looked for the next gig." He realized she was pulling his chain. "Oh, you just said that for a reaction."

"I can't tell you the circumstances, but she did not die a natural death. Two gang members were seen leaving the scene where it happened and I think it may have had to do with drugs, but I don't know for sure. Did she work from here or at home?"

"She worked at home mostly, since we didn't have any real support here. I don't have investigators to help my writers, so she had to do the heavy lifting herself. We gave her a laptop and a box on our cloud so she could back up her files if needed, but her copy would all be on her laptop. If you found that, you would have her story, I would assume."

Sanchez thought this was leading nowhere. "Did you talk to her about her story? Do you know any names that were involved? Was it about gangs and illegal drugs? Anything you can tell me would help."

"Well, I can't tell you much because it's potentially our story, but it had to do with prescription drugs, not the usual street drugs—cocaine, heroin, marijuana—that sort of thing."

Sanchez saw a roadblock going up that would prevent any cooperation between the *Phoenix Tribune* and the PD. "What do you mean it may be your story if you didn't pay her?"

"Assuming she wrote it on our computer, then that would be on our property. I think it's common law. Ownership by possession." He smiled thinly. "Besides, if we don't have her password, we can't even get into her files on the cloud."

"That sounds unscrupulous," Sanchez said.

"Hey, I don't make the rules. But that's standard practice in the business. She intended to publish her work in our paper anyway, so it's not that unusual."

"Well, can you help me or not?" she asked tersely. "I need to know why someone would kill her in a brutal way. It looks like she was killed for something she found out."

"I'm afraid I can't help you. It's company policy." He looked smug. "But you can tell me what happened, can't you? I mean, she was one of ours."

"I don't know if you can say that. In any case, it's against department policy to discuss active investigations. I'm afraid I can't help you."

She stood up and briskly walked out of the office and through the bullpen-like work area. As she pushed through the front door of the building and stepped onto the blistering hot sidewalk, she had an idea that might just let her get her hands on those files.

***

Bordou stood by with a pair of Ridgid bolt cutters that looked like they were industrial strength. Sanchez was on the phone verifying that they had indeed received the warrant to open up Nick Carter's locker at the Maraxx Pharma gym. One of the evidence team guys stood by to log in whatever they found in the locker once they hacked into it.

"OK, guys," Sanchez said. "We got the paperwork. We can enter now." She looked at the somewhat rested Bordou. "You have the honor, Jeff."

He positioned the huge jaws of the cutters around the thick shaft of the combination lock and gave it some muscle. There was a loud clack, and the lock snapped open. He removed the remains of the lock and said, "Just in case, you'd better step back."

Bordou opened the latch on the full-length locker and was surprised by what they saw. The locker was crammed full of small cardboard boxes and plastic bottles of medications. Sanchez stepped back so the evidence guy could take photos. When he was finished, she reached for a large bottle of pills and read the label out loud: "Oxycodone, thirty-milligram tablets." She scanned the bottle. "There are five hundred pills in here and—let's see—at least five bottles of the stuff. And we have boxes of syringes here." She pulled one box out to read its contents. "Anadrol-100. What's that? A steroid?"

"Yeah, I think so," Bordou said. "Geez, he sure has a lot of drugs—for sale, I guess."

"Well, this puts him in a different category than just a sleazeball making sex videos. Now he's in the drug business." She pointed at all the boxes. "And look here, guys. Most of these boxes have *Maraxx Pharma* printed on them. Some have *MERCK*; some have *Randman Labs*."

The evidence man spoke up. "I can catalog this all for you now, if you like. And bag it, of course. Then we can make a list and estimate the value of this stash. It will be thousands for sure."

"OK," Sanchez said. "I guess that's the best thing to do here. Thanks, Harry."

She and Bordou walked away. "Now we can go and talk to Megan Faux," Sanchez said. "She apparently showed up this afternoon."

"She's in her office expecting us," Bordou said with a grin. "I can't wait to hear what she has to say about the videos."

They walked toward the rear of the gym where the hallway led them to Carter's office and another one farther down that Faux used. The door was open a crack, and they knocked as they heard Faux on the telephone inside.

"Who is it?" she called out. "Hold on. I'm on the phone."

Sanchez wasn't shy about leaning close to the door to hear the conversation. "She's setting up a special workout with someone," she whispered to Bordou. She was so intent on eavesdropping that Faux almost caught her when she opened the door.

"Oh," Faux said. "Come in. I was expecting you to stop by sometime this afternoon. Have a seat." She moved a stack of papers off a chair so they could both sit down.

Sanchez watched Faux and admired her grace as she moved between the desk and chairs. Faux had an athletic build that was very attractive, not the overmuscled look that some bodybuilders had from years of pumping iron. She was tall and lean with toned arms displaying impressive biceps. Her face was long and lean with a narrow nose and mouth. She wore no makeup but exuded an animal presence that caught your attention. She had obviously had a boob job.

"Now, where's Nick?" Faux asked. "I heard he's disappeared again."

"Again?" Sanchez asked. "Has he disappeared before?"

"Oh yes," Faux said. "Last year, he just up and left for a few days because he had some cash flow problems. I think he owed someone money."

"Do you think that's what happened this time?" Bordou asked innocently.

"Oh, no." She smiled cleverly. "I heard that two guys dragged him off on Monday night. I talked to our night guard. He showed you the video, didn't he?"

"Yes, we saw the video. Did you watch it too?" Bordou asked. When Faux nodded, he probed further. "Do you know who the men were?"

"No, I don't," she responded. "They aren't anyone who works here or who's a gym member. I know most of them by sight."

Sanchez tried to be subtle about what they had found. "Well, Miss Faux, a female reporter was killed here the same night Nick was kidnapped—or at least escorted away from the gym. Did you know her or know what she and Nick might have talked about?"

"The woman? No. I don't know anything about her."

"Do you know about the extra cameras that are here in the gym? The ones Nick used to make videos?"

"No, I don't."

Sanchez was blunt. "Well, you're in one of them, entertaining a man on a bench."

"Really?" Faux became angry, her face flushed. "What has that little pervert been doing now?" She seemed surprised and upset at the news. "I told him to cool the video shit, OK? But he must have kept it up without telling me. I told him I'd report him if he did it anymore."

"So you knew about the cameras? How'd that happen?" Bordou asked, his face tight and doubtful.

"Look, at one time, we had the idea to video people doing their exercises as a way to improve their performance and style. Some people want to look good while working out, and some just want to make sure they have the right form. We had a few weight lifters who wanted a way to document their best lifts— that sort of thing. At first, we just moved a tripod around to set up the scene or the piece of equipment they would use. Then Nick decided that we needed a couple of cameras in the walls for more of an overview. He began to record some of the ladies without their consent, so I shut him down."

"How about you and this guy?" Sanchez asked.

"Look, Detective." Faux sounded embarrassed and exasperated. "Nick and I dated for a while, and we made a few videos of us together in his office. It was for fun. The sex was good, and it seemed exciting to record it, OK? Both of us have had clients who came on to us, and sometimes it led to another type of relationship." She stopped and looked angry. "And yeah, I've made it with a client or two in the gym after hours. One guy thought it would be kinky to do it on the vault one night, so we locked the doors, and, well . . . But I never recorded that kind of thing."

"But Nick did?"

"Yeah, I guess . . . Anyway, if he shot me with someone, I want that video back. I didn't make it voluntarily and don't want my client to know it even exists."

Sanchez wasn't sure she fully believed the woman, but some of her emotions seemed real. She had appeared genuinely surprised to hear there was a recording of her having sex with a client. She did not seem that surprised that Nick had secretly recorded her. She also was clearly holding information back, but Sanchez didn't know what.

"So what else does Nick do on the side? He seems to have several recordings of women."

"I'm not sure what else. Why?"

"How about prescription drugs?"

"What do you mean?"

"Steroids and painkillers."

"Oh, that kind of stuff. Well, every serious bodybuilder uses roids and painkillers of some sort. It's more common than you'd think." Faux looked at Sanchez carefully. "Why? What else?"

"Is he selling steroids to people?

"No, not that I knew." Now Faux looked distressed. Her face took on a hard edge. "Oh shit! He is, isn't he? That little bastard." She looked at Sanchez and then Bordou with steel in her eyes. "Wait till I get ahold of that moron. I'll beat some sense into him."

"Not if we can find him first." Sanchez stood up and handed Faux one of her cards. "He may have gotten in over his head. Maybe he pissed someone off in one of the gangs."

"You know, there was a guy who came in here a few months ago to see Nick. He didn't look like anyone we normally deal with here at the gym. He was Hispanic and looked real—I don't know—rough. I wonder if Nick was dealing with him. Maybe he was selling roids."

"Could you identify the man if you saw him again?" Bordou asked. "Maybe he was one of the guys that hauled Nick off on Monday night. I'll get enhanced photos from the surveillance footage to show you. You can look at the two men again. Maybe we'll get lucky."

"Sure, if it will help. Maybe the jerk owes them money. In that case, he may show up with a broken arm. I've heard stories about how gangs handle deadbeats."

"Say, I had the impression from the young woman he was seeing that he lived here in his office." Sanchez paused. "Does he have an apartment too?"

"I don't know now. He has some cabin in the mountains, but I don't know where it is. He took me there once, but we drove there at night, so I couldn't describe how to get there."

Sanchez stuck out her hand to shake with Faux. "We'll be in touch about ID'ing the men. I'm afraid your sex video is now part of the evidence for this case. I'll see if we can suppress it and keep your name out of it."

"Thanks. I've got to get ahold of that tape to see what's on it. Can I see that when you come back with the recording of the men? I'd like to know what he shot."

"OK, we'll see what we can do." Sanchez looked at Bordou to see if he had any questions. They left the gym and walked out to the parking lot.

"Do you believe any of that?" he asked.

"I'm not sure what to believe. She seemed sincere about the sex video, but I don't think she is as innocent as she pretends to be . . . You?"

"I don't know what to believe, but I'll let you show her the video. I don't want to be there when she sees it all."

"Roger that," Sanchez chuckled.

They went to their separate cars. Sanchez waved as Bordou drove off, and she started her vehicle to get the air-conditioning running. Then she dialed Alvera on her phone. "Hi, Clara. How are you doing today? Are you at work?" she asked.

"Lori, I'm just ready to begin a deposition. I'm fine, but can I call you back in an hour and a half?"

"Sure. That works. I want to catch you up on the case when you're ready, OK?"

"Yes, that would be fine."

"How about a drink after work?"

"I missed yesterday, so I'm going to run real late tonight. Maybe tomorrow. Got to run."

Alvera was as busy as usual. Sanchez was used to her friend having a haphazard schedule when she was involved with a trial. She just hoped Alvera was dealing with her loss and not just burying it with work. Sanchez had been there before.

She rested her head on the steering wheel and thought about all the things she had to do.

***

Montero was singing Lolita's praises about how she had made an important contribution to the PTSD session. "I tell you, Lori, this girl is amazing. She did a backflip right there in the middle of the therapy group circle. Everyone was impressed."

Montero, Sanchez, Lolita, and Jeff and Kathy Bordou all were sitting around the restaurant table awaiting their dinner. They were at the renowned Salvador's Grille on McDowell Road—Montero's favorite Guatemalan restaurant in Phoenix. He and Sanchez had ordered their favorite roast chicken with Salvador's special sauce while the others had ordered new dishes to try. They sat in a long booth with Lolita between Sanchez and Montero, facing the Bordous.

"It was a lot of fun, really," Lolita said warmly. "They were a nice bunch of guys, and the women too. I'm so sorry they got messed up while serving our country."

"Yeah, some of us have been luckier than others in the Middle East," Montero said. "But I served with guys that got shot up pretty bad. Our company didn't see a lot of IEDs in those days."

"If you ever go out to the VA hospital again, let me know," Lolita said. "I'll go with you."

"Well, I might take you up on that, Lo. I'll go out again on Thursday. You could come with me and meet some more of the vets that way. I'll do a general round of visitations then, but you would be very welcome."

"OK."

The food arrived, and they each began to eat hungrily. They spoke about the food and ordered more drinks. Then Montero asked how the investigation was going.

"We've made some progress," Sanchez said. "We had a surprise today." She looked at Lolita and considered what she could say in mixed company. She didn't want to upset the girl but wanted to ask her a few questions. Maybe it would be best to wait until after dinner so as not to put her on the spot.

While she was pondering this, Bordou made a slip of the tongue. "We found a big stash of drugs today in one of the lockers—the one Nick Carter had." Then he looked up and saw Lolita's face. "Oh shit, Lo. I'm sorry."

Sanchez glared at her partner. "Bordou!"

"He had drugs in his locker?" Lolita looked concerned. "He told me he only had enough for himself with some sort of prescription."

"Sorry, Lo. It was more than that. He must have been dealing to clients and gym members." Sanchez tried to lessen the surprise. "Megan Faux implied he sold some drugs on the side and that it's common on the bodybuilding scene."

"He lied to me. When we first started working together, he said he didn't believe in roids and performance-enhancing drugs." She looked really upset and angry. "I found some in his desk once and asked him about them, but he said they were left over from a client. He must have just hidden his stash from me so I wouldn't know." She stared at her plate of food.

"Are you OK?" Sanchez asked.

"Yeah. It's just you think you know someone, and then they do something stupid. It's hard to deal with, you know?"

Bordou said, "I'm sorry. I didn't think how it might affect you."

They went on with the meal, and conversation shifted to other topics. Lolita snapped back from the news about the drugs, and she was soon laughing again.

After dinner, Sanchez took Lolita home with her for the night. Once in the apartment, Sanchez brought up another topic related to the investigation. "When we were talking to Megan, she said she didn't think Nick had an apartment in town. Do you know if he did or not?" she asked.

Lolita looked up from her cell phone to answer. "He didn't have an apartment that I knew of. But what do I know? Maybe he had one but didn't want me to know about it." She looked very subdued, unlike her usual cheerful self.

Sanchez approached the next detail carefully. "She also said he had a cabin up in the hills somewhere, but she didn't know where. Do you know anything about that?"

Lolita sat up straight on the couch and looked at Sanchez. "Yeah, I do. It's up near Payson in the national forest. He said his family had owned it for a long time. It was his grandmother's place."

"Oh good. Have you been there?"

"Yeah, once. We went up for a weekend. It was old and run down, but it was in a secluded part of the forest." She seemed to have good memories of the trip and smiled. "It was right after I first started training with him. We went on hikes and had pizza and wine." She looked cautiously at Sanchez and leaned in to whisper, "That weekend was the first time we made love. It was lovely."

Sanchez watched Lolita and realized she was in love with Carter—at least to some extent. She didn't want to push the girl too much and decided she and Bordou would have to keep new information from her to avoid hurting her any more than Carter himself had done. *Where is that guy?* she thought. *Is he still alive?* She thought the gang thugs may have beaten him over bad debts. But if that was the case, he should turn up somewhere. The question was, where?

Lolita whispered again. "He took a picture of us together— you know, doing it." Then she blushed. "Even a video of us in bed. I have a copy on my phone. I've been looking at it today. I guess I miss him." Her eyes were tearing up.

Sanchez wasn't comfortable with this conversation. She kept her voice down. "He did what? He can't do that. Not with a teenager. It's called child pornography. And him sleeping with you is illegal. Don't you get that, Lo? He was taking advantage of you."

"But he loved me. I know he was older, but it was OK," she pleaded with Sanchez. "It was consensual, so that's all right, isn't it?"

"No, Lo. It's called statutory rape because he's older and you're sixteen. You know that, don't you?"

"No, I don't agree. I'm an adult." Lolita looked like she would argue with her.

Sanchez didn't want to get into a fight over the law. She sat up straight, looked around the room, then brought her eyes back to Lolita. "Hey," she blurted out in a normal voice, "could you find the cabin if we drove up there? I mean, from sight?" She felt excited. She had a fresh thought about the case. "We've looked all over for him in the rental and real estate listings but haven't found anything anywhere in the state. Maybe he went up there to hide out."

"Maybe—I think so." Lolita brightened up at the idea. "Yeah, I bet I can find it. We drove in and out a few times, so I remember the road."

"OK. Here's what we're going to do." Sanchez was very upbeat. "I'll clear my day. In the morning, we'll drive up to Payson and look for the cabin. If Nick is there, we'll solve a few aspects of this case that have been left hanging. We'll know he's OK, find out who the two men were who took him away, and find out if those guys killed Josie Vale. Or at least eliminate a few variables." She paused as Lolita seemed to brighten up. "What do you say?"

"Yes, I'm game. Let's do it. Maybe we'll find Nick." She seemed cheerful again.

Chapter 10

Wednesday morning, April 3, 2019
Camelback Mountain, Arizona

The dynamic duo of Sanchez and Lolita were on the road by 8:00 a.m. the next day. They stopped for a quick breakfast at a McDonald's on the way out of town and were sipping coffee in the Interceptor with the windows down while cruising along State Route 87, heading north toward the fabled Mogollon Rim. The rim was the southern edge of the Colorado Plateau that formed the high, rugged landscape of northern Arizona and parts of Colorado, New Mexico, and Utah. Payson was located just south of the rim at about a five-thousand-foot elevation where the desert heat was left behind and the cooler mountain air was refreshing.

Sanchez hadn't been up in that part of the state for about two years, so she was enjoying the idea of an outing that got her out of the city for the day. She had the radio turned up on a local rock station that Lolita had picked, and they were just having a little fun on a clear, warm spring morning.

"You crawled into my bed again last night. Why? There were no strange noises in the living room again, were there?"

Lolita looked chagrined as she answered, "I was just lonely, I guess. I felt really isolated on the couch—you know—in a new place and all."

"We can't sleep in the same bed, Lo. It just doesn't look

right." She looked at the girl's pensive face. "Well . . . I guess it's OK under present conditions as long as we don't tell anyone about it. OK?"

"I guess. I didn't do anything wrong." She looked miffed. "Besides, your couch doesn't have any springs. It's hard to sleep on."

"Now you're criticizing my furniture. Be careful there. I've had that couch for like ten years or something. It has emotional value."

Sanchez's cell phone rang. She wondered if it was Bordou trying to track her down about the case. He had called earlier to report some new findings on the drugs. Apparently, the ones with the Maraxx Pharma labels were counterfeit. That threw the case into another direction altogether.

The phone screen read *Teller*, meaning her boss, Captain William Teller, was calling. That usually was not a good thing since he had a way of interfering with her investigations and making extra work for her. She considered letting it go to voice mail for a moment and just cruising on her planned mission. But he would track her down somehow. It might be better to just answer the call. She picked up her phone and slid over the green button.

"Hello, Sanchez here."

"Where are you? I've been trying to get ahold of you."

"I'm on the way to Payson to look for a missing person, sir. Why? What do you need?"

"What I need is for you to turn your car around and head over to Camelback for a crime scene. We've got a DB that appears to be related to your Maraxx Pharma case. I need you on it right now."

"Wait, who's the vic this time? Why me?"

"Bordou is in court this morning, so he can't cover it, and most of the other detectives are tied up on other cases. The vic is an Elon Grosse. He's the VP of marketing over at Maraxx Pharma. He's believed to have killed himself last night. It's not clear what happened yet, but I need you down there to handle it. No missing person today. Consider this an emergency. You got it?"

Sanchez felt like she had been kicked in the gut. She had undertaken too many of these high-pressure assignments lately. She needed a break. Now this.

"OK. Text me an address. I can be there in about thirty minutes if traffic doesn't completely suck."

"Thanks, Detective. Here comes the address."

She braked hard and pulled onto the shoulder of the road. She sat there and wondered what she would do with Lolita now. She cranked the wheel hard to the left and watched for an opening to power into a U-turn.

"What was that about?" Lolita asked.

"I've got to handle another case, pronto. Hang on and tighten your seat belt, Lo. We're going Code Three."

An opening occurred in the passing traffic, and Sanchez punched the gas pedal to begin a powered turn that burned rubber and squealed the tires as the back end flashed around in a smoking one-eighty. The car fishtailed at the end of the turn as the outer rear tire slid onto the gravel shoulder of the highway. She pushed the speed up as they came out of the turn and proceeded to drive fast back toward Phoenix. She threw the switch to engage the siren and reached out the window to place her magnetic red bubble light on the roof.

The Interceptor got its name from the massive horsepower of the engine, which Sanchez had modified recently—460 horsepower. With Lolita shrieking with delight and holding on to her door for dear life, they reached a hundred miles an hour in seconds. That wouldn't last long before they got into traffic, but it felt great while it lasted.

Sanchez grinned like crazy as Lolita shouted, "Whooo! This is cool!"

It *was* really cool!

***

They arrived at the address in a very upscale neighborhood near the Phoenician Golf Club just southeast of Camelback Mountain. Sanchez asked Lolita to wait in the car as she ducked past a clot of patrol cars that nearly blocked the street. She was the first detective to reach the scene, so it was up to her to decide how they were going to handle the situation, whatever it turned out to be.

The Grosse residence was one of the older homes that had been extensively remodeled recently to add more ground-to-ceiling windows and two extra bays to the garage. It had Frank Lloyd Wright-style architecture, with long clean lines and fabulous landscaping. Much of that was dryland planting and gravel to keep the water bill under control, but some of the backyard was lush. Montero would have loved the cactus garden.

She walked up the driveway and was intercepted by an older patrolman she knew from a previous case. He was John Benjamin, a sixteen-year veteran on the force. He was called Big John because he stood six feet two and had a hearty laugh like a lumberjack. She didn't get the association with big timber, but he was a friendly and helpful guy.

"Hey, Detective Sanchez. Good morning," Benjamin said. "They roped you into this job too?"

"Yeah. Just got the call," she said. "What's the story? Were you first on site?"

"The cleaning service came in this morning before eight and found the resident—this Mr. Grosse—hanging from a beam in the living room." He chuckled. "Apparently, she freaked out and ran into the street screaming, just like in the movies. She said she didn't touch anything, and I had one of our guys take a statement right away. She's over there if you want to follow up."

"Maybe later. Can you show me what you found inside?"

"Yeah, sure. Follow me," he said. He turned up the driveway and lumbered along the concrete to the sidewalk and the front door. It was a fancy maple double door that was carved into a floral scene. Benjamin pushed open one side, and they stepped into a large entryway with a ten-foot-high ceiling. They stopped to don rubber gloves and plastic booties to avoid contaminating the crime scene.

To the right, there was a staircase leading upward. A great room lay to their left. It was nearly twenty feet high and had a pitched roof with exposed oak ceiling beams that were polished to a high gloss. A river rock fireplace dominated the back wall, and the front was all glass looking out onto the street and a fabulous view to the south. Near the back wall, there was a single crossbeam that spanned the room about four feet from the fireplace, apparently a structural necessity that the architect had added to stabilize the walls. *Well, you see odd things in remodels*, she thought. There were several hunting trophies arrayed along the far wall—elk and deer that must have been the owner's kills.

The room was sunny and cheerful except for the body hanging by its neck from the middle of the crossbeam. A man of middle age hung on a rope like another trophy, unmoving, his eyes bugged out in death. He did not have the benefit of a taxidermist to close his mouth and spruce up his looks. He hung there with his mouth twisted to one side and dried blood on his chin and neck. He wore normal business attire—blue short-sleeve shirt, dark slacks, and a loosened tie—except he didn't have any shoes on. His feet, which were clad in black Gold Toe socks, were dangling free.

"We waited for you to come before cutting him down. He was obviously dead, so we had no need to check a pulse," Benjamin said. "I wanted you to see the setup for yourself. He had the rope tied off to this bracket on the fireplace and looped over the beam from there."

Sanchez walked cautiously around the acrid wet spot on the rug directly under him and examined the bracket and rope. "This looks like that kind of polypropylene rope they use for boat tie-ups." She poked at the knot with her BIC pen. "The knot is sort of weird. I think it's a trucker's hitch. The rope looks used, so it wasn't just purchased for a suicide."

"Is that what it is? Never seen one before." He leaned in to examine the knot more carefully.

"Truckers use it to tie down their loads. You can tighten it easily by pulling on the end—see?"

"Yeah, I guess. What had me confused is this: How'd he get in position to hang himself?" Benjamin asked. "He would have to climb up the stonework, then let go. He had to swing out to hang there. See, his feet are only about two feet off the floor."

"Right, and there's no chair nearby that he could have stood on beforehand."

They stepped away from the body and scanned the room. "Where are his shoes?" Sanchez asked. "Why'd he take them off?"

"Yeah, good question," he said. "Hey, it looks like the CSIs are here. You want them to cut him down yet?" He pointed out the front window where a few people were gathered on the street. "People can look in and see him."

"Oh shit," she said. "Let's get photos here and see if we can tape off that viewpoint for now, John. I don't want a bunch of looky-loos out there. When CSI says they're ready, we'll cut him down." She stared at the dead man. "And I want to see that rope up close—and the knot. It just seems out of character for a suicide."

Benjamin started for the door, then stopped and said, "Oh yeah. His name is Elon Grosse. According to a neighbor, he works at Maraxx Pharma."

Sanchez walked back to look at the dead man again. He looked vaguely familiar, like she had seen him in a photo. She pulled out her cell phone and scrolled down to an email that Bordou had sent her the day before. He had attached still photos of the faces of clients who were caught on video at the gym. She opened the attachments and was surprised. The man in one photo looked like the man hanging from the beam. He was the guy that Lolita couldn't quite identify yesterday. So it had been Elon Grosse doing the nasty with Megan Faux.

Sanchez walked around carefully, looking for any kind of note Grosse might have left that might explain why he had killed himself. She also looked for his shoes. Nada.

She walked to the door and talked to the lead CSI woman and let them get started, pointing out information she especially needed. Once they had gotten underway, she walked out the door and over to her car to see how Lolita was doing. She found the girl asleep in the car with the sun on her face. She looked completely innocent. She decided not to wake her up yet.

Sanchez walked back to the crime scene and had Benjamin

tape off the area because she could not tell yet if this was a suicide or a suspicious death. She hoped to learn more as soon as the body was lowered to the floor.

She searched the rest of the home. It was something of a mess. The kitchen was cluttered with unwashed dishes. The trash can was full of signs of the man's eating habits, like Chinese takeout boxes and fast-food wrappers. Grosse ate out a lot, or at least brought food home often.

Sanchez prowled into other rooms to see what else she could learn about the man. In his upstairs office, she found several receipts thrown in the trash can. She dug in them to see what he was buying lately. There were dining receipts and parking stubs from the Wild Horse Pass Hotel & Casino in Chandler and the Golden Coast Casino out by Globe. The guy must have been a regular gambler. She wondered how much he owed in gambling debts. If he went gaming often, then he may have been a sharp cookie looking for entertainment, or he had been compulsive, and that usually meant he had lost big-time.

He had photos of a large sailboat hanging on the wall of the office. In fact, he had several smaller photos scattered about, each of a different scene—the boat tied up in a marina, one of him by the wheel with a blonde, another with the same woman sitting on a chair on deck, one on the open sea, and one with him in the cabin. So he had been a sailor, and he had loved the sea.

She made a preliminary search of the bedroom. It was obvious that he had lived alone—no women's clothing in the house at all. The bed was unmade, and the sheets looked like they were ready for a wash. And yet the house was not a complete trash pit. He did have a cleaning service after all.

She wondered what the story was here. Was he divorced? That might explain the large house and old photos of a woman with the boat. But he had no one living in. And he gambled.

Sanchez decided to talk to the cleaning lady and the neighbor right away. She hurried outside and caught the neighbor just as she began to retreat to her home next door. Her name was Mary Connelly.

"Mary, thank you for offering to help," Sanchez asked. "We need to find out if Mr. Grosse lived alone or had next of kin we could contact. Do you know about that? Was he married at one time? Kids?"

"Oh my. I'm so upset." She seemed distraught but also like she wanted to talk. "Poor Elon lived alone. Well, ever since his wife, Elizabeth, left three years ago." She rolled her eyes. "They got divorced because of his gambling debts. He was one of those compulsive people who liked to take a chance on cards. I never understood exactly what happened, but he was really down in the dumps after she left him."

"I see. Did she keep his last name, or does she now use her maiden name? And were there any kids we should contact? Any siblings?"

"Oh now, let's see." Connelly screwed up her face and looked like she was trying to recall ancient memories. "I think he had a brother in the Chicago area. That's where they lived before moving here for his job. They didn't have kids. That was a point of disagreement, apparently. She wanted to have kids, and he just worked and gambled all the time. They were a nice couple at first, but then things seemed to just change."

"Did he have any friends that you can remember? Anyone else I should contact?"

"No, I can't think of anyone else. But he did have visitors some nights. I don't know if I would call them friends, though. They would shout sometimes. I remember one time it was about money. They had to have some money right then, or they would—well, I couldn't hear the rest. I know that one time I heard some glass breaking during one of the arguments."

"How about last night? Did you hear anything?"

"No, nothing unusual. Once I go to sleep, I don't hear anything. I have one of those CPAP machines, and I can't hear anything once I turn that thing on."

"OK, one last question," Sanchez said. "Did he travel a lot? I heard that he was a salesman. Did he go out of town very often?"

"Not anymore," Connelly said. "He used to travel a lot, but he told me last year that he did most of his meetings over the phone now. One of those GoToMeeting things—like that. And he did stay home a lot more than he used to."

"Well, here's my card if you think of anything else, OK?" Sanchez began to walk away.

"Wait," Connelly said. "I can't believe he would commit suicide. He told me last week he was finally able to replace his sailboat. Why kill himself if he had that coming?"

Sanchez turned around and met Connelly's gaze. "Good question, Mary." She shrugged her shoulders and walked away toward the Interceptor.

She only got as far as the crime scene before Benjamin flagged her down. "The CSIs are ready to take the body down now. They want you to be there."

She followed him up the sidewalk and inside the house. As soon as she arrived, the lead scientist signaled for one of his people to cut the rope at the fireplace. Two other men dressed in white Tyvek suits held the dead man as the first one lowered the body on the rope. They placed the DB onto a plastic sheet on the floor and began inspecting it, photographically documenting every detail. The lead scientist inspected the throat carefully and then signaled for Sanchez to come over to examine the rope and see how it had cut into the man's neck tissue.

"The rope cut really deep, so he wouldn't have been able to breathe, and I think it would have cut off circulation the way it dug into his skin and deeper tissue." He moved the rope somewhat to get a better view of the knot that had been used to tie the rope around his neck. "This is just a simple slipknot, so when he placed weight on the rope, it cinched up tighter and tighter."

"So it's a common knot? Anyone could tie the rope this way?" she asked.

"Yes, I guess so. Nothing fancy here."

"OK, thanks for your help. I think I'll list this as a suspicious death until we have more information to work with. We'll need an autopsy."

"OK, Sanchez. I'll pass that on to the coroner."

Sanchez took one last look around and then pointed out a few things to the CSI crew that she wanted documented. Then she left the house. It was still only 10:30 a.m.

As she slowly strolled down the sidewalk, she thought to herself, *This doesn't seem like a suicide to me.* Elon Grosse was a sailor. If he had hanged himself, he would have used different knots. It was that simple. And they still had not found his shoes. And there was no note so far. But that could have been left on his phone, if they could find it. There were a number of things here that didn't seem right.

The other aspect of this death was that it was inexplicably tied together with the crime scene at the Maraxx Pharma gym. If Elon Grosse was the man in the video, then he had been involved in illicit sex. He had money troubles and had some irritable associates that had come to his house to harass him about money he owed. But what did he have to do with gangs and drugs? That seemed to be the driving factor in the murder at the gym.

She decided to call the company's offices and ask some preliminary questions. She asked Google to get her the phone number and dialed it. She got the receptionist and asked to speak to someone in personnel. When she was put through, she immediately asked to speak to a supervisor. As she stood there in the hot sun, she thought of what she would say. Finally, an officious-sounding woman responded.

"Hello, this is Janice Williamson. How may I help you?"

The imperious voice was an immediate turnoff, but Sanchez kept her attitude in check. "This is Detective Lori Sanchez with the Phoenix Police Department. We're investigating the death of Mr. Elon Grosse and need to ask a few questions."

"Oh . . ." The woman seemed completely caught off guard. "Mr. Grosse is dead? Oh my God . . . I'm not sure I can help you. What do you need to know?"

"First of all, I need to confirm that he does in fact work for Maraxx Pharma and find out his title there."

"Oh yes. He was one of our vice presidents—vice president of government sales. He was with the company for years."

"What exactly does the title mean? Did he only sell to certain types of agencies or customers?"

"Yes, that's it. He did the big corporate sales to agencies like the army, navy, GSA, VA—all of those places."

"Wait, did you say the VA, as in Veterans Affairs?"

"Yes, they are one of our biggest clients. Why?"

"Do you sell pharmaceuticals to the VA hospital here in Phoenix too?"

"Yes. As a matter of fact, we do," Williamson said. "Is that important?"

"Maybe. And what kind of drugs does Maraxx Pharma sell to those agencies?"

"Oh, I think everything—opioids, insulin, IV fluids, antibiotics."

"I see," Sanchez said. "I need to come by and talk to someone in charge about his recent activities and clients. Would that be possible tomorrow morning? Who would be the best person to talk to about Mr. Grosse's role at the company?"

"Well, my boss is Jerold Idiani. He's personnel manager here at Maraxx. I can make an appointment with him for you if you like. He can answer most of your questions, I think."

Sanchez replied yes and waited while Williamson arranged a meeting time for the morning. They settled on 9:30 a.m. at the Maraxx Pharma offices. She made a few more calls, including one to Captain Teller to give him a progress report and to relay her suspicions about the death. He said the facts were too thin to go on, but let her proceed as she thought best. Finally, with all her phone calls complete, she returned to her car and looked around for Lolita.

Lolita was sitting on the grass of a neighbor's lawn. Sanchez sat down next to the girl and sighed.

"Sorry it took so long, but I had to make assignments."

"Yeah, it's OK. I'm just let down that we can't go searching for Nick today." She seemed disappointed.

Sanchez reflected on the situation. She had blocked out the whole day to drive to Payson and was disappointed herself that they had aborted the trip. She didn't have another block of time free this week to make it either because of other commitments.

"You know what, Lo?" she said. "We still have time to drive

up there and have lots of daylight to find the place." She eyed Lolita to see if she was interested. "What do you say?"

Lolita smiled right away and asked, "Can we go Code Three?"

They both laughed and climbed into the Interceptor. Sanchez turned their rocket ship around to head out of town. Once on the open road, she opened the throttle up, and they cruised along merrily.

She was enjoying the ride but couldn't help thinking about this new case and how it must tie into the murder at the gym and Carter's kidnapping. They were dealing with violent men here— men who would do anything, kill anyone to get what they wanted. And Lolita and Alvera were witnesses and therefore potential targets. She made up her mind then and there that she had to protect these two women from harm. She would have to solve these related cases quickly. It was now her challenge to solve the murders and protect the innocent.

Chapter 11

Sanchez and Lolita made good time cruising through the Tonto National Forest on their way to Payson, admiring the scenic landscape. They had a pleasant conversation about a recent camping trip Lolita had made last fall with her dad up in these woods.

Sanchez had to inform Alvera about the latest developmments in the case so she wouldn't worry. Alvera had been keeping a low profile since that night and working from home as much as possible. Today, she had asked one of the other attorneys to handle a small matter that required a court appearance and that had gone smoothly. As far as Sanchez knew, Alvera had not told anyone about her meeting in the dead of night. Sanchez and Bordou had managed to keep Alvera's name out of the records by labeling her a confidential witness, but that wouldn't hold up if someone really wanted to know who the witness was or if the case went to trial.

Sanchez called Bordou to ask what was new on the gym case. He relayed information that had been gathered at the crime scene. The DNA results for the semen collected from Vale would not be analyzed for at least a week due to the workload at the state lab. They did have a usable fingerprint match at the scene. It had been taken from the apparatus that Vale had been tied down to—the vault.

"The print matched a guy named Devon Jones," Bordou said. "He's in the system because he has a history of drug-related charges in downtown Phoenix. He's a member of the Southside Crips. He's originally from LA but has graced this city with his presence for about three years."

"A model citizen, no doubt." Sanchez was not as familiar with the Southside Crips organization in Phoenix as she was with the Westside Gang, with whom she had dealt often in the past. "We'll have to check him out and figure out why he's involved with the gym. If he was following Vale, that may be the tie."

"We're still working through the videos. I had to get some help from vice to scan the files. It may take a while to wrap that up." Bordou sounded a little sluggish over the phone.

"Hey, Jeff, did you get any sleep yet since this all got going?" she asked. "You sound less chipper than usual."

"I got some, but there's just a lot to process." He tried to sound more upbeat. "We're almost through the bulk of this stuff, so I'll probably take a day off once that's done. But I have three other cases to work too. Can't let them slide."

"Sounds good," she said, appreciative of the amount of time required on this sort of case. "Hey, did we get a listing of the drugs in that locker yet? I wondered if most of them were from Maraxx Pharma."

"Yeah, we got the listing. I have a hard copy here on my desk somewhere. Just a sec." She heard the sound of papers being rustled through and mild complaints about where everything had disappeared to. "OK, here it is. Yes, Maraxx Pharma and Randman Labs. Why does that matter?"

"I think that there may be a connection between this so-called suicide and the gym. The dead guy is Elon Grosse, and I think he's the guy we see on one of those videos. I need to get a better ID, but I think it's him."

"Well, that's interesting. So you and Lo are headed up to Payson to check out the cabin if you can find it?"

"Roger to that. I'll let you know what we find. Talk to you later."

Next, Sanchez called the sheriff's office in Gila County to confirm that they were going to be looking for the cabin as planned. She told the deputy she was to work with, Nando Littlehorse, that they would call him as soon as they figured out where the cabin was. He would then join them to investigate the property and try to find Carter.

They arrived in Payson at 12:30 p.m. and stopped for a quick lunch at the Beeline Cafe right on the main road through town. Lolita was sure that Carter's place was east of there because she remembered the road heading that way, Highway 260.

They drove a few miles and then passed through the cluster of buildings known as Kohl's Ranch. They backtracked when Lolita didn't recognize the road farther east. They exited at Kohl's Ranch and tried the road leading north from there, but she didn't think it was that way either. When they reversed course and drove south on a gravel road, she was sure they were getting close.

They followed the road southeast along a creek, passing several turnoffs that looked like rustic private drives. Lolita had no idea which one led to Carter's cabin because they all looked very similar. They had no choice but to try each one in turn and see where it led.

After an hour of driving up dirt roads that were little more than trails, they hit pay dirt. They drove a half mile into the forest until they reached a small clearing with a dark cabin in it. The front of the cabin was log faced, but the other walls looked newer with standard siding. It had a narrow front porch with a dilapidated railing, and the whole affair was covered with brown, weather-beaten tar and gravel shingles. They stopped as soon as they entered the clearing, but the dirt road skirted around to the right.

"I don't see any cars here," Sanchez said. "Is there another way in or out from here?"

"I don't think so, except trails. This is the only way we drove in," Lolita said.

"And you're sure this is the right cabin?"

"Yeah, but if I could get closer, it would help. There was one of those carved bear statues by the parking area that said, 'Go away.' It made me laugh."

"OK," Sanchez said. "Let me drive up just a little more for a better look. I don't want to spook anyone hiding out in there."

She carefully and quietly inched the car forward to get a better angle on the right side of the cabin. She drove halfway around the clearing, and then they could see a little wooden bear standing next to the cabin. Through her binoculars, Sanchez could see the sign saying to go away. They had the right cabin.

"Let's sit here, and I'll tell the deputy that we've found the right cabin," she said.

With that, Sanchez called Littlehorse. He said he would be there in half an hour, but that she should drive out to the gravel road so he could identify the turnoff. Otherwise, he said, the driveways all looked the same.

Just as Sanchez ended the call, a black Nissan SUV appeared from the rear of the cabin. It came roaring down the dirt driveway with two men in the front seat. They drove straight toward the Interceptor as if they were going to ram it, dust billowing in their wake. The passenger stuck his hand out the window holding a black weapon. It was a MAC-10, and he began to shoot at them as the SUV closed on them. Bullets flew all around and one smacked the fender of the Interceptor.

"Get on the floor and stay there!" Sanchez shouted as she threw the car into reverse.

She punched the gas, and they shot backward along the dirt driveway toward the edge of the meadow. Another bullet hit the car and ricocheted off the windshield.

Sanchez banged along the undulating road until they reached the point where the driveway entered the meadow. She drove the car backward into the edge of the trees on the outside of the turn and stood on the brakes to stop the vehicle before it hit a pine tree. A cloud of dust swirled around them as she dove out of the car on her side.

"Stay down, Lo! I got this."

The driver of the Nissan was apparently blinded by the cloud of dust the Interceptor had churned up because he swung too tight a turn and ran up and over an old tree stump on the inside of the turn. The SUV came to a grinding halt and began to throw a stream of dirt out behind it as the driver gunned the engine in an attempt to drive off the stump. The passenger realized they were stuck right by Sanchez's car and opened fire again, shooting at Sanchez rather than the car. The driver rammed the Nissan into reverse and then tried several times to free the vehicle from the stump.

Sanchez rolled away from the Interceptor and pulled out her Glock to return fire. She had no real cover except for the grass and a small rock, but she took up a prone position and laid into the SUV with a few rounds. She knocked the glass out of the smoky rear window on the right side and sent a slug through the passenger-side door. It must have hit the shooter because he shouted in pain and held fire for a few seconds.

The Nissan's driver apparently locked into four-wheel drive and was able to get his other tires to dig forward. The SUV suddenly lurched off the stump and roared away toward the gravel road.

Sanchez leaped up and fired three more rounds through the back window as the Nissan sped away. She let them go and tried to make out the license plate number, but the dust precluded that opportunity. She holstered her weapon and hurried over to the Interceptor's passenger side, where she snatched open Lolita's door. The girl already was crawling up from the floor and appeared unscathed.

"Holy shit!" Lolita said. "Is it over yet? Can I come out?"

"Yeah, it's done." Sanchez pulled her from the car. "They got away. You OK? No injuries?"

"No. I'm fine." Lolita looked down the road at the dissipating cloud of dust. "Aren't we going to chase them? They're getting away."

"No, I don't think we can. The car is hung up on a log. We're stuck here until we get help."

Sanchez and Lolita both crouched down to look at the undercarriage of the car. Sure enough, a log was jammed against the rear axle, lofting one wheel off the ground. Sanchez got in the car and tried to move it, but one rear wheel spun freely. She radioed Littlehorse that they had encountered unfriendly people at the cabin and warned him they had turned right once they had reached the gravel road.

The two women took their water bottles and walked out to the gravel road to flag Littlehorse down when he arrived. It was pleasant sitting in the shade on a sunny afternoon near the Rim after a near-death experience.

Littlehorse arrived after forty-five minutes, and Sanchez directed him back to the cabin. This time they quietly drove right up to the cabin in his vehicle. They verified that no cars were present and that the cabin seemed uninhabited. As a precaution, Sanchez asked Lolita to remain in Littlehorse's squad car until they were sure it was safe.

"But if Nick is here, it *will* be safe. And he knows me, so he won't do anything weird," Lolita pleaded.

"Well, I'm just being cautious, so stay put, OK?" She gave Lolita the eye that she meant it. She watched Littlehorse as he carefully approached the cabin. He was a tall, dark-skinned man with short black hair cut in a variation of a crew cut. He was quiet and had intense dark eyes set in a long, bony face. He looked to her like a hunter stalking prey.

"I don't think anyone is here," Littlehorse said.

He walked first with Sanchez behind him. Both of them had their hands ready to draw weapons if needed, but there appeared to be no threat. He passed the little bear and put one foot on the first step. Then he stopped and sniffed the air.

"Better hold up right there, Sanchez. I smell something odd. Let me check it out." He looked back at her, and she nodded. "It's something putrid. Could be a dead animal inside. Maybe a live one too."

He tiptoed across the porch to the door and sniffed some more. He made a face as if he had smelled something disgusting. He was about to knock on the door but then stopped and bent down to peer through the window next to it. He squinted as he looked inside and then turned toward Sanchez. He motioned her to carefully come forward.

When she got close, he said, "Pull out your Maglite, and look through the window. Let me know what you see. I think we've got a problem."

Sanchez bent down and shined her light inside. It took a moment to figure out the layout of the cabin. A table just inside the window limited her view, but she could see that the door led into a large room with a fireplace on the far wall. There was a wooden chair in the middle of the room facing away from her. It looked like something was on the chair. There were other chairs scattered about the room and no movement inside, so it seemed unoccupied.

She got a whiff of a strong odor, an odor she had smelled before. She pulled away from the window in surprise. Death. It was the smell of a dead animal all right.

"There's something weird about this, Deputy. There's something dead in there, and it smells like another crime scene I worked. We may have a dead body."

Littlehorse nodded his head. "I think so too. Let me borrow your light a minute." He reached for her flashlight and tried to get a good look at the back side of the door. Then he backed away from the door. "Get back," he said.

He led her off the porch and around the side of the cabin. Lolita started to open the car door, but Sanchez pointed for her to stay inside.

The deputy walked quickly around the back to look for other windows. He found one in the rear of the cabin and shined the light inside. The putrid smell they had noticed at the front of the cabin was much stronger here.

"OK," he said. "I got a weird vibe off the front door. I think we should enter back here." He kept shining the light around the room and stopped on the chair in the middle. "Some people up here booby-trap their places against trespassers. I think I see wires on that front door. Here, take a look."

He handed the light back to Sanchez. "Really?" she said as she looked through the window.

"Pot growers or survivalists do that kind of thing. Someone with something to steal. They don't want people nosing around their stuff."

He took out his handgun and used the butt of the revolver to break out the glass from the window. He reached inside to unlatch the frame and open the window. Then he stuck his head inside to look around and shouted, "Police! We're coming in." To Sanchez, he said, "Hold on a minute while I check this out."

He bent down and crawled through the window. After thirty seconds or so, he called out, "Come on in."

Sanchez crawled through the window and was immediately overcome by the reek of a dead body. She nearly gagged at the smell and could easily have retched right there if she hadn't been prepared. Then she saw the object of their investigation strapped to the chair in the middle of the room, with Littlehorse standing next to the chair.

Nick Carter! She couldn't tell for sure it was him due to the state of the face and body, but she assumed it was. He had apparently been tied up in the chair and beaten to death. They dared not approach too closely because of the pool of dried blood and body fluids surrounding the chair.

She moved closer and saw that Carter's face was largely missing. After beating him to get him to talk, his assailants had shot him in such a way that much of his face was blown off and lay scattered across the floor of the cabin. In short, there was blood everywhere.

"Now look at this," Littlehorse said. He pointed to the front door, which had a wire running from it to the trigger on a shotgun that had been tied off to a separate chair. It was rigged so that when someone entered the cabin, the wire would pull the trigger and shoot whomever was in the doorway. He unfastened the wire from the shotgun and turned the chair to point the gun at the opposite wall. "I don't want to touch the gun until forensics has a look at it. The perps must have untied it and then set it up again when they left. They might have left fingerprints."

Sanchez inspected the shotgun setup because she had never seen one like it before. Then she moved to the body and quickly looked it over. She surveyed the room and saw that whoever had been there had torn the place apart looking for something, probably the reason they had tortured Carter. Then she followed Littlehorse out the front door onto the porch for some fresh air. They both stood there breathing deeply to purge their lungs of the stench.

"I'm glad I had you here today, Deputy," she said. "If we'd arrived ten minutes later and not run into those guys, I would have walked right into that shotgun. Thanks, man."

"We have different types of outlaws up here on the Rim than you're used to in the city. Some of them are just strange in their outlook on life."

Lolita ran up onto the porch and was about to step inside when Sanchez intercepted her and threw her arms around her. "You can't go in there, Lo. You don't want to even look inside. Nick is dead."

Lolita screamed and tried to break free from her bear hug.

"No! No! He can't be dead. Not Nicky."

Sanchez fought to keep the teenager from struggling. "No, Lo. It's better not to see. It's pretty bad, and you don't want to remember him like that."

She muscled Lolita off the porch with some help from Littlehorse. She kept her in a bear hug until Lolita stopped fighting and then held on to her in sympathy. The girl thought she loved this guy. It was bad enough that he was gone, but she needed to keep her memories untainted by this tragedy.

Littlehorse called in the murder, which he dubbed "a suspicious death" for Lolita's benefit. Soon, three more deputies arrived, and they taped off the cabin and its surroundings. Gila County had a small forensics team that got to work right away.

Sanchez deposited Lolita in the car, by now a sobbing mess of a young woman, and then advised Littlehorse what would be of interest to her investigation. She walked over to the Interceptor and talked to Lolita for a half hour, mostly holding her while she cried and let out her anxiety and fear. She told her that everything would be all right, mostly listening to her talk about how much she had loved Carter. Sanchez couldn't really say anything negative about the guy. He had been into dangerous things and now he was dead. But in Lolita's mind he was her lover and friend. She couldn't tear that down while the girl was in such pain.

When the crying stopped, Sanchez let Lolita go and stepped away. Then she began making a series of phone calls to people who would be interested in their findings. It looked like it would be another long night.

***

Sanchez did what she could to help get the investigation going into Carter's death. It was Littlehorse's crime scene, so she only had a marginal role. She agreed to help in any way and to provide any resources that might be helpful to Gila County. The investigators would keep in touch daily as the work continued.

A sheriff's deputy with a pickup truck attached a heavy chain to the Interceptor's tow point and yanked the car off the log that was jammed against the rear axle. With that, she departed Payson at 5:15 p.m. and drove back to Phoenix.

Lolita had progressed from upset to morose to depleted. She had run out of tears for Carter and settled into silence on the long drive home. Sanchez made a few more phone calls as they drove, but otherwise they didn't say much. Sanchez didn't want to tell the girl that he was no angel. She knew that, of course, but there was no point going there.

They stopped for pizza at the local Al Forno and tried to cheer each other up. Two glasses of wine improved Sanchez's spirits, but they didn't lift Lolita's. They reached Sanchez's apartment at 9:35 p.m. and crashed for the night.

After a few minutes on the couch, Lolita crawled into Sanchez's bed, sobbing quietly. They both fell asleep with Lolita's head on Sanchez's shoulder.

Chapter 12

Thursday morning, April 4, 2019

Phoenix, Arizona

The next morning, Sanchez dropped Lolita off at Montero's house. He and the girl were going to drive out to the VA hospital for the morning to visit with veterans again. After lunch, Montero would drop her off at her home, where her father was to arrive at about 2:00 p.m. The girl was looking forward to seeing her dad after all that had happened this week.

Sanchez had a meeting at 9:30 a.m. with the personnel manager at Maraxx Pharma to discuss Elon Grosse's work and death. She wasn't exactly clear as to what she might learn from Jerold Idiani, but she hoped he could tell her much about Grosse's activities within the corporation.

When she arrived and was kept waiting for the frustrating fifteen minutes needed for Idiani to demonstrate his importance, Sanchez entered his office ready to unload on someone, preferably him. She sat in the offered chair just as he lifted his telephone receiver from its cradle. She glared at him, and he lowered the receiver to its resting place.

"Oh, good morning, Detective Sanchez. I was just about to order us some coffee. Would you like a latte?" He smiled in a genuine manner, and Sanchez bit her tongue.

"Yes, that would be nice," she said. "I haven't had my quota of caffeine yet today. Thank you."

He made a short call to his secretary for the coffee service and settled into his plush leather Sealy executive chair. His chair may have cost more than Sanchez's car, and she was aware of it.

"As you have heard by now, Elon Grosse is dead," she said calmly. "It appears to be a suicide. I wondered if you could tell me about his work and anything that may help with the case?"

"I supposed that you would want to know about his recent work, so I had Miss Williamson prepare a summary of his sales load and recent schedule of calls. Normally, there would be a travel schedule too, but lately, he had done most of his client calls remotely. He didn't travel on business at all for the last month or so." He handed her a sheaf of papers that were neatly stapled together.

The coffee arrived, and Sanchez lost focus for a few seconds while savoring the taste of the latte. It may have been the best cup of joe she had ever tasted.

"Oh, thank you . . . Is that normal for him to not travel?"

"More and more of our business is done that way by phone or one of the meeting software apps. It's more cost-effective, given the amount of time one can spend in airports these days. I found that when I was doing sales management, I would travel but still did half my communications by phone from the airport concourse waiting for my next flight. It's a lot easier now if we do it over the computer because we can share files and images so easily. It's almost like sitting across the desk from your client once you get used to it."

"OK. I guess that makes sense." She looked at her notes. "Do you know of any reason why Mr. Grosse might have taken his own life? Was he under greater pressure than usual here at work?"

"No, not really." He seemed to search his memory for clues. "He did have one of the easier clients to deal with.

Government contracts usually last a few years, so he wouldn't have been marketing them hard until the next contract came due. But I seem to recall hearing that one of his clients was unhappy about our handling of their work. He was working hard to deal with those issues."

"What kind of issues?"

"I think they were unhappy with our product's quality control. I would have to look into it for you. That could put a huge amount of pressure on a contract manager because so much money is on the line."

"What does that mean? I guess I don't know how your business works." She wasn't sure she understood what exactly a quality-control issue would be. "Can you explain it to me in layman's terms?"

"I can try, but let me call someone else in who actually worked with Elon on the problem. She can explain it better than I," Idiani said as he lifted the receiver on his phone again. He tapped in a number and spoke briefly to someone. Then he returned his attention to Sanchez, who was in coffee nirvana.

"I asked Natasha Stillwater to stop in to see us. She is VP of Finance and has dealt with Elon on this matter. She can tell you the details, at least as far as she can without revealing too much company business." He smiled and added, "This is a very competitive business. A few cents on an item can make or break a contract, so I assume you will be discreet with any information you learn here." He raised his eyebrows and waited for Sanchez to nod in understanding.

"No problem," she said. "We deal with confidential information all the time. We just use the info that's relevant to our case."

There was a knock on the door, and a middle-aged woman

with prematurely gray hair stepped through the door. She was average in height with a decades-old hairdo, a brownish Ann Taylor plaid business suit with a crew neck jacket, and black pumps. Her face was friendly and showed the signs of a stressful job. Being the financial officer would take a brutal toll on anyone.

She stepped up to Sanchez and shook hands in a matter-of-fact way. "I'm Natasha Stillwater. You can call me Tash if you like."

Idiani smiled at her and stood up, coming around the desk to talk. "This is Detective Lori Sanchez with the police department. She's investigating Elon Grosse's death. I hoped you could answer some of her questions."

Sanchez picked up the conversation there. "Yes, Tash." She smiled at the older woman and continued. "I understand you were working with Grosse on a problem he had with a client. Could you say more about that?"

Idiani said, "I'm sorry, Detective, but I have to go to another meeting. Tash can help you with anything you need and find anyone else that may be of assistance. It was a pleasure to meet you." He shook hands with Sanchez, nodded his head at Stillwater, and walked out the door.

Stillwater said, "I'm so sorry to hear about Elon. He was a nice man. A little confused, I think, since his wife left him, but a nice sort."

"Well, that's what I'm looking for. It looked like he committed suicide, but we haven't found any note from him suggesting he might kill himself." Sanchez saw Tash's face change when she mentioned suicide. "Didn't you hear that he may have committed suicide?"

Stillwater looked uneasy. "No, I only heard that he died last night. Suicide is a shock to me." She glanced around the room. "Listen, could we not talk here? I would prefer it if we talked in the cafeteria or somewhere quiet. It would help me gather my thoughts."

"Sure, wherever you'd like." Sanchez sensed that she was uncomfortable in Idiani's office. "You lead the way."

They walked to the elevator, rode down to the first floor, and turned left down the hallway to a small cafeteria that was nearly empty at this time of day. They each took a cup of coffee and a pastry from the counter and walked outside onto a small concrete terrace where there were small tables. They had the whole terrace to themselves, and it was still cool enough to enjoy being outdoors.

"Some of the offices are recorded," Stillwater said. "I'm not sure if Mr. Idiani's is, but I thought it would be better to speak out here." She looked at Sanchez and smiled. "We have an audit going on right now, and there have been rumors that some people may be doing something they shouldn't. I can't say more, but it's made my life a real misery because the audit is focused on the bookkeeping end of the business."

"Oh, is someone skimming funds from sales?"

Stillwater raised her eyebrows and looked worried. "Partially, yes. And some product has gone missing. At least, it looks that way so far. No one seems to know what's going on, and it's making everyone nervous."

"Was Grosse involved in any of this audit?"

"Yes, in some ways. But not in the same way." She struggled to find a way to say more without disclosing too much. "Elon had a client who said the drugs we were sending him were substandard. But his shipments were all accounted for, and the accounts balanced." She took a sip of coffee. "In his case, the pressure was to find out how that was even possible. I mean, the drugs all were shipped from our warehouse in Mesa directly to the VA with our own trucks and personnel. They came from the same batches shipped to other clients without any complaints. It doesn't make sense."

"When you say the VA, you mean the hospital here in Phoenix, right?"

"Elon was under a lot of pressure to figure out what was happening and to fix things with his contact at the VA, Jack Diller. He was furious and threatened to cancel our contract." She looked worried. "Clients can do that contractually if they can make a good case. Elon was beside himself to fix the problem. But he seemed to not be able to find out what the problem was."

"I see," Sanchez said. "Do you think things were bad enough that Grosse would kill himself? I mean, that's a huge step—suicide."

"I don't know. I thought he was happier lately than he had been for the last three years—since the divorce. It devastated him. He lost a lot in the settlement—even his boat. He really loved that boat."

"I saw pictures of it at his home. It looked nice."

"Things seemed to be looking up for him lately, though. He said he finally had his financial matters under control. He even told me last week he was going to buy a new boat in San Diego. So he must have come into some money somehow."

"I understood he was a gambler too. Is that right? Maybe he finally hit the jackpot." Sanchez wanted to get Stillwater to say more. She had the feeling that she and Grosse were more than just coworkers.

"But that's the funny thing. He had really cut back on the gambling through some self-help group. I don't think he did it much anymore."

"Maybe he inherited money? Did he have any family with money?"

"Oh no. He had a brother in Chicago, but he was just middle class like most of us. He wouldn't have much to give Elon or even loan him—two kids in college, I guess."

Sanchez made a mental note to look into Grosse's bank accounts to see where his money was coming from. Based on what Tash was saying, it did sound like the guy might have had enough troubles to consider suicide. "But did he seem like the type who might kill himself? He had a boat to look forward to, and his worst money problems appeared to be over."

"No, I just can't see him doing that. He seemed happier lately. Not despondent or suicidal in any way."

Sanchez thanked Stillwater for being so helpful and encouraged her to call if she could think of anything else that might aid the case.

She walked to her car and drove out of the Maraxx Pharma parking lot thinking that she might be onto something here, which might also address the prescription medicine troubles that Montero had mentioned about the VA hospital. She might be able to help him out by following leads from the Grosse suicide. That would let her kill two birds with one stone and therefore save her from expending lots of her own personal time on the VA situation—time she had precious little of. She smiled at the thought of paying off her quo to Montero, making good on her promises, and making him happy. It was worthy of an early lunch today, she thought, or at least an early happy hour later. But first, she had to show up at the office and placate Captain Teller, who hadn't authorized her to drive up to Payson, and especially not with a juvenile. She would catch up with Bordou while she was there.

***

Montero and Lolita had a good day at the VA hospital. They worked their way through three wards of veterans who had a variety of ailments, from automobile accidents to cancer treatments. The veterans all appreciated their visit, and many seemed especially thrilled to meet the young Lolita. She seemed to remind the older men of their grandchildren or daughters when they were younger. She even challenged one younger veteran who was recovering from a farming accident to a handstand contest. The guy had complications from a broken tibia, but he told her he could hold a handstand longer than she could. He won.

At noon, the two left in good spirits and had a simple lunch of tacos at a food truck outside the hospital. It was a pleasant day, so they sat in the warm, but not yet hot April sun.

"These guys are great to be around," Lolita said. "They seem able to handle just about anything."

"Yeah," Montero agreed. "But there's something wrong here. I asked a few of them about their meds and got a range of answers. Four said the meds don't work for them anymore. When they were first prescribed they worked fine, but lately, they just aren't effective—especially the pain meds. They said you could really tell whether you got a good pill or a bad one by the pain you have. Sometimes they take a pill and nothing happens at all—they think they're taking a sugar pill. There's a lot of dissatisfaction with the treatment they're getting."

"I heard that too," Lolita said. "One guy said he could tell which pill was good and which was bad by their appearance. He said the good pills had a shiny finish and the ones that didn't work didn't, but they come in the same packaging. It's strange."

"I'm going to look into this more, and Lori has said she

would help with it. Our veterans deserve better than this."

"I wonder if it's just happening here or in other hospitals too." She finished her meal and glanced at her cell phone. "My dad should be landing about now. Maybe we should drive home so I can be there when he arrives. It'll be great to see him again." She smiled cheerfully, having pushed Carter's tragic death down in her psyche far enough to have a normal day.

"Right," Montero said as he finished his drink. "Let's get you home, Lo. And thanks for coming out with me today. The guys really like you."

Chapter 13

Thursday evening, April 4, 2019
Phoenix, Arizona

Montero met Sanchez at the Alamo Bar for happy hour that evening. He entered and pulled up the barstool next to her, ordering a Dos Equis Ambar beer as he did so. He had already endured a long day but had given in to her suggestion that they meet and talk about the situation at the VA hospital. He wore his clerical shirt and black pants but had removed the detachable collar from the shirt so as not to broadcast that he was clergy. Sanchez was dressed in the same blue shirt and black slacks he had seen her in that morning. She was drinking a golden margarita made with Sauza Gold tequila. She said she was celebrating something.

"Are we celebrating something significant?" he asked in a joking manner. "Is that why you upped your game to a margarita?"

"Why, yes, we are celebrating. It turns out that that suicide guy we found this morning works for Maraxx Pharma and was in charge of government sales. He was in trouble with the hospital for supplying lower-grade prescription drugs. But I have no idea how or why that could happen. I'm celebrating because I have a clue. Not much to go on, but a starting point in paying off my quo to you." She smiled widely. "So cheer up. The next drink is on me."

"Well, that may be good news."

"Of course it's good news. All I need now is the motive for why a guy who had gotten out of debt recently, seemed cheerful, and had just purchased an expensive sailboat would go and commit suicide."

Her smile, he knew from previous experience, was her attempt to be ironic. "You don't think it was a suicide?" he asked.

"No, I don't." She sipped her drink and scanned the room for anyone who might be listening. "He may have had some reasons to be depressed, but I don't think he did it."

"And why is that?"

"Knots."

"Nots? Like in no?"

"Knots like in tying a rope in a knot. I don't think he tied the knots in the rope."

Montero stared at her with a blank face. "But why is that? It seems like a little thing to base such a statement on."

"Well, the knots were ordinary knots; the kind that anyone would tie if they were in a hurry." She grinned sideways at her friend. "This Grosse fellow had a sailboat for years. He must have known all about knots and which ones to use in different situations. I don't think someone with that experience would tie his hanging rope to the chimney with a trucker's hitch knot. He would use a clove hitch or a couple of loops, and the noose was just a simple slipknot."

"Why not use a slipknot?"

"There are slipknots, and there are slipknots. I just expect that he would have spent more time on tying the knots for his own death. It seems like he would have thought about it and selected the knots carefully."

"I don't buy it. Maybe he just drank too much and decided to end it all. He might have done the simplest thing under those conditions," Montero said calmly.

"I think he would have done more than the minimum. But then there are the knots that were used to tie up Nick Carter. His wrists were tied with slipknots, but he was tied into the chair with a trucker's hitch, like the perp wanted to tie him up tight with a knot that he could tighten as needed."

"I guess I don't know my knots very well," Montero said. "Show me a trucker's hitch. I think I know what you mean, but I'm not sure."

"OK," Sanchez said. She looked around for something to use to tie a knot. Then she leaned over and started to unlace her right tactical boot. "This should work."

When she had freed the bootlace, she tied a slipknot onto the railing of the bar. "See? Pretty simple." Then she tied a trucker's knot, making a slip loop on the running line first and then placing the leading end of the rope through the loop. She was able to cinch the rope by pulling down on the lead and tying it off to the rope itself. It was a knot that could be tightened as much as needed, which was why truckers used it to tie down their loads.

"OK, I know this knot. We called it a load cinch, but it does the same thing. We tied off our gear with it on the Hummers," Montero said. "It can also be used to raise or lower a load like a single-pulley lift. It lets you multiply the power you use on the load."

"Oh, I hadn't thought about that," she said. "If you used it right, you could use it to lift a man's weight off the floor and then tie the rope off."

"That makes sense too." Montero suddenly looked grim. "So

maybe Grosse didn't kill himself. How could he cinch off the line if he hanged himself?"

"So you still think I'm crazy?"

"Oh, I never thought you were crazy—maybe reaching a little, but now I see why you have doubts about suicide."

They sat there in silence for a minute and ordered another round. This time, Montero had a margarita too. Sanchez was lost in thought, but Montero broke the silence.

"I went up to the VA today with Lolita," he said. "We visited three wards and talked to the guys and women. Lo really cheers them up."

"She's quite friendly and listens well. Did you drop her off with her dad?"

"Yeah, he was there when we got to the house." Montero smiled. "He was very emotional. We talked for a few minutes, and I suggested he hire security for the next few weeks until we get this case solved. He took the advice seriously. Then I left them to catch up."

"Well, I'm glad they get along. I think she's a lonely kid some of the time."

"She really talked you up to her father. Told him how you took care of her."

"Glad to do it," she said with a sip of her margarita. She smacked her lips. "So, what did you find out at the VA? Any more about the drug problems?"

"I talked to a few guys and am going to follow up with them tomorrow. There's apparently one vet who's been spying on the staff to see if they are part of the problem. I arranged to meet him tomorrow." He looked at his watch and made a face. "Say, would you like to eat here? I need to get back soon for a call, but I'm getting hungry."

"Sure. Let's see if the food lives up to the legend I have etched in my memories."

They both laughed at the thought.

***

After dinner, Montero drove home and dealt with a matter related to his parish. He had a call from someone at the archdiocese who questioned some of his expenditures incurred while visiting the VA hospital and the state prison in Florence where he often drove to meet with prisoners who needed counseling. He explained the cost was necessary for his mission to comfort those who were incarcerated and found themselves in circumstances outside the normal operations of other parishes. He was told he had to prepare further documentation and submit receipts for a few trips to Florence. He was also advised to make fewer trips to visit the prisoners, whom he considered to be the prime population that he ministered to.

After the phone call, he felt disappointed. He poured himself a shot of tequila and walked out onto his patio. The evening temperature was quite pleasant now that the sun had set, so he settled into a lounge chair to contemplate the circumstances of the call. It was another clear message from the archdiocese that they were less supportive of his mission. He felt that they were letting him know that they might curtail his freedom to operate as he had been. They had recently suggested that they might have to transfer him to a traditional parish position that would be more helpful to their goals.

Montero knew what that meant. They were letting him know that they were displeased by the attention he had drawn to himself and the church during his recent activities. Those activities included getting involved in the plight of several dozen

Mexican refugees whom he and Sanchez had protected from attack by a local gang. Their involvement in the crisis had made the news in a big way, and that had embarrassed the church. Furthermore, he had been involved in a gun battle. Even though it had been self-defense, the church leaders felt it reflected badly on them.

Montero tasted his tequila, Sauza Hornitos Reposado, an exquisite sipping drink. He would have to repair his relations with the church and the man he reported to. Initially, the concept of a nontraditional parish had been appealing. Who knew what had gone wrong? But his superiors had told him to not get involved with the Phoenix Police Department because they felt it put the church in opposition to its traditional role. How could helping people or the police be a problem? He didn't intend to get into shooting situations. They simply happened due to circumstance. Well, they were hard to explain once or twice.

He sat there and wondered where this would all end up. In any case, he had a new mission, and that was to help the veterans deal with the latest set of problems that affected their healthcare. That was something that should remain low key and not embarrass his superiors.

He looked up at the moon and prayed for guidance.

***

Sanchez drove home from the Alamo Bar feeling pretty good about the way her case was turning out. It was complicated, but the few threads of evidence she had uncovered suggested that she was making progress. At this early phase of any case, hope of progress was always a good sign. Now she needed to put in the time to pull all the pieces together and see where they led. Then she had to figure out the holes in the case and seek a way to fill in the gaps in her knowledge. She had to accomplish that with good old-fashioned police work.

She walked through the door of her apartment and realized that she had the place to herself tonight for the first time that week. That meant she could get some work done before crashing for the night. She took her boots off and shuffled over to the air conditioner to pound on it to stop a clattering sound. The unit seemed to rebel by blowing hot air at her. She called the apartment manager's number and left another message that her place was like a sauna. She hoped he would one day do something to fix the troubled machine.

She sat down at her computer and checked emails to see what had happened since she had left the office that morning. Sure enough, there were three emails pertaining to her cases. She opened the report from the CSI team for the Grosse crime scene first.

She scanned the report with interest. It told her that the victim had an elevated level of alcohol in his system, but not enough to be considered drunk by any means. He did, however, have a high level of oxycodone commensurate with a habitual user who had chronic pain issues. The team had checked with his physician and found that he had been in a car accident two years before and had been prescribed a heavy dose of the drug for pain management. His prescription had expired a year and a half ago. Sanchez wrinkled her nose at this information. He therefore had found another source for his dependency on the drug. The question was, who was his source?

Another note entered by the CSI team was that a large bottle of oxycodone had been found in his home, consistent with his use of the drug for pain management. However, it bore a Maraxx Pharma label, but no prescription was printed on the bottle. He apparently had been self-medicating and getting his medicines directly from the company.

She read further and learned that there were some questions about the suicide. The forensics team had noted that Grosse had abrasions and contusions on his body consistent with a beating. He had several severe bruises to his ribs, head, and abdomen. In other words, he had been beaten severely before his death by hanging. Further determinations of his injuries would await the coroner's examination in a day or two.

Sanchez sat back in her chair and considered this evidence. The victim had made the effort to beat himself up before he had hanged himself in an awkward and illogical manner? Not very believable.

A thorough search of the premises had not revealed a suicide note. In addition, his shoes were not found, and no cell phone or laptop computer had been discovered. This was unusual for a man contemplating suicide. It raised the question as to where these items were and why they were not present in his home where he conducted most of his business. A search warrant had been obtained to search his office and a storage unit he had rented. No other information about his death had surfaced.

Next she moved on to an email about the break-in at Josie Vale's apartment. They had found fingerprints there, but none that were obviously from the break-in or that corresponded to the gym crime scene, probably because the thieves had worn gloves. She tried to visualize in her memory whether the men she had encountered were wearing gloves or not. She couldn't be sure, but thought that the one with the gun had worn blue goves. They had run other prints through the usual databases and found only those of the victim, plus Clara Alvera. That was a tough break.

The investigators had determined that her laptop and phone had been taken, along with some papers. Nothing really new there. The partial license plate corresponded to a stolen car that had turned up the next day in Chandler. It had been wiped down, but they had found one fingerprint on the doorsill. It had matched Devon Jones's prints.

Sanchez wrote a response to the CSI leader, thanking him for the information and mentioning that Alvera knew the victim and had been to her apartment before, so nothing surprising there. Maybe it would cut off a few questions.

The last email was from Deputy Littlehorse in Gila County. His team had been busy with their own crime scene, and he was letting her know it would be a while before he had much for her. He did confirm that the dead man was Nick Carter. They had taken prints from him and had ID'd the body as his. The initial search of the premises had not turned up anything new. They concluded that Carter had been brought to the cabin to be tortured and killed. They still had to process the rest of the evidence.

She sat back in her chair and thought about what she had to work with. The common thread in all cases was Maraxx Pharma, either because of the gym or the drugs. Gang members, one associated with the Southside Crips, apparently had followed Vale to the gym when she had met Carter. She had met with him, and the gangbangers had killed her, kidnapped him for further questioning, and he had wound up dead. So that told her that Vale had uncovered information that was worth killing for. What was it? It must have concerned drugs and the gang. But the only drugs Maraxx Pharma was involved with were prescription drugs.

Maybe Vale had found out that the gang was either stealing drugs or selling them. That would be a new area for any of the gangs to infiltrate, but they did sell oxycodone in small quantities already. If one of the gangs was getting into pharmaceuticals in a big way, then that would be something new. It also would provide plenty of motive for the gang to stop any story that Vale had been working on.

Sanchez walked over to the evidence box that she had placed on the coffee table next to the couch in the living room. She had been so busy that she hadn't dealt with the evidence inside. She had given Alvera her file back to take to the office but had not read Vale's diary yet. And Alvera's other personal items were in there for her to decide what to do with. She lifted out the small bag containing the vibrator. She could see no reason to enter the little rascal into evidence. The same was true for the rest of the personal effects. She would give them back to Alvera the next day.

The last evidence bag contained Vale's diary. Sanchez took it out of the bag wearing rubber gloves and started to leaf through it. She decided to start reading the entries from the week before Vale's death to see what she could learn.

It turned out that Vale was a very emotional person, who apparently had been enthralled with Alvera. She freely talked about what they had done and how she had felt. Some of it was embarrassing for Sanchez to read about one of her best friends, but Vale seemed to have been a very sweet woman who hadn't been afraid to express herself in her diary pages. She had written about how her research for the *Phoenix Tribune* was coming along from an emotional level but had been careful not to say much in the diary what the story was about. Sanchez assumed that she was separating her professional life and research notes from her personal record of living.

In any case, Sanchez felt awkward reading about her friend's relationship. She decided she would enlist Alvera to read the diary and have her report back anything that may pertain to the case. If the diary had no real value for the investigation, Sanchez might just enter it as evidence at a later date and let it slip through the cracks in the evidence process. She could save Alvera some embarrassment that way and still not violate rules of evidence.

She texted Alvera on her cell that they should meet the next day, asking to set a time at her home. As soon as she sent it, she realized that she probably shouldn't give the diary directly to Alvera even if she was an assistant DA. It would be better to make her a photocopy to read and comment on. That would create a paper trail that Alvera may not like, but it gave Sanchez a trackable copy.

She set about making photocopies on her HP printer. She found the process really boring and cracked open a bottle of Tecate Ambar beer to soothe her mood. She also changed into her sleeper togs and turned on the radio for some tunes. It took an hour with a couple of time-outs, but at last she had prepared the copy she needed for Alvera.

She ended the evening with a shot of Hornitos and listened to the radio. After making some adjustments to her pillow, she fell into a deep and refreshing sleep.

Chapter 14

Friday morning, April 5, 2020

Florence, Arizona

Montero had an idea that he wanted to check out. It had to do with someone he had met while ministering to prisoners down at the Arizona State Prison Complex in Florence. He had met an inmate who had been convicted for murder. Apparently, he had been considered an accomplice in a murder to cover up an embezzlement and grand larceny operation in which he had been involved. He had claimed to Montero that he was a victim of circumstance and had no hand in the killing. The state of Arizona had thought otherwise.

Montero drove east on the Florence-Coolidge Highway in his white Toyota pickup, with the window rolled down listening to music on the radio. He was more wary now of the need to document his expenses and reasons for travel to his far-flung parishioners and other clients he served. He considered downloading one of those cell phone aps that would record mileage and track expenses on his credit card. But he felt that that level of documentation was excessive. He would work out a system that wasn't so onerous.

Today, he listened to a traditional style of Mexican music called Banda, performed by a popular ranchero-style group with several brass instruments. He hummed along as he contemplated his impending visit with Hector Speaser, the murderer he had befriended to some degree. It would be an interesting morning if he could get the old man talking. That was always the trick to these types of conversations.

Speaser was a criminal mastermind when it came to counterfeiting products and the long con. He was initially convicted of wholesaling counterfeit music CDs on a large scale from a storefront in Mexicali. Later, he had begun to move fake liquors within Arizona, where he substituted the contents of some varieties of expensive tequila and whiskey. He was sent up to state prison a number of years ago for bootlegging. He had always been at the higher end of the operation and had often gone free because he had covered his tracks well, letting the people further down the food chain take the heat while he destroyed records that would tie him to any illicit dealings. The Bureau of Alcohol, Tobacco, Firearms and Explosives finally had nailed him in a sting operation five years ago for the murders his partners had carried out in relation to the cover-up. He had been serving a life sentence since that time.

Montero parked the truck in the shade of a yellow paloverde tree to keep the vehicle from burning up in the Arizona sun. He walked into the visitors' entrance and signed in as a regular, using his state-issued ID for that purpose. Shortly after, he was led into a small visitors' room where Speaser was waiting in a steel chair.

Speaser was a tall, wiry man with longish gray hair, a mustache with similar shading, and a long, narrow face. He had bright brown eyes that peeked out from behind wire-rimmed glasses and seemed out of place in his otherwise placid face. He wore an orange prisoner jumpsuit and white tennis shoes. He smiled when he saw Montero enter the room and take the chair opposite from his. A model prisoner, he did not have to be handcuffed to the table in front of them.

"Guillermo, it's good to see you. Been a long time," he said in a friendly tone. "How've you been?"

"I've been well, Hector," Montero said. "How about you? You seem thinner than the last time I was here."

"The food here is not the sort of gourmet experience I had expected, but I have few other complaints." Speaser chuckled. "What brings you to this hot and dusty corner of hell, my friend?"

Montero enjoyed the fact that Speaser usually liked to get right to business. "Well, I came to ask you for information. You're an expert on counterfeiting operations, and I think I've encountered one in Phoenix."

"What sort of product are you looking at?"

"Pharmaceuticals—oxycodone, Vicodin, other painkillers, and steroids, as far as I can tell," Montero said calmly. "I wondered if you could tell me how this sort of thing is done. You know—off the record."

"Of course off the record, but as you know, they listen to everything we say in this room, so it is not so off the record as you might like." He laughed good-naturedly. "Pills, not capsules?"

"Mostly pills," Montero said as he leaned forward and put his arms on the table. "I work at the Veterans Affairs hospital in Phoenix with injured and ill veterans. A number of them have told me recently that the effectiveness of their meds has changed. One man showed me a tablet from the new supply of oxy that he had been issued and compared it with another one from an older batch that had worked just fine. The newer pill didn't have a smooth surface like the old one did. He thought that was proof that the pill was a fake. Other men have observed similar defects in the medication."

"So they're less effective but not complete duds, huh?"

"Yeah, I guess. Some say the pills don't work at all anymore."

"OK, Guillermo, here's a general overview of the possible ways drugs can be counterfeited or remanufactured that might fit your case." He sat up, leaned forward, and pointed to the notepad Montero had brought with him. "You might want to take a note or two because it can get complicated." He nodded his head as if pulling his thoughts together.

Montero took out his pen and sat poised to write down any important information that might come from the conversation.

"You're talking about replacing or making a retail product to sell or substitute into the marketplace. First, you have to realize that pills are the easiest thing in the world to make. You can buy an automatic pill-pressing machine for a few thousand dollars on the Internet. So if you have the raw powder, you can make your own pills for a hundredth of a cent per pill. The cost is in getting your ingredients right and then packaging the product to look right, of course."

"You make it sound easy," Montero commented as he made a few notes.

"Well, the concept is easy, but the devil is in the details, as they say." Speaser snickered. He seemed to be having fun blue-skying how he would conduct such an operation. "Let's look at your options to get your pills made and on the market. One, you can steal and resell the drugs. To do that, you need documentation of the source of your drugs. People will ask for that if you aren't dealing on the black market. So you change the records of sale or create new sales documents if you want to sell the pills as legitimate products.

"One scam that people use for small quantities of drugs is to pay patients for their extra pills or their whole prescription. There are all kinds of pill scams like this, and you can find doctors who will write prescriptions for confederates for you. You pay them to go to a pliable doc and get the prescription, and then you take the script or the pills, whichever is easier. But this is all small-time stuff. It's done every day by dozens of people in a city the size of Phoenix."

Montero wanted to get down to the VA case as quickly as possible. "Suppose I wanted to operate on a larger scale and place the drugs in the retail market. It would have to be a pretty good product to slip it in unnoticed, wouldn't it?"

"For that sort of market, you need to either divert real product from a manufacturer or make a good copy with great packaging. Well, most likely." Speaser hesitated. "If I wanted to do that, I would look for someone at the factory or warehouse whom I could bribe to give me some product. That way the product is the genuine thing, and you aren't likely to raise questions about its quality."

"You mean the warehouse at the manufacturer, right?"

"Yes, or at an outfit that receives a lot of the product, or a transshipping facility such as an Amazon or Target warehouse where they store a lot of the stuff. If you take only part of each shipment, few people will notice a problem. You're talking about the VA, right? They must order tons of these drugs and have to redistribute them from a warehouse to various locations. Or you work the Big Pharma company itself."

"OK, what else could I do?" Montero asked, now very interested in the possibilities. "You said something about substituting products. How would that work?"

"If you had some of the real pills, you could sell them separately and then refill the bottles with fake pills or a lesser grade of the same pill. You could buy a cheap generic form of the drug and pass it off as the brand-name product. You can make a good profit that way. Packaging gives your fake the veneer of legitimacy." Speaser laughed. "I did that with liquor, and it worked well. I also diluted the booze and sold it same as the good stuff. They do that in India a lot. Hell, in China too. Ever take one of those tour boats and a little man stands there and sells you Jack Daniel's black label for five bucks a bottle?"

"I've seen that in Shanghai." Montero laughed.

"Well, there you go." They both chuckled at being taken at least once by some sort of scam. "And the final thing you could do is order the drug in powder form and press your own pills." Speaser smiled. "Or, even easier, you can have them pressed in quantity in China or India and have them shipped to you. Then you bottle them and label them. Voilà, you've got a brand name to sell. You can even invent your own brand if you spend some time trying to make it look legit."

"How about putting my pills in someone else's bottles? Can I make fake labels and bottles?"

"Sure, but you can buy the empty bottles very cheap online. Then you can find a lot of people on the dark web who will print up any label you want if you give them a sample to match. It's done all the time. Counterfeit labels are easy to buy."

"I'll be darned," Montero said. "I didn't think that it would be so easy."

"Well, the hard part is having the distribution channels to sell the stuff once it's produced." Speaser rubbed his chin as he thought. "You'd need someone to move the product for you unless you have those channels."

Montero suddenly felt unsure of himself. "Would any gangs be able to move that kind of product? Our situation may involve a gang."

"Gangs push coke and heroin already. Some do a few prescription drugs as well. But not at a large scale, as far as I know." Speaser's face suddenly went slack. "I'd better not say any more about it, then. If a gang is involved, I don't want to be the one to suggest what they could do." He looked at Montero and whispered, "In here, I have to be careful. You know what I mean."

"Oh right," Montero said. Then he leaned forward and whispered, "Well, I really appreciate your help with this background info. I had no idea this sort of thing goes on."

"You'd be surprised."

Speaser shook hands with Montero, and they signaled that Speaser was ready to return to his cell.

Montero visited four other inmates at the prison before he drove back to his home near Camelback Mountain. As he did, he reflected on his conversation with Speaser. He needed to share what he had heard with Sanchez and Bordou to see if any of those options made sense to them as far as the current case was concerned. Certainly this new information gave him a direction to follow up on at the VA. But he had a lot to do before he could solve anything.

***

Sanchez sat down on the plush sofa Alvera had recently added to her apartment and tried not to spill her coffee on the beautiful white designer cushions. She looked around for a place to set the coffee cup and finally lurched for the coffee table that was just too far away to reach without standing up. Normally, she would have set the cup on the new wool Fabrica carpet, but was afraid even one drop of coffee would leave an indelible mark of her carelessness. She guzzled her coffee and set the cup back in the kitchen.

"Would you like another cup of the new Bolivian blend? It's good, isn't it?" Alvera asked.

"Yeah, it's really tasty," Sanchez said. "And the couch is nice too. But aren't you worried about spilling something on it? I mean, it will show just any spill."

"I thought about that but went with white anyway. It's the new look for formal living," Alvera said brightly. "But you didn't come here to talk about my sofa, did you?"

"No, Clara," Sanchez said quietly. "I came to talk about the case. I brought you some of your more personal things." She grinned. "And a copy of Josie's diary. I want you to go through any relevant parts of it and let me know if you think it will help us with the gym murder and the apartment break-in."

Alvera looked a little sad at the mention of Vale's death and glanced down at the white wool carpet. She was silent for a few moments and then raised her gaze to meet Sanchez's. "Did you read any of it?"

"I started to—the last week of it to see if she said anything about what she was working on or about the meeting. I didn't see anything that jumped out as being useful in the case. But I did see a lot of emotion and personal information that I wasn't comfortable reading. I mean, if it's important to solving this case, I'll go through it in detail. But I felt like I was intruding on you and Josie by even looking at it. So I decided that I would ask you to look through it over the next couple of days and see if there's anything relevant. I know it will be hard on you to read her personal thoughts and feelings, but better you than me." She looked at her friend to see how she was taking this upsetting request. "If it's too painful for you, I can find someone else to do it. A professional that has no idea who you are."

"I think I can do it if I don't have to rush. It will be hard, though." Alvera began to tear up and stared at the floor again, her shoulders shaking slightly as she tried to suppress her emotions.

Sanchez slid off the sofa and sat next to her friend with an arm around her shoulders to comfort her. She felt awful having to ask for this favor. But how else could she proceed? She pulled Alvera over in a hug and felt her shake with grief.

"I don't want to hurt you, Clara. But it's a relevant document that we have to go through. Who else to do it but someone who knew her the way you did?"

"I know, Lori." Alvera raised her head to look at Sanchez's face. "You're my friend, and you know how I feel. I'll do it out of respect for Josie, my dear friend and lover." She tried to smile a little. "You're the only person I've trusted with my secret, and I appreciate you protecting me and Josie from whatever could happen—the judgment that could taint our relationship. I think you, of all my friends, are the one who understands us."

Sanchez was afraid that this was getting too emotional. She had hoped to keep it on a professional level. She tried to take control and move on.

"So anyway, I wanted to bring you up to speed on the investigation." She slid off Alvera's seat and back onto the sofa. "There are a few unresolved issues regarding Josie's apartment. We didn't find any notes about what she was working on. Do you have any ideas about that?"

Alvera sat up straight and tried to focus on the question. She was able to do that most of the time—suddenly turn very professional even if she was preoccupied by grief or other troubles.

"Well," she said, "she never went anywhere without her phone, so I assume the thugs that killed her took that at the gym along with her purse. She usually carried her laptop with her for work. She kept it in the trunk of her car so it wouldn't be stolen. That way she could sit down in a café and type. And they got her laptop. But like I said before, she didn't keep paper notes or drafts of her work more than a day or so, and then she would shred them. She kept it all on her computer."

"But that's just it. We did find her car in the parking lot, but it had been trashed." Sanchez thought of how there were still so many loose ends in the investigation. "She must have had some original documents she would keep as evidence if she found them. You'd think she would have hung on to some things for safekeeping."

Alvera's face was neutral, which Sanchez hoped signaled she was deep in thought and not about to get emotional again. She hoped her friend could deal with the grief, even though her loss was so recent.

"You know, I only cry about Josie when you're around, Lori." Alvera looked at her. "It's because I can talk about her with you and you understand. I don't fall apart like this at work. Just when I come home. That's why I try to keep busy."

"I know, Clara. Have you talked to Bordou or Montero lately? Maybe you could use a night out with friends."

"That would be nice. I can't just hang around here and feel miserable." Alvera's face changed. "Say, I do remember one time we were driving to lunch and Josie needed to make a stop at a bank in Midtown. She said she had to lock something up. She had a safe-deposit box at the Wells Fargo on South Central Avenue."

"Wait, really?" Sanchez was excited. "That's great! What a break." She pulled up an email on her phone and began thumbing through the list of inventory that CSI had logged at

Vale's apartment. "Shit, they didn't find a safe-deposit box key in the apartment." She looked up at Alvera. "She didn't carry the key with her, did she? That would seem odd to do . . . Or did she have any other places she would hide a key?"

"She had a few quirks there. She hid some things in her sock drawer inside socks. Most people don't dig into the socks themselves, I guess. We could go look for it if you want." Alvera looked as though she would like to get out of the apartment.

"OK, let's do it. But if we find it, we need to get ahold of a warrant to enter the box itself."

"I can arrange that pretty easily this afternoon," Alvera said.

They left the apartment and rode the elevator down to the garage where Sanchez had parked her car. On the drive over to the apartment, Sanchez asked, "You wouldn't know what the password for her computer was, do you? If we do find it, we'll need that."

"Sure, it's Cleo30956031. She liked Cleopatra as a historical figure—strong woman."

"What was her Internet provider?"

"She was on cox dot com, the local provider."

They drove directly to the apartment and entered the home. Alvera led the way into the bedroom and pointed to the bottom drawer of a dresser that the CSI team already had searched. Sure enough, Sanchez found the key to a bank storage box and few other small keys.

"Well, we have a key. I want to drive by the bank and make sure it's a Wells Fargo key before we ask for a search warrant," Sanchez said. "Why don't you come with me for that? Then you can work on the warrant app while I check out another angle on the computer."

"Sounds good to me." Alvera looked around the room

wistfully, and then they left and locked the door.

"This may be just the lead we need to find out who killed Josie," Sanchez said. She pulled the Interceptor out from the curb and punched the gas pedal just for fun.

Chapter 15

Friday afternoon, April 5, 2019

Phoenix, Arizona

Sanchez sipped a Coke at the Arby's on East Baseline Road near the Mountain Park Plaza at 4:30 p.m. She was meeting a guy she knew who could do things for her that no one else could. Well, maybe they could, but not quickly and clandestinely. She needed to have a problem solved rapidly. It was a computer problem, and she hadn't managed to find anyone in the department who had an idea of how to solve it. It was frustrating.

She had gone through the proper channels with her question: Can we somehow locate a laptop computer that had gone missing and communicate with it? It wasn't a difficult question, but apparently the answer was not obvious. She had asked the boys in the technical section about it, and they had referred her to the child sex crimes unit because they had reason to try to locate people whom they might lure in with a child pornography sting operation. Her conversation with them had gone nowhere because none of those guys had been able to help her. Furthermore, they had thought that using the computer link to ID someone might potentially break privacy laws. That was why they lured their targets out to some seedy hotel to catch them in the act. At the end of a long runaround, she was told to contact the FBI at Quantico, Virginia. She did so and got a voice recorder at their special investigations unit. Apparently, the FBI took their Friday afternoons off early.

She felt she had to at least try to locate Vale's laptop before whoever had stolen it had destroyed it or tampered with the data on it. She was operating on the idea that if the gang got a hold of it, they would try to read what it contained. After all, they wanted to know what the reporter had on them, right? So they would feel compelled to try to open the files. They would need the password. They would likely try a number of them and then be stymied. If they left the machine on for very long, the battery would run out of juice. If they had stolen the battery charger, they could plug it in and keep trying password combinations. Maybe they were still trying that approach, or they may have found a hacker to break in.

Sanchez had checked with the team who had searched Vale's home. No charging unit had been found there. Maybe Vale had carried it in her car along with the computer. Maybe the thieves had taken it with them and Sanchez's imagined scenario was happening as she sat sipping soda. If the computer was plugged in and turned on, maybe there was hope she could make contact with it.

She was afraid to get her hopes up, but she needed to know if the right person could do what needed to be done. She needed to hack that laptop, and she knew only one man who might be up to the task.

Mummer.

Just then, a short, slightly overweight, gnomelike man with a beard entered the restaurant, and, after checking that he was not being watched, he sauntered her way. He smelled of coffee and something akin to compost with maybe a trace of patchouli blended in. He was in his forties, wore bifocals, and worn but comfortable clothes. He sat down at the table across from her.

"Hi, Sanchez. Mom says hi too." It was part of a short ritual they performed each time they met. He smiled with tan-colored teeth beneath a gray mustache—a new look since she had seen him last. "Explain what you want to do again. I'm not sure I got it over the phone."

"Hi, Mummer. Say hi to your mom for me too. Here's the deal: Someone stole a laptop from a friend of mine, and I want to find it. Even if I can't locate the actual computer, I want to know if it's possible to remotely locate it and talk to it. Can that sort of thing be done?"

"Well, maybe," he responded in a whisper. "It would have to be turned on or in sleep mode. What kind of computer is it, and what's the op system?"

Sanchez dug in her pocket and produced a slip of paper that contained the computer brand, model, operating system, and web browser software. A second line had Vale's email address and passwords. She slid it across the table and looked to see if anyone was watching.

"Aha," he said. "Windows 10 and Edge. No problem with those. But most people just leave it in sleep mode if they have Windows 10. So the machine may be accessible if it was logged on to Wi-Fi somewhere."

"Suppose it's asleep?" she asked cautiously.

"How do you think Microsoft sends you those updates?" He acted like it was obvious. "The machine sends a signal to Microsoft looking for updates and then downloads stuff to it. But they have the access codes for that tied to the machine and the Windows registry. We may also be able to access it via email since you have the address. We have to see if it's trying to get online somewhere."

"Can you do that?"

"Maybe. I'll need some luck, but it should be possible." He grinned at her. "This will be interesting. I haven't done this before."

"Well, can you let me know how much it might be? I'm paying out of my own pocket again."

"No worries, Sanchez. You know I have reasonable rates for you."

"As usual, speed is helpful." She gave him an encouraging look. "I knew that you could do it if anybody could."

He smiled at that and stood up. "I better go and get started then." He nodded and walked out the door, checking for any interested parties as he went.

Sanchez watched him go. Her phone beeped that she had a message from Bordou: *Have papers from safe box. Will bring to HH.*

Thank God for Bordou. He had gotten the warrant with Alvera's help and entered the bank security box. Now they had something to work with. She would get a preliminary look at the docs during happy hour, the *HH* in the message.

She sat there and thought about her situation. She had planned to spend the weekend with Tom Smith when he got back in town, supposedly this evening. But he had called after lunch to say he would be spending an extra day in Boston because he had the opportunity to attend a concert there with friends from his short course. So she had an extra day to grind forward with her workload. It was too bad. She had been looking forward to being with him tonight.

She decided to go home and change before meeting her friends at Taco Guild on Osborn Road at five. It was a new meeting place they were going to try. Bordou had suggested it based on a dinner he and Kathy had eaten there. She would have to hurry to make the happy hour rush. She ducked out of the Arby's and headed west.

***

Sanchez had gotten to the restaurant early enough to sneak a look at the materials retrieved from the security box. She and Bordou sat at one side of a high-top table reading while drinking their beers. The others—Kathy, Montero, Alvera, and Sandoval, her buddy from the precinct with her new boyfriend, Carlos— were spread out over their table and the other high-top they had pulled over to form a single surface. Conversation raged around them.

"These are mostly bills of lading for shipments of different drugs that were shipped from Maraxx Pharma to different clients," Sanchez said. "This one is for a shipment to the VA hospital here in town. Several items have been circled, but I don't know why or what it means. And these are photographs of pallets of pharmaceuticals that are being loaded onto a truck at night. I don't understand what they mean either. It's too out of context for me."

"And here's one from a warehouse in Chandler to the Maraxx warehouse here in Phoenix," Bordou said. "This one involves shipments of Randman Labs drugs. Maybe they consolidated shipments at Maraxx for some reason."

"I wonder why Vale was interested in shipments of drugs."

"I don't get it either. The fact that the packing slips and photos are of Maraxx Pharma goods suggests there's a problem with their shipping control or something like that." Bordou scratched his head. "I don't know if this helps us solve our murder."

"I don't know either." She placed the documents back in the

envelope and turned toward their friends. "I guess we'll figure it out later. We must be talking shop too much. Kathy's motioning you over. Let's party while we can, shall we?"

They both turned to talk to the others. Alvera seemed to be enjoying her conversation with Sandoval and Carlos, laughing and listening to some fishing tale. Sanchez concentrated on that conversation for a while and had to admit that Carlos told some very funny stories. Soon everyone was hearing about how he had lost his new cell phone last week and it had miraculously reappeared later. She moved over next to Montero to catch his attention.

"We need to talk after dinner about Maraxx Pharma and the VA," she said.

"OK, no problem," he whispered. "But where's Tom? I thought he was going to be back by now."

"Long story, but he stayed an extra day to do things with people from his short course. He'll get in tomorrow night." She smiled at her small crowd of friends. It was good to get together like this at the end of the week. The FAC, or Friday Afternoon Club, was a sort of ritual for them lately.

They all moved off to eat dinner at one large table inside the restaurant and had a wonderful time. By ten o'clock, the gathering broke up, and everyone drove home for a good night's rest. Sanchez and Montero stayed on for one more Sol.

"I learned some interesting things today down at Florence," Montero said earnestly. "I know a man there who was in the counterfeiting business. He told me a lot about how someone could create counterfeit drugs and replace legitimate ones."

Sanchez was all ears, setting down her beer to focus on what Montero had learned. "Really? Was he into the prescription drug trade at one time?"

"No, but he assured me that the approach to counterfeiting is similar for most products on the market. However, there are many variations of the business." He took a sip of beer and smacked his lips. "He gave me some ideas of what we need to check out in order to understand what's going on at the VA."

"Such as what?"

Montero pulled a sheet of paper from his pocket. It contained the notes he had made while talking to Speaser. He scanned them briefly and then explained them to Sanchez, pointing to his notes.

"Based on what the guys tell me at the VA, someone may be substituting an illicit version of their drugs for the real thing. Let's take oxy as an example. The new drug is not as effective as the old pills they used to get. One guy showed me one of the old pills and one of the new ones. They looked exactly the same, except that the new pill didn't have the same finish on it—it wasn't polished like the original."

"OK, but maybe there was some difference between the batches of pills. Maybe that's just a random cosmetic thing," Sanchez commented.

"According to Speaser—assuming there was a substitution—it would likely happen in one of two ways. Either someone intercepted the real pills and replaced them, or they just made a complete replica from scratch, including all the packaging materials."

"But how do you do that? These are all registered pharmaceuticals with patented formulas, aren't they?" Sanchez thought this sounded too unlikely. "Someone would have to copy the formula and be able to package them to look exactly alike, right? How could they do that?"

Montero shook his head. "I'm not sure how, but I believe

Speaser when he says it's doable. He said you can buy a lot of this stuff on the dark web, already made by counterfeiters who can do it. I guess the difference is in the quality of the brand-name drug versus the copy. I guess that's how generics do it, but they're legally able to get the formula from the brand name, so it's not a mystery they have to reverse engineer."

"Sounds dangerous to me. Imagine if you take a pill for angina and it's not the right medication." She looked at him and grimaced. "But you may be onto something. We have to find out if there really are fake drugs showing up at the hospital and, if so, where they're coming from."

"I may get up to the VA tomorrow," Montero said. "Maybe I can enlist a couple of the guys to dig around and see what they can find out about the drugs and any quirks in the packaging. There's a nurse that's sympathetic to the guys' situation. He might help."

"I'll look into what the hospital itself is doing about the problem. Apparently, Maraxx Pharma is doing its own investigation about trouble there—drugs misplaced or something. I can ask for more details there too."

"Do you think that this drug scheme could be the reason Vale was killed?"

"There must be big money involved, so it might be. Maybe Josie Vale was onto something big—I mean really big." She finished her beer and stood up to go.

"Most outlaws would think a few million dollars would be worth killing for," Montero said.

"In any case, we need to learn more about the drugs being dispensed at the hospital, and I have to figure out these bills of lading we found in Vale's safe-deposit box. Let's talk again tomorrow."

They walked out the door together and drove their separate ways.

Chapter 16

Saturday afternoon, April 6, 2019

Phoenix, Arizona

Sanchez felt despondent as Bordou drove his unmarked silver Dodge Durango on their mission to the Golden Coast Casino out in the desert. She was upset because the department had confiscated the Interceptor for a few days to evaluate whether the shooting had done anything to degrade its safety. They also hoped to recover the bullet that had struck the car to use as evidence against the perpetrators in Gila County. That was a good thing, but it meant that she would be without her favorite wheels for at least a day. She had pressured one of the mechanics to hurry the evaluation so that she could get her car back as soon as possible. In the meantime, they were using Bordou's cruiser for transportation.

The pleasant-looking casino lay out near Globe, an ancient mining town that had seen better days. Globe was located about forty miles east of Phoenix on the edge of the Apache reservation. For a little more than a hundred a night, you could stay there playing the slots or cards until the wee hours of the morning having fun and spending money. If you were really good, you could just about break even and get a nice dinner out of the occasion. It turned out Elon Grosse had spent many evenings there working off his bank account until he had run out of money. But he apparently had kept on playing and accumulated some debt, as well as some persons of interest.

"It sounds like this is a long shot, but we have to cover every loose end," Sanchez said in a disappointed voice. "I guess the guy had outstanding debts in lots of places. His friend at work said he had come into money recently. He had ordered a boat, for Pete's sake. I found out yesterday that it wasn't just a boat like you'd float around in at the reservoir. It cost a half-million dollars used. Who would put that much money into a chunk of fiberglass to use on a weekend? He put fifty K down!" She was getting a little worked up at the class distinction between her miserly pay and Grosse's.

"Well, these guys are fat cats in the corporate world, so they pull down a big salary." Bordou was more sanguine about the pay disparity. "But that's still a lot of cash for his leisure time. Maybe he won big at the casino or something."

"We'll find out in a little while. It would change things if he owed some loan shark a big chunk of change."

"Let's see. If he had big debts, then he may have been pressured for money. That's motive for a beating or robbery, but not usually for murder."

"Yeah, I know most bookies would rather beat the hell out of you instead of killing you. Why kill the golden goose and lose all that income?"

They pulled into the visitor lot in front of the casino, and found one parking space with partial shade so the car wouldn't catch fire in the late-morning sun. They walked into the front door and flashed their badges when greeted by a hostess who was waiting for them to arrive. She ushered them to an elevator, and in short order, they stepped into the casino business manager's office. The hostess waited to see if they would like coffee or soft drinks and then vanished when her boss entered the room.

"Good morning, Detectives," the manager said. "My name is Joe Abraham. I'm the operations manager here at Golden Coast. How can I help you?" He indicated seats on the sofa and sat in a soft chair nearby. "It's good to see you again, Detective Bordou. How have you been?"

"Well, thank you," Bordou replied. "You seem well yourself."

"Yes, I'm feeling better since those bad men were captured. My people appreciate your assistance in the matter." Abraham was a member of the tribal council for the Apache reservation. Bordou had helped arrest some men who had stolen money from the casino and, therefore, from the tribe. He had tracked them down in Phoenix and made the arrest. Abraham had worked with him on the case.

Abraham was a man of medium height with a muscular build. He appeared to have Apache heritage and wore a silver and turquoise bracelet on each wrist. He was in his forties, Sanchez guessed, and had a wide face with prominent features. His dark eyes flashed with intelligence, and he seemed genuinely happy to talk to them, not the sort of reception they were used to. Bordou's influence made things easier today.

"Thanks for meeting with us," Bordou said. "We appreciate your offer to cooperate with our investigation into Mr. Grosse's death. We hope that your security cameras may point us in the direction of solving his suspicious death."

"I've arranged for my security office to play back any of the public-area videos we have." He smiled graciously. "Let's walk to the security office right away so you can get started."

He stood up and led them along a hallway and down a flight of stairs to that office. As they walked, he said, "You know, Mr. Grosse had been a member of our Elite Club for two years and was a regular player at our casino. It was a surprise to hear of his death. We are sorry to lose him as a customer and as someone we viewed as a friend to our resort."

They entered the security office and a man named Yazzie sat down at a computer monitor to play back footage from the casino's cameras. "I've been scrolling through the inside cameras to find your man Grosse and picked him up at one of the blackjack tables at eleven thirty-eight p.m. on April second. He had come in at ten p.m., purchased two hundred dollars in chips, and had been playing well for a change. He was up a couple of hundred dollars when this man came up to him and started talking."

Yazzie stopped the frame of the camera as a burly man walked right up to Grosse and started what could only be called a confrontation. It began with their faces close, and then the aggressor started to poke his figure into Grosse's chest. "This guy is called Malo by our staff. He's a big-time money man. He waits until people are really down on their luck and drunk and then approaches them with a loan. Terms up to fifty percent. But he may not tell them that up front."

"Yes, this man has been a thorn in our side. The door is not supposed to let him on the premises. Still, he sneaks inside to bother our guests." Abraham looked grim. "We would rather work out terms with our guests that are mutually beneficial." He smiled slightly to show he was being facetious. The casino backed regular players to a point. They didn't want their guests to get in so deep that they would stop coming in to play.

The video kept playing and they saw Malo start shouting at Grosse. One of the casino security guards came into the frame to tell Malo that he should leave. The guard grabbed Malo by the arm and escorted him out of the area.

"The guard threw Malo out the front door, and that was that." Yazzie pulled up a different window representing a different camera. He scrolled ahead for a minute while the others watched over his shoulder. "This new video system we have uses facial recognition software. It makes it easier to track a given person through the casino. Here's Mr. Grosse leaving the casino a little after midnight on the morning of April third. He walks out to his car in the number two parking lot." Yazzie turned around to explain. "That's where you park yourself if you don't use the valet." He turned back to the screen. "Here we see him using his remote to unlock his car, and then Malo rushes in from the shadows to attack him."

The video was dim, but they could clearly see Grosse's face under one street lamp. He was totally unaware that he was about to be attacked. Malo blindsided him with a club of some sort—possibly a baseball bat—and hit him several times while Grosse held up his arms to fend off the blows. Malo turned into a maniac for a few seconds, but he knew enough to not hit his mark on the head with the bat. Instead, he rained down body blows. He stopped when Grosse fell to his knees. He was clearly shouting at Grosse the whole time—*Probably telling him to pay up*, Sanchez thought. Then Malo searched Grosse's pockets and stole the money he had won at the blackjack table. He left the scene.

Grosse staggered to his car and slowly climbed in. After sitting in the vehicle for a few minutes, he drove out of the parking lot, presumably toward home.

"How much did he win that night?" Sanchez asked. She knew that casinos monitored their customers' winnings regularly to track the company's profit and loss.

"He had a good night," Abraham said lightly. "He was up

twelve hundred thirty-eight bucks when he left the building. He had even cleared up a small debt with us before he left."

"So Malo robbed and beat him as a warning. Then Grosse drove himself out," Bordou said.

Sanchez picked up the story. "And it turns out he had an alarm at his house. He arrived there just before one a.m. when he keyed in the alarm code. But he forgot to reset the alarm once he was inside. The coroner estimated his time of death at two a.m."

Bordou completed the thought. "So someone came into the house unnoticed and strung him up by that time. Whoever it was might have been waiting for him to arrive and simply followed him into the house."

"But I thought you said he committed suicide?" Abraham asked.

"That was the initial theory, but there are some facts that don't mesh with that scenario," Sanchez commented.

Yazzie made a copy of the videos for them to take as evidence, and Sanchez completed the documentation while Bordou talked to Abraham. They shook hands all around and walked to the car in the steadily warming day. The shade they had counted on had slipped off the car, so the vehicle was stifling when they got inside. *Thank God for air-conditioning,* thought Sanchez.

They both opened their windows, and Bordou got the car moving as fast as possible. They hit the road back to Phoenix, and the air conditioner finally caught up with the heat. They closed the windows with a sigh of relief.

"I'm taking Kathy out to a dance tonight. You and Tom should join us," Bordou said as he cruised westward. "When does he get in, anyway?"

"His plane touches down at four thirty p.m., give or take.

I'm going to pick him up, and we'll go home," Sanchez said with a smile. "It will be good to see him. But I'm not sure he'll be up for dancing after the long flight."

"Oh yeah, that's a good point," he said. "Maybe another time, like dinner later this week?"

"Sure, that might work. I'll be tied to the office all week working on these cases."

"Me too. We're still waiting on some forensics to come back—DNA and chemical testing of those pharmaceuticals we found. We had to verify their contents to be sure of what we have. The lab guys have a way to verify if they are legit or counterfeit drugs."

"That sounds good because I have a feeling we're dealing with a drug ring of some kind."

"And your guy Grosse had a really bad day when he was at the casino." Bordou glanced at her out of the corner of his eye.

"I've got a meeting with the ME in an hour," she said. "He's coming in to show me something he found during his exam. He said it could change the direction of the case."

"I wonder what it is."

"I'll know soon enough. I'll call you if it's a big deal."

***

Sanchez walked to the basement of the building on West Jefferson Street to the medical examiner's office. She had been there several times before to observe autopsies or discuss their findings. It was a fairly new facility inside, even though the exterior was a little dated.

She entered the lobby and approached the guard to sign in for her meeting. She didn't know the guard and he was busy with another visitor, so he just waved her through to the stairs. She walked down and found the assistant ME waiting for her in the main storage area. He already had Grosse's body laid out on one of the wheeled tables for her to examine.

"Hi, Sanchez," Lars Vigorsen said with a grin. "I have your guy here." He pointed at the table and shuffled toward it. "The ME said this was a potentially sensitive case, so I should show you this personally before we issue our report."

"OK, great. I appreciate the heads-up that there's something unusual," she said as she followed him to the table. She prepared herself for the unsettling display of a dead body. She had seen enough of them to not be shocked anymore, especially after the ME crew cleaned them up. But it was still disturbing to see what used to be a living human being lying there—a lifeless cadaver. "So what'd you find?"

Vigorsen pulled the sheet back just enough to expose Grosse's upper body. His shoulders and arms showed considerable blue and purple bruising that was consistent with the beating the man had received from Malo in the parking lot. He had few bruises on his head, Sanchez noted. That too was consistent with what she had seen on the video of the attack. His neck, however, was one giant bruise. The bruising was not only right where the rope had hanged him—it was on his head and one side of his neck more than the other.

"As you can see, he was beaten on the body by some blunt instrument, maybe a ball bat or pipe." Vigorsen pointed to individual injuries. "They must have hurt, but didn't kill him."

"I have a video taken outside the Golden Coast Casino that shows him being attacked by a man with a baseball bat," she said. "The assailant did not hit him in the face or head, as far as I could see."

"Now it gets interesting," he said. "Here, you can clearly see the marks left by the rope he hung from. Some blood was present, and there's a lot of bruising. That's consistent with strangulation as the cause of death."

"Oh, so he died by hanging?"

"I didn't say that," he said and then brought out an X-ray of Grosse's neck. "First, look at this bruising all around the front of his neck, especially on this side here." He pointed. "We don't believe that that bruising was caused by a rope. It looks more like someone used his hands to strangle the victim."

"Really?" Sanchez was intrigued.

"Furthermore, we took an X-ray that shows clearly that his hyoid bone above the Adam's apple was broken, as well as his larynx. That's consistent with manual strangulation rather than hanging."

"But we found him hanging from a rope that had been thrown over a beam in his house."

"It may be that whoever choked him to death then hung him up to look like he committed suicide. That would be consistent with his injuries." Vigorsen looked very grim as he said this. "Detective, I think you have a murder on your hands."

"I thought that might be the case. A few things just didn't add up." She leaned in to examine the neck carefully. "And he was hit back here on the head too?"

"There are several injuries to his face and head that may have been inflicted by fists or a heavy but soft object like a towel with a weight in it. We saw that once in a gang beating where the perpetrators apparently didn't want to leave obvious marks on their victim."

"Well, thank you, Lars. When will we see the official report?"

"Next week. We're overwhelmed by investigations and everyone is on overtime, so the ME is going crazy to get things done and stay within the budget. You can imagine the pressure."

"Yeah, I hear you. Well, thanks for the show-and-tell. I appreciate it."

She walked out of the building to her car. *So I was right,* she thought. *It was a faked suicide. I'll have to sit on that info for a day or two and use it to my advantage.*

She climbed into her borrowed department car, an older Dodge Charger, and headed for the airport, running a little behind schedule. As she approached a traffic light that was about to turn red she punched the accelerator to speed through it. The Charger leaped at the touch of her foot on the gas pedal. It roared in response, and she flashed past other cars.

She grinned like an idiot and pushed the Charger all the way to the airport. Maybe this car wouldn't be so bad for a couple of days after all. *It's got some ponies to it.* She arrived at the airport terminal a few minutes before Tom Smith staggered out of the arrivals area to meet her.

Chapter 17

Late Sunday afternoon, April 7, 2019

Phoenix, Arizona

Montero parked in his usual spot in the VA parking lot where he could push about half the truck into the shade of a large steel sign. In theory, it would help keep his vehicle from getting any hotter than necessary. This was a game that Phoenix residents played every day during the hot months. Even if the shade only lasted a couple of hours, it seemed worth the effort to at least try to escape the heat of the day. It also kept your car's paint from fading as fast as it would in full sunlight. The other trick he had to keep his car drivable on hot days was to drape a towel over his car seat so that it wasn't blistering hot when he came back to sit on it. The seat would be at an ambient temperature—maybe 105 degrees—instead of match-lighting hot.

On a Sunday morning like this, there were fewer workers around the hospital, but a lot of visitors came to call on patients who had the misfortune to be bedridden. He looked forward to conversing with a couple of people who had said they would help him with his research into drug management at the hospital.

He had considered going through official channels within the hospital administration to learn more about their own investigation into the misappropriation of drugs. But after a few inquiries, he had been shut down by an officious attitude and a level of secrecy he hadn't expected to find at such a facility. He was told that the hospital was already doing its own investigation into drug-related issues. In fact, there were two: one into alleged diversion of drugs from the pharmacy and one regarding mislabeling of products. Management would not tell him anything about either one because they were "ongoing investigations." He had learned online that there were two additional inquiries being conducted at the federal level by the Office of Investigations within the VA. One involved potential negligence for the delay that most veterans encountered in scheduling appointments and other management issues. The other looked into malfeasance in funding.

So far, none of them had helped answer why the drugs seemed impotent and why there were occasional shortages of medicine. Knowing how long any government investigation could take, he had decided to act on his own with help from a few good men.

He checked in and found his way up to the ward where Mike Polosso was housed for treatment. Polosso was an older fellow, a former navy man, who had said he would help him. Polosso had been in and out of the hospital with an affliction that had not been clearly diagnosed at first but had turned into a recurring infection of his joints due to his hip replacement operation. He had received intravenous antibiotics three times and was in for observation after the last treatment. He was familiar with the way things worked at the hospital and knew how to circumvent the organization and personnel when needed. He had enlisted one of the nurses to help him figure out the drug problem.

Polosso was a burly man with thinning, sandy hair, short of height, and quick-tempered. He had a wide face that showed signs of mistreatment dating back to when he had boxed in the navy and later, never winning any titles even though he was considered a good fighter. He was clean-shaven with light-blue eyes and a crooked nose that pointed to the left. Too many left hooks, he had said. Polosso was not afraid to nose around the nurses' station or the pill cart to see what was what. He had also infiltrated the pharmacy, which happened to be located on the ground floor of the building where he was currently housed. He showed Montero a few photos on his phone that he had taken of the conditions within the pharmacy during his last surreptitious visit.

"OK, look here. See how these bottles are sitting out on the counter like this?" he asked as he pointed to one photo. "These things are supposed to be locked up at all times, not left out like this during a lunch break. If I can get in there with a camera, then someone else can get in there and take some pills or replace some."

"I see what you mean," Montero replied as he looked through the photos. "What are these other photos of?"

"This is a photo of the lock on the room where they keep the controlled goods—you know—methadone, oxy, Vicodin, morphine, and stuff like that." He took the phone back and scrolled through the photos. "Here—this is a photo of one of the techs going into that room to get a large bottle of oxy . . . Here he is coming out with the bottle, one of the five-hundred-pill bottles they dispense from. At any one time, they may have thirty different bottles lined up on the workbench as they make up prescriptions for individual patients or the pill cart. The cart's what the nurse on the floor uses to carry all the drugs for patients on her rounds through the ward."

"So they're just out there while the the staff is working. How about when someone goes on break?"

"They usually leave them there while they step out. I think there's supposed to be at least one person present at all times.

But you know how it goes. People get sloppy about the rules."

"What else have you learned?" Montero asked.

"Well, I don't know exactly what's happening, but I've seen two things I don't understand." Polosso dug around the phone for another set of photos and showed one to Montero. "One is that they bring out bottles of drugs, say oxy, and pour from one into another. I don't know why they would do that unless they're just dumping two partially filled bottles into one to save space. The other is that some people seem to stop and open a drawer next to the storeroom just before they enter it and take something from it. I couldn't see what they were doing from the angle where I was standing."

"Why is that important? I don't get it."

"The only thing I can come up with is that there is a key in the drawer or something like that. Overnight, they engage an electronic lock using a keypad, but during the day, they go in and out so often that I think they disable the keypad to save time."

There was a knock on the door to Polosso's room, and a man stuck his head in. "Hey, Mike, are we doing this?" he asked.

"Yeah, come in, Luis. You guys know each other, right?" Polosso asked, looking between the two men.

"Yeah, I know Luis," Montero said. He had met Luis Marstaite several times before and had discussed the drug issue with him. Marstaite was a nurse who usually worked in this building of the hospital. He was a young, wiry man the same height as Polosso with black hair and brown eyes indicating a French or Cajun family heritage. He had an accent that Montero couldn't place but thought it might be from bayou country. They shook hands.

"We better move if you wanna do this," Marstaite whispered. "The guard outside the pharmacy just went on lunch break, so we have at least thirty minutes for an in and out. Are you still up for it?"

"OK, man," Polosso said. He turned to Montero with an expectant look. "We set things up to go into the pharmacy now when none of the pharmacy staff was working. We can look things over and see what we can see." He seemed very sure of himself. "You want to come along for a look-see?"

Montero was surprised by this turn of events. He had expressed an interest in learning what went on in the drug management end of things but hadn't planned to go into the pharmacy itself. He wasn't sure whether he should participate in this incursion into a restricted area. It could be dangerous if they were caught.

"Wow!" he said. "That's a surprise. I don't know if I can do that."

"I'm sorry we caught you off guard, Guillermo, but this is the opportunity we have been waiting for. Sunday is the best day to get in there unnoticed," Polosso said quietly. "I tell you what: Why don't we go down, and you can stand by and be a lookout while Luis and I go inside? Luis has authority to be in the front portion of the pharmacy anyway. It's only going into the back storage area that's off-limits to him."

Montero thought about this option and decided he could try that, especially if it would gain them information about how the drugs were actually used within the VA. He agreed to go with them.

The trio walked out of Polosso's room and took the elevator down to the ground floor. There were few visitors wandering the halls at that time and hardly any staff either. They made their way to the pharmacy on the west end of the floor and around the bend in the hallway. Just past the bend, they stopped and Montero agreed to stand on alert there. He keyed Polosso's number into his cell phone so he could alert to the old navy man of any potential danger. Polosso set his phone to vibrate so he could receive the warning undetected.

"OK. We'll go ahead," Polosso said. "Keep on your toes."

"Right. Be careful," Montero responded.

Polosso and Marstaite continued down the hall. They reached the door of the pharmacy and looked over their shoulders to be sure the coast was clear. Marstaite placed his magnetic ID card up to the scanner, and the door unlatched. They slipped inside and quietly closed the door.

Fortunately, there were several windows that faced the hallway, so Montero could follow their actions from a distance. He moved to a position across the hall that allowed him to watch the two intruders in the pharmacy and still keep an eye on approaching people. He watched them moving around inside, taking photos, examining bottle labels, and reading order sheets for prescriptions. After five or six minutes, the two men opened a drawer next to the inner door leading to the storeroom. Montero noticed the surprised expression on Polosso's face when they looked inside. Polosso held up a key for Montero to see and then used it to unlock the door. It opened, and they stepped inside the storeroom.

Now Montero was worried because he couldn't see what his cohorts were doing. He checked his watch. He began to sweat and wiped moisture from his forehead as he alternately watched the time pass by and kept an eye on the hallway. Seven minutes quickly passed.

Then Montero's phone vibrated violently in his pocket. The screen said simply: *Polosso.* He answered.

"Montero, you have to see this. Come down here, and I'll let you in the door." Polosso hung up the phone before Montero could respond.

He looked down the hall and saw Polosso come out of the storeroom and over to the pharmacy's front door. He waved his arm and motioned for Montero to come forward. Montero had no choice but to jog along the hall to meet him. Polosso pulled him in and led him immediately to the storeroom. Once inside, Polosso closed the door.

"Look at this. They've been substituting generic oxy for the real thing. You can see the difference in the pills here." He opened a bottle of Maraxx Pharma oxycodone and pulled out a fifteen-milligram pill; then he opened a bottle of Randman oxycodone and removed one pill from it. He set the two pills next to each other on the counter under a lamp and handed a magnifying glass to Montero. "Look at the sides of the pills."

Montero took the lens and studied the two pills. The Maraxx Pharma pill had shiny sidewalls but also had a small X on one side. The Randman pill had a cruder finish on its surface and lacked marking on either side. The two pills were clearly different. Montero was convinced because he had seen similar pills before when had he talked to another veteran a few days before.

"All right; they're different," Montero said to Polosso.

"But over here . . ." Polosso stepped farther along the bench to where several prescription pill bottles had been filled. "The paper order said that this patient is to receive brand-name oxycodone, but when we opened the bottle up, the pills inside were not Maraxx pills but the generic replacement from Randman. So someone in the pharmacy is substituting pills. We checked five other prescriptions and found similar results."

"I've seen enough here," Montero said. "I'd better get out of here and back on guard. Good work, guys."

He opened the storeroom door and peeked outside. He saw a man in uniform—clearly the guard—walking casually along the hall toward the pharmacy. He ducked back into the storeroom.

"The guard's coming this way," he whispered. "What do we do?"

Marstaite answered, "Just stay put and be quiet. He'll probably walk past to his usual post up the hall. We'll wait him out."

They all stood silently waiting, nervous as hell and hoping the guard wouldn't notice anything that would bring him into the pharmacy. After two minutes, they heard nothing outside the storeroom. Marstaite opened the door a fraction of an inch and peered through the crack.

"He's gone," he said. "Montero, you'd better get back out there. We'll take some photos and then join you in about five minutes."

Montero didn't wait to argue. He stuck his head out the door and swiveled it to look up and down the hallway. The coast was clear, so he tiptoed out of the room and through the pharmacy door. He felt a little shaken by the close call but took up his position at the bend in the hallway. He stood by and watched the windows in the pharmacy.

After another five minutes, Polosso and Marstaite exited the storeroom and quickly stepped out into the hallway. They joined Montero and took the elevator to the floor where Polosso was staying. Once inside his room with the door closed, they burst out laughing and shook hands.

"That was too close for comfort, my friends," Montero said jovially. "But now let's look at the photos you took and see what we have."

Montero left the VA hospital feeling like they were finally

getting somewhere. But many questions remained. Why were the technicians substituting drugs, and why use a generic at all? The only reason he could come up with was that someone was skimming the pills and selling them on the black market. And was the Randman brand an acceptable replacement for brand names like Maraxx Pharma? What other drugs were involved?

He quietly drove home in the late-afternoon heat. He needed to talk to Sanchez to solicit her input and see where this all could lead.

Chapter 18

Sunday evening, April 7, 2019

Phoenix, Arizona

"All of the shipments that are documented in these bills of lading came into the VA receiving dock from either Maraxx Pharma or Randman Labs, according to our accounting people," Sanchez said to Bordou and Montero. "That's the upshot of the papers that Vale had in her bank box."

Sanchez, Montero, and Bordou were sitting on the veranda at Montero's home, sipping their cold Tecate beers. They had met at Montero's insistence to figure out what the new information about the drugs meant. It had been a warm day but it was cooling off nicely as a cold front swept into the Phoenix area and dropped the temperature from the day's high of ninety-eight degrees to a mere seventy-eight. Even small weather gifts were appreciated by the locals.

Montero recounted his early afternoon exploits to his two friends. "We saw bottles and cartons from other manufacturers in the storeroom. But the majority of the bulk bottles were Randman and Maraxx Pharma ones. I have these samples from a vet on the ward: three oxy pills from Randman and three pills from Maraxx. They were given to me, so they weren't stolen; I want to make that clear. They didn't come from the pharmacy itself." He glanced between the two of them. "Lori, I want you to find a way to have them analyzed to see if they are legitimate drugs. I know it's irregular, but I need to know if we're chasing random mistakes by employees or if there really is drug substitution going on at the hospital."

Bordou rolled his eyes and said, "OK. I was going to send samples in from the different bottles we found in the gym locker. I could slip them in as extra samples in that order, if that would work."

"Yes, yes." Montero sat up and grinned. "As long as we can track them separately, that would be good."

"I talked to one of our guys in the narcotics unit in the state troopers' office about Randman Labs," Sanchez said between sips of beer. "He said that they are relatively new on the market. They've made a few generic drugs for years but have shown up everywhere lately producing many of the high-demand drugs— real profit makers. Their main office is in LA with manufacturing in Burbank, I think he said."

"So they're a legitimate company then," Bordou commented. "A generic drugmaker."

"I guess they decided to get into new lines of products, according to what the narcotics guys told you." Montero stood up and walked to the kitchen while he talked. "I wonder who else makes these generics that are in use so much now. I can check around with people I know in the business and see what I can learn." He collected three Tecates from the refrigerator and brought them back to the patio, where he handed one to each of his guests. "I'll try to learn more about this company— Randman—too."

"I already searched for them online and only found a corporate page that talked about their history," Sanchez said. "They have been around for thirty years and had to file for bankruptcy four years ago. Two years ago, they gained a significant loan from an unknown source and merged with another drugmaker called Novarios, S.A., a Spanish company. They kept their name and expanded operations then."

"Did you find any other discussion about them or the quality of their drugs?" Bordou asked.

"Not yet," Montero said. "But I'll do more digging around."

"I can follow up with my guy at narcotics and see what he may not have told me," Sanchez said as she checked her phone. "Just a minute. I have a message from my computer friend. I'd better call him back."

She got up and shuffled through the sliding glass door into the house. She thought about calling Smith too to see how he was doing on his first night back on duty. He was an officer with the Arizona State University police force. He had been assigned to weekend duty because he had been gone for the week. *No good deed goes unpunished*, she thought. He worked the shift from 6:00 p.m. until 6:00 a.m. the next morning. She would see him for an hour before she had to report for duty.

She dialed Mummer. "Hello," she said, using no names. "You called?"

"Yeah, I got something for you. Can we meet?" he whispered like he often did on the phone. He was sure his line was tapped, even though he changed burner phones every month at the latest.

"You mean now?"

"Yes," he responded. "The usual." Before she could say anything, he hung up.

"Shit!" she said to herself. *He must have something hot if he wants to meet right now.* She placed her beer on the counter and stood up straight as if that would immediately ward off the effects of two beers. She considered her options. It was her day off, so she had worn her shorts and a tank top to Montero's place, and fricking flip-flops—not her usual gear for work. She still had her utility belt and Glock in the car trunk, so she could handle most situations without too much difficulty. Meeting Mummer was no real problem; but if he had actionable information right now, then she might not be ready for what would follow.

She walked out to the patio with a grim face and stepped between the two men. They stopped talking and noticed her level of agitation right away. She held up a hand as if she were directing traffic for them to stop and listen. She wouldn't do that unless something important had happened.

"What's the matter?" Montero immediately asked. He had worked with her in tough situations and saw that she was now on alert.

"I got a call from my Internet guy. He said he has something for me right now. I have to leave and see what it is." She looked at each of them in turn and then added, "I asked him to locate Josie Vale's laptop. There's a slight possibility that her machine can still be reached if it's online. I think he may have found it, but I'm not sure. He hung up right after he said he needed to meet."

"What does that mean?" Bordou asked. "That he has a location?"

"I think so. If that's the case, we may have to assemble a team and go there before the machine runs out of juice or is turned off. I won't know anything until I talk to him." She pointed to her clothes. "I can meet him like this OK. I usually wear casual for our meetings, but I may need backup if I need to move fast." She shifted her glance to Bordou. "I may have to check out a location right after we meet. Can you be on standby in case something happens?"

Bordou was caught off guard, but he was used to working

with Sanchez, who sometimes had an unpredictable way of making things happen. He was her partner, so he had no qualms about jumping in when she needed his help.

"Yeah. Where do you want me—on overwatch for the meet?" Bordou asked.

"I have to approach him alone," she said as she thought through the scenario. "He can't know you're anywhere nearby. So maybe I can have you wait a block or two away, within quick response but completely out of sight. After that, I'll have to leave the meeting and then contact you if we have actionable info. Does that work for you?"

"I guess. Let me call Kathy and let her know I'll be running late." He picked up his phone, stepped away, and made the call.

"Can I do anything to help?" Montero asked.

"I don't know yet, Guillermo. If we get a location, I might need to check out an address. Are you going to be here for the evening, or were you going out?"

"I'll be here. Call if you need me."

"Thanks," she said and bolted for the door. "Bordou, I'm going to gear up," she called as she left.

In the driveway, Sanchez used her remote to open her car and then used an extra key to unlock her trunk. It popped open, and she scanned her equipment in the fading daylight. She picked up her utility belt loaded with all her usual gear, then set it back down. She didn't need all that now—maybe later. She opened a Velcroed compartment in a duffle bag and withdrew her backup piece—a .45-caliber Springfield Armory XD-S handgun. It was also her concealed carry weapon. She tucked the compact holster inside the back of her shorts and pulled her top down over it. It would be a little uncomfortable driving that way, but she couldn't gun up in public, so this would have to do. She closed the trunk just as Bordou stepped out of the house and walked to her side.

"Give me a holding position nearby, and I'll just wait for your call," he said.

"Why don't you wait at the KFC on East Baseline and South Central? You'll be only a few blocks away. Keep your phone on." She looked at the loyal Bordou and said, "Hey, I'm sorry to screw up your Sunday, but this might be important. I'll have to buy you a beer for acts above and beyond. OK?"

"I'll hold you to that, partner." He grinned. "I'm out of here." He climbed in his Durango and backed out of the driveway.

Sanchez pulled her Charger onto the street and headed south on a side street to East Lincoln Drive. There she turned west and followed the road to the Piestewa Freeway, where she merged with southbound traffic. She punched the gas pedal to get up to speed and then decided she didn't want to draw attention by speeding. She backed off to only ten miles above the speed limit like everyone else.

She followed the freeway south until it joined I-10 South in the spaghetti-like mess of the I-10 and I-17 interchange. She always was amazed by the weird expanse of concrete with its multiple lanes and confusing signage. She exited onto I-17 westbound soon after that and drove west to the South 7th Street exit that she was all too familiar with from one of her previous high-speed car chases. She took the exit ramp and followed the frontage road west to South Central.

She checked for any tails she may have picked up. Seeing none along the way, she felt secure in her meeting with Mummer. She only had to drive a couple of miles south to get to East Baseline Road and then east to the Arby's where Mummer would be waiting in the shadows for her to arrive.

She pulled into the Arby's and checked for any suspicious cars, especially any with people sitting inside. Assured that the scene was clear, she exited the car and walked slowly into the restaurant, where she ordered a Diet Coke. She found an empty table at the back and sat down to wait for Mummer. Their customary procedure was for her to sit and he would scan the area for any threats that were probably conducting electronic surveillance as well, especially for the FBI. She knew that he had to keep a clean slate with the law to avoid breaking his release agreement on a hacking charge. Sanchez felt guilty asking him to do some of the things she had him do, but he was the best at the game.

She texted Bordou that she was in place and waiting for the subject to arrive. Bordou did not know the hacker's real name, and she wanted to keep it that way in case anything went wrong.

Her relationship with Mummer was a strange one. They had come to a simple arrangement: he helped her with her more complex computer problems; in return, she served as his escort on his monthly gambling excursions to earn money at the casinos. She knew where he lived and had even met his mother, a sweet lady. He was a remarkable blackjack player. He didn't own a car, so she drove him and acted as eye candy while he gambled. He usually gave her 10 percent of his winnings for being his friend for a few hours. It was strictly platonic, and she kept him from being distracted by other people while he was concentrating on the game. But, of course, she couldn't divulge any of this information to anyone.

When he finally arrived carrying a shoulder bag, he sauntered over to sit across from her at the little plastic table. Looking agitated, he said, "We better go outside to your car to talk."

They got up and walked outside to Sanchez's car. Mummer

hesitated for a moment. "Where's your car?"

"My old car was wrecked last year, remember? This is the unmarked police car I use. My new car is at home—the one we used to go to the casino the last two times."

"Oh. Is it monitored in any way?" He was extremely nervous about being tracked by anyone.

"No," she said soothingly. "It has a GPS locator, but I turned it off for our meeting."

"You can do that?"

"No problem. I had one of our techs put a switch on it so I didn't have to worry about being tracked by the Sinaloa Cartel. They still have a grudge against me, you know."

"You make a lot of enemies, don't you?"

"I seem to get criminals angry, yes."

They stepped into the car and closed the doors. Sanchez started the car and the air conditioner at the same time. Cool air began to flow through the vents and brought the temperature inside the vehicle to a manageable level.

"That feels good. Let me start my laptop," Mummer said quietly while he fidgeted with the machine. "I have a location for you. It hasn't moved since this morning."

"Oh great!" she said. "That's great news. How'd you locate it?"

"That was easy once I learned which version of Windows she used." He rotated the computer so Sanchez could see the screen and looked over his shoulder to be sure no one was watching.

"How did you do it?" she asked.

"Well, her laptop was one of several that her newspaper company bought two years ago. They all have LTE cards in them. I was able to get into the newspaper's files and find the number on her card. The card makes it easy to locate a stolen machine. Companies use them to track their employees all the time." He punched a few keys and then looked worried. "I used their locator function to find the computer." He leaned forward and squinted at the computer screen. "Just a minute."

She saw a concerned look creep over his face. "Why? What's happening?"

"The machine says its battery is low. I thought they must have it plugged in to be active this long. But maybe they've unplugged it."

"Oh shit!" Sanchez said. "Are they changing location?"

"No, I think someone unplugged it. Yes, it says so right here. It's running on the battery."

"Holy crap. What can we do?"

"Well, it doesn't look like it's moving, just turned off. We still have its GPS coordinates."

"Can you tell how long it's been at that location?"

"No. If we actually had the machine, I might be able to elicit that from its log." Mummer seemed content with his work. "Say, Lori?" He looked nervous. "Would you like to do a casino run with me next Friday? I'm running low on cash, and I need to make some money."

"That's a good point." She twisted sideways in the seat to look at his face. "What do I owe you for this?"

"It only took a few hours. It was mostly waiting for the machine to respond." He looked sheepish. "Maybe two hundred would be nice." He looked embarrassed to ask for the money.

"Oh Mummer, my friend. That's not enough for something so complicated." She eyed him sympathetically. For a reclusive genius, he had no idea what his skills were worth. "I'm going to pay you three hundred, and I can give you . . ." She looked in her wallet. "A hundred and twenty now. That's all I have on me tonight. I didn't expect you to call so soon." She handed him the cash.

"That's good, Lori. We can settle up on Friday, OK?" He looked hopeful and stuffed the cash in his pants pocket.

She knew that he enjoyed their gambling outings as much as she did. For him, it was a chance to actively use his mind and make some income. He never pushed his ability to the point that a casino would challenge him or throw him out for his skilled play. And he enjoyed the attention of the crowds that would eventually gather and admire his prowess. She enjoyed it because it was just fun to watch him win so easily. It also allowed her to dress up and be an anonymous lady of mystery for a day—and sip a cocktail or two on the house.

"OK. I'd better go and see where the computer is."

"It's in an apartment near West Indian School Road and North 45th—apartment 116, I think." Unlike the discovery of its digital presence, Mummer seemed bored by the actual location. "Call me if you need more help." He handed her a slip of paper with the address on it. Then he opened the car door and looked right and left before carefully stepping outside.

Sanchez said, "See you later, and thanks," as she examined the slip of paper. By the time she looked up, he had vanished into thin air.

She pulled out her cell phone and started the car at the same time as she dialed Bordou.

Chapter 19

Sunday evening, April 7, 2019

Phoenix, Arizona

"I've got an address we have to check out on the west side," Sanchez told Bordou over the phone. "I'm on my way to you, and we can take one car. What do you think?"

Bordou responded quickly, "OK. You can fill me in on the rest when you get here." He hung up his phone.

Sanchez drove down Baseline in his direction, trying to work out how this could go down. If it was an apartment in a complex, then they would have to tread lightly until they had a reason to enter the unit. They didn't have enough evidence to get a search warrant. They didn't have enough information to get other police personnel involved yet either. They would have to observe the apartment for a while and hope for a break.

She pulled up next to Bordou's Durango, transferred the equipment she would need, and switched vehicles. He got rolling right away as they talked and headed north on 7th to the I-17 freeway. He turned west at Sanchez's instruction and continued that way for a few miles as the highway changed direction from east-west to north-south. That took them through the central industrial district west of downtown Phoenix.

"The computer is in apartment 116 of the Cluster Apartments. They're located right behind a tire shop. We'll have to pull in and see what the layout is once we're there."

"OK. So, the machine is turned off but still transmitting a location. How's that possible?" Bordou asked as he piloted his SUV through the nearly empty streets of the city.

"I don't understand it all myself," she confessed. "Apparently, Vale's computer has a tracking chip in it, and a lot of computers purchased for company operations like the newspaper have that capability so they can track employees and find machines that have been stolen. Sort of like a LoJack for computers. Somehow, my Internet guy tapped into the device's communications and read the GPS coordinates of the computer. That also gave him its current IP address so he could talk to the machine directly and see what its status was."

"Is any of this legal? It sounds like hacking."

"I don't want to know. But our guys back at the station had no ideas about how to find the laptop, so I had to use outside means." She gave Bordou a serious look. "If it helps us solve a murder, then I'm OK with it."

Bordou looked over at her and raised his eyebrows. "Don't tell me any more about it or this guy. I don't want to know."

"Well, don't worry. I'll keep you out of it. But think of him as a confidential informant. We pay them for information they hear on the street, right? In a way, he's just another type of informant, but his street is the Internet, not some chunk of pavement."

"That's a stretch, Lori. And in this case, he may have hacked a private computer."

"Half of our CIs probably gain their information through illicit means, and we don't question them about their sources too much. We even protect their identity in court. Journalists can keep their sources secret, even if they pass on illegally leaked information. So I feel I'm on some solid ground here."

"OK. I'm going to take the diagonal on Grand Avenue to save time."

"No, don't. It's too scrambled right now with all the new construction going on. Just stick with this up to Indian School. Road crews haven't screwed with that intersection for a while." Sanchez hated it when cities messed with traffic flow. They usually just created a more complicated series of ramps and overpasses that confused drivers and made their maps look like knots of spaghetti.

Bordou exited to West Indian School Road, and they soon approached North 44th. From there, they circumnavigated the entire apartment complex to see how it was laid out. They located the correct building that had the apartment in it and parked across the road where they could observe the main entrance. Sanchez stepped out of the car and walked nonchalantly in her flip-flops into the lobby to see if the coordinates that Mummer had given her for the building made sense. It looked like he was accurate about the apartment number and its location.

The name on the mailbox for apartment 116 was Jessie Hernandez. Sanchez left the building after testing the inner security door that residents had to open for entry. That was easy enough to get past on a late evening. Next she walked around outside to see if she could look into the first-floor apartment through the windows. She stayed on the sidewalk to avoid attracting attention and scanned what she thought were the windows of 116. There was only one light on in what looked like the living room, and she saw only one head inside. *Good*, she thought. *At least there aren't a bunch of drunken guys standing around comparing the size of their pistols.*

She slid into the passenger seat of the Durango and reported what she had found to Bordou. He had an idea that might get them into the apartment.

"Let's search for the guy's name in the database. Maybe we have an outstanding warrant on him." He typed into his mobile laptop and searched the department records and warrants. After a few minutes, he said, "Aha. He has several parking tickets outstanding. A bench warrant was issued for failure to appear in traffic court." He kept on reading and clicked a few keys to expand his search. "Look at that." He pointed to the screen for Sanchez to lean across and read. "He has been arrested four times and convicted once for receiving stolen goods. Electronics mostly. Spent two years in Chino in California, where he was released early under their new reduced sentencing rules. Studied computer service technology while inside. Part of their training and rehab program."

Sanchez wrinkled her nose. "That doesn't make sense. I was expecting him to be one of the gang's muscle guys. This doesn't seem right for the hits we've seen."

"Maybe he's just the fence for the others. They may have sold him the computer or asked him to look at it to see what's on it."

"It's password protected," she said as she thought about the computer. "That may be why they still have it running: to find out what's on it."

"So is that enough to knock on his door and check out the apartment?" Bordou asked. "It seems pretty thin to me."

"Well, it's legal," she replied. "It will get us in. If he has stolen property inside, then we can arrest him on that."

"OK. Let's check out how many guys are in there. I don't want to walk into a bunch of drunken gangbangers with guns."

"Roger that," she said. "I'm not dressed for that level of

confrontation." She turned to face him and grinned. "But I bet I'm dressed well enough to ask to use the bathroom."

Bordou looked at her and shook his head. "Not a good idea without backup, Lori."

She was out of the car before he could object further. She marched as fast as she could in her flip-flops to the door of the apartment house. She scanned the list of occupants on the mailbox and selected a name to use in her rouse. Gloria Gomez had an apartment a few doors down from 116. She would use that name. Then she dialed up Bordou on her cell phone and told him her plan. "I'll leave my phone on speaker so you can hear what's going down. I should be in and out in five minutes." She tucked the phone into her pocket and pushed three apartment buzzers to get inside.

Within forty seconds, two people had buzzed back to see who was there. She said she was a resident but had forgotten her keycard. The first one to respond punched the button to unlock the door. She yanked the door open, stepped through, walked steadily down the hall to the door of 116, and boldly knocked. She heard movement inside the apartment, and then the door opened a crack.

"Yeah, who are you?" Hernandez, a young, thin, dark-haired man dressed in a T-shirt and blue jeans, looked her over with one eye as he held the door open by a one-inch slit. Once he saw her shorts and face, he opened the door wider for a better view.

"Hey, I'm sorry to bother you, man. I came to visit Gloria, but she's not home. But I gotta pee *real bad*. Can I use your bathroom—just for a minute? I'd really appreciate it." She smiled prettily and squirmed a little like she really had to go.

He stared at her and said nothing for several seconds.

"Please, I need to go," she repeated in a pleading voice.

"Huh. OK, I guess. Gloria's not home? I thought I saw her a while ago."

"No, not now."

Sanchez stepped inside as soon as he had opened the door for her. He pointed to a hallway, and she rushed toward it like it was life or death. She found the bathroom and hurried inside, where she locked the door. Sanchez did have to use the bathroom, but when she saw the state of the grungy room she decided she could wait a little longer. Instead, she searched the medicine cabinet for prescription drugs. She hit pay dirt. There was a pharmacy-size bottle of five hundred oxycodone pills from Maraxx Pharma sitting on the shelf. There was an assortment of other prescription drugs as well, none of them with a prescription attached.

She flushed the toilet and left the room. Hernandez was sitting on the sofa in the living room tapping the keys on a laptop computer when she returned. It was a silver Acer with a blank screen. A photograph of a blonde woman was taped onto the lower left deck of the keyboard.

She moved closer to see the image while saying, "Nice computer you have there," as noncommittally as she could, showing interest but trying not to act nosey. She leaned over to look at the photo and watched his eyes shift to look at her cleavage as she did so. She got a good look at the image. It was a photo of Clara Alvera's smiling face.

She jumped back in surprise. She hadn't expected that. She straightened up and realized Hernandez had reacted to her move.

"Sorry," she said. "Is that your girlfriend?"

"Ah . . . no, someone else. Say, would you like a beer or something while you wait for Gloria?" Apparently he had decided to hit on her. She must have appeared to be a good target of opportunity.

"Thanks for the use of your bathroom, but I really need to go." She turned and moved to the door as he quickly jumped up from the sofa. "I'll call Gloria later."

She got to the door and opened it just as Hernandez put a hand on her shoulder. "Hey, don't hurry off. We could have a beer and maybe listen to some music."

She shrugged off his hand and was out the door before he delivered a second offer. Her flip-flops slapped the bottoms of her feet as she hustled toward the main entrance. He apparently gave up and slammed his door. She left the building and walked to the Durango as she turned off her phone.

"He has the laptop. He must have gotten it from the guys who broke into Vale's apartment. I saw it. It had Clara's picture taped to it." Adrenaline was still pumping through her veins from the brief encounter, and she took a few deep breaths. She wasn't used to being undercover anymore, so the acting had taken a toll on her confidence. She had survived an impromptu scene, but hadn't expected it to hit her so personally. "And he has illegal drugs in his bathroom. He's our man and he's alone. We'd better take him now before it gets more complicated," she added breathlessly.

"Are you OK? You sound rattled." Bordou put a hand on her shoulder. "Hey, Lori, take a minute and breathe." He sounded concerned and was the voice of reason, as he often was in these situations.

She knew he had her best interests at heart, but she wanted to strike while the iron was hot. Still, she was much more wound up than she had expected to be. Maybe it was seeing Alvera's photo that had upset her so much. It was as if Alvera herself had been kidnapped, not just her image. And Alvera and Josie Vale looked so much alike. It was disturbing.

"Let's get this done," she said. "We have one perp. I didn't see a weapon in the house, and my perception is that he isn't likely to be dangerous. But we have to assume he has a weapon handy and will resist any arrest. When we go in, I can go first and confuse him for a few seconds when he opens the door. Then we pull badges and do standard procedure. Does that sound OK to you?"

"OK, but I'll put on a vest in case this gets rough or he has someone else in the apartment. I think I should enter first because you aren't in uniform and have no protection." He gave her the look he did when he knew his argument was right. "I think I should knock and gain entry and you should be my backup for those same reasons. Plus if we trick him into opening the door with you as eye candy, he might claim entrapment or something like that."

"Wait a minute—" she said.

He didn't let her continue. "Let's not mess up a simple arrest and possibly taint the evidence we collect, OK?" He stared at her as she began to rebut his statement. "Don't argue with me on this, Lori. You don't want to screw things up, do you?"

She was angry now. He had undercut her approach, but she knew he was right. Maybe she wasn't thinking straight because she was upset. She wanted to argue but fell silent after she began to bluster a bit. She took a deep breath and nodded her head. "Shit!" she whispered finally. "You're right. We'll do it your way. It makes sense about the evidence."

Bordou punched her lightly on the shoulder. "Wyatt Earp Sanchez is still showing her head sometimes." He laughed and she joined him.

"Hey, you aren't supposed to call me that anymore." She

grinned at the reference to her shoot-out with cartel heavies two years ago.

"Let's do this, Wyatt," he said as he stepped out of the car. He walked to the trunk and pulled out his bulletproof vest—bulletproof for handguns, at least. He checked his sidearm, a .40-caliber Smith & Wesson M&P Pro that held fifteen-plus-one rounds, a venerable weapon for street use. He replaced it in his holster and gave Sanchez the thumbs-up. She slipped on her utility belt and holster.

Their plan was simple: ring a bell or two to gain entry to the building like Sanchez had done and then go and knock on the door of apartment 116. When they did, they heard a voice inside say they were coming. Then Hernandez opened the door to see a large police officer with a blond crew cut holding out his badge. Hernandez gulped loudly and tried to close the door, but Bordou had a foot shoved in the doorway by then.

"Jessie Hernandez, you are under arrest for failing to appear in traffic court on February twentieth of this year! Open this door, or we'll have to tear the thing down." Bordou began to push heavily on the door while Hernandez pushed back.

"No way, man! I ain't done nothing wrong. You got the wrong man!" Hernandez shouted.

Sanchez stepped up and threw her weight against the door, and that made the difference. Hernandez was thrown back, and the door opened wide. Bordou stepped inside and rushed the suspect, turning him around and pinning him against the wall while Sanchez searched him and cuffed him. Bordou read him his rights.

"I'll clear the place," she said as she swept the room with her Glock gripped in her right hand and her left supporting her grip. She swung the pistol from right to left as she proceeded down the hallway and into two bedrooms and the bath. No one else was present.

"All clear!" she shouted to Bordou. "I'll call it in, and we can get someone to help with the perp and the evidence." She got on the phone.

Bordou moved Hernandez to a chair across the room from the couch and sat him down to keep an eye on him. He took Hernandez's wallet from his pocket and confirmed the man's identity: Jessie Hernandez; born June 3, 1996; black hair; brown eyes; height five feet, nine inches. He held on to the wallet and searched through Hernandez's other pockets. He found a set of keys, some cash, and a computer thumb drive. He placed these objects on the coffee table.

"Where'd you get the computer, Jessie?" Bordou asked. "Who's the chick on the keyboard?"

"She's my girlfriend, asshole." He nearly spat out the words in anger.

"And the machine?"

"A friend gave it to me. It's really nice, isn't it?" Hernandez said sarcastically.

"Who's your friend? The one who gave it to you?"

"I'm not saying any more to you cops." He glowered and stared at Sanchez as she finished her call. "Who's that little bitch, anyway? She came in here and pretended she needed the bathroom. She tried to frame me. She's a real bitch, ya know."

"Yeah, yeah. So who gave you the computer?" Bordou persisted. "Better tell me, or you'll get in even deeper trouble than you're in now. Right now, we have you for a bench warrant, resisting arrest, and receiving stolen property."

"Go fuck yourself!" Hernandez shouted. He tried to spit at Bordou but managed to only get his shirt front wet. "I ain't saying nothing more until I have a lawyer."

"That's probably the best thing to do. You know why?" Bordou smiled grimly. "Because the woman in the photo—the one you called your girlfriend—is dead. That makes you the prime suspect for her murder, you dumb son of a bitch."

It was a white lie, but it shut Hernandez up.

Chapter 20

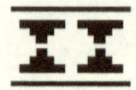

Monday morning, April 8, 2019

Phoenix, Arizona

Sanchez looked exhausted on Monday morning. There were small bags under her eyes, noticeable to her at least, if not to others. She examined her tired features in the mirror. Where was the young, beautiful, vivacious woman she used to be? She was in there somewhere, but she didn't see herself that way today. She needed some rest from this constant running from case to case, clue to clue, crime scene to crime scene. She needed personal time, time with Smith, sleep, sex, fresh air. A week on the beach in the sun with a margarita—a grande. She needed to get back to that dream she had had of herself on an air mattress floating in the sunlight . . . Oh well. Maybe tomorrow she could catch a break.

It had been a long night between processing the apartment and Hernandez's car, and seeing him off to holding. She had verified that the computer was Vale's by typing in her password and seeing the machine come alive. Now she was at Clara Alvera's apartment sharing her discoveries with her over a cup of coffee.

"The technical team said that Hernandez must have been trying to guess at the password, but after one hundred and forty-seven tries, he still hadn't gotten into the machine," she said. "The perps may have given him the computer to figure how to crack it but had been unsuccessful. In any case, the contents of the drives are intact, and I have a copy of Josie's Word files and spreadsheets."

"That's good news. Now maybe we can find out what she was investigating," Alvera said. "But before we get into that, I wanted to tell you I went through her diary and didn't find anything significant about her investigation. She seemed to keep her professional life and her private life completely separate." She smiled wanly. "She was quite a woman."

"Well, that was probably smart of her to do that. It protects her work and her friends as well," Sanchez said. "Nothing else of interest?"

Alvera let out a loud breath. "Well, there is one other thing I found. I guess I'd better tell you." She smiled at her friend in an odd way. "She apparently knew Nick Carter better than I thought." She hesitated.

Sanchez saw that there was something probably disturbing that was about to come out. "Well, spit it out, Clara."

"She and Nick were lovers before she met me."

"Oh geez!"

"She was very needy that way. And I guess he was good in bed," Alvera went on.

"Geez, Clara. I don't want to hear about it." Sanchez was frustrated. "That complicates things. Now we know how she knew him and maybe developed him as a source." She turned to stare at Alvera. "Shit. I wonder if he made a sex video of her too."

Alvera looked grim faced and whispered, "I wondered the same thing. I hope not."

Sanchez sat on the sofa and studied her friend's face, which now exhibited a neutral expression that she could not interpret. "What are you thinking?"

"We need to find out if there's a video of the two of them together. I hope there isn't, but I have to know." She looked up at Sanchez. "For a number of reasons."

"You want to keep her sex life out of the tabloids, for one."

"Right. And she and I look so much alike . . . well."

Sanchez finally got it. "People might think it's you with Nick and not her. Shit! I never thought of that." She looked Alvera up and down. "Wow. That would be weird."

"Can we find out about the video? Can we stop those men from watching all those videos until we find out?" She hesitated again. "Before they think I'm some kind of porn queen?"

Sanchez had to stop to digest that comment. Then she started to laugh. "Oh Clara. That's pretty bizarre. I'll never get that image out of my head."

Alvera was angry then. "It's not funny. It could ruin Josie's reputation and mine too. We have to know if there's a video or not."

"You're going to run for public office, aren't you? That's why you're acting so strange about this stuff, isn't it? It would ruin your chances."

Alvera looked very glum at that point. "The DA has talked to me about running for his seat when he moves on to his senate campaign. It's not for two years, and who knows what could happen by then. I'm thinking about it."

"Oh Clara, I didn't know." Sanchez considered this new information and chuckled. "So none of this can come out—can it?"

"No."

"I'll see if I can intercept the guys at vice and have them pause the review of the videos." Sanchez felt odd doing this. It might be considered interfering with an investigation, and she didn't like it. But Alvera was her best female friend. What else could she do?

"Thank you, Lori."

"Well, the videos aren't central to the case, so a review there may not make any difference."

She looked at her friend for a moment, and an understanding passed between them. It was a unique favor, but they both knew it injected a significant change into their relationship.

"OK," Alvera said quietly. "Now let's talk about the other info you have."

Sanchez was happy to move on. "Here's what we found on the laptop. Josie had not yet written an article, but she had notes and what looks like a draft of the lead into her story."

She read from some pages she had printed out for review. "Recently discovered information has revealed that Maraxx Pharma has been delivering fake prescription drugs to its customers for months and has made a fortune in the process. Investigative reporter Josie Vale has found that drugs manufactured by Maraxx have been diverted for sale to the black market and low-quality generic drugs have been substituted to many of their major clients, such as Veterans Affairs and the Department of Defense Procurement Division, and . . . Sanchez looked up at Alvera. "Wow! Josie could write, couldn't she?"

"No kidding. She was really onto something, by the sounds of it. I wish I could have helped her." Alvera had that lost look on her face again. "No wonder someone wanted her dead."

Sanchez scanned through her notes on the pages she had printed out for review. She summarized the highlights out loud. "She says that Nick was her source for the information on Maraxx. That she met him and discovered the story from conversations with him. He obtained some info for her, probably the bills of lading we saw. He also spied on the shipping department for her and learned that a guy named George Martin was the person switching out the shipments." She raised her head and commented, "That gives us a lead to work with and something I can bring up to the people I've been talking to at Maraxx Pharma.

"So Josie knew Nick, and he told her about the drugs being diverted from Maraxx." Sanchez stood up and started pacing back and forth as she thought it out. "He must have known about it because he must have gotten some of his drug supplies from someone in Maraxx also. Maybe this George Martin. Somehow some gang members—apparently from the Crips— found out about her investigation and tracked her to the gym when she was meeting with Nick."

Alvera got up and walked into the kitchen. She returned to the living room with a pot of coffee and poured some into both of their cups. "And they tortured her for information and maybe for who her source was." She stopped and sipped her coffee, her face grim again. "She wouldn't have told them it was Nick. She was stubborn that way, but maybe they figured it out from body language or something. Anyway, they killed her and then hauled him off to question him elsewhere."

Sanchez picked up the story. "They took him up to the cabin in Payson and beat him to death. Why go all the way up there? Did they already know he had a cabin? Or did he have something they wanted and he told them it was there? If so, what was it?" She stopped pacing to drink some java as her brain began to clear. "Did he have evidence that could be used against them? Or did he owe them money? Whatever it was, they thought he kept it at the cabin."

"Did the deputies find anything unusual there? Have you heard more from them lately?" Alvera asked.

"Not lately. I should call Littlehorse for an update. Maybe there's still something hidden up there."

"So whatever that was all about, they came back to Phoenix to loot Josie's apartment."

"But they didn't find anything that night, so they came back two days later to search the cabin again. That's when Lo and I showed up."

"They must have decided Josie knew too much, but maybe they wanted to know how far she had gotten? So they stole her phone and computer to have a look-see. But they couldn't get into the computer—they hit a dead end," Sanchez said, now pacing again. "So they don't know how far Josie got in her investigation. We know, but they can only guess. They may be in a panic wondering who knows about their operation."

"And how is Elon Grosse involved? Who killed him?"

"That's a mystery," Sanchez said, stopping to pick up her coffee cup. "He was killed in a different manner. Why a hanging? And why two nights later?"

They both stood there thinking. He didn't seem to fit into the pattern of the drug thefts, but he did work for Maraxx.

"Let's look at the bills of lading again. Do you have those with you, Lori?" Alvera looked like she had an idea.

"Yeah, I have images on my phone. What are you thinking?"

"Well, we know that George Martin was involved in the shipments, right? He and maybe someone else in the shipping department basically stole the Maraxx drugs, according to Josie, and substituted other drugs. But to be a big story, a lot of shipments and a lot of drugs per shipment must have been involved. Like boxes or pallets of boxes. To move that much merchandise around, they would need purchase orders and bills of lading. Those might lead us to other people involved at Maraxx."

"OK. Let's look." Sanchez scrolled through the screen on her cell phone awhile and finally opened one of the documents. "Here's one for a Maraxx shipment to the VA. Here's one for receiving a shipment from that other warehouse. Nothing interesting on either one."

"Who signed them?"

"Oh, let's see . . . One is signed by Martin. One is signed by what looks like N. Stillwater. She's in finance. Why would she be signing one of these?"

"Maybe the shipping people needed a signature and she was the only person available. That happens sometimes in big outfits."

"OK. Here's one signed by Martin again. And one signed by E. Grosse? I think that's right. That's a big shipment. This has both Maraxx and Randman products listed on it. And here's another signed by E. Grosse. What a terrible signature. And . . . *Holy shit!*" Sanchez said loudly. "The rest are all signed by Grosse."

Alvera's head snapped up when she understood what it meant. "He was involved in the substitution scheme also. The gang members needed a higher-up to sign off on the sales and shipments. Maybe Grosse was the insider who authorized it all."

"So in their haste to find out who was talking to Josie Vale, they interrogated him and must have killed him, either deliberately or during their questioning. He was a loose end."

"Lori, I think you found the motive for his death and tied the cases together. These people sound like vicious killers. And they're eliminating loose ends."

"And maybe witnesses. Now I'm worried about Lo. Suppose they find out she was at the gym and might have seen something? Her father is leaving for a couple of days again, and she's back in school. She'll be home alone—well—with some sort of security coverage, but I don't know how tight it is."

"Yes, that is a concern. They might come after her and even George Martin if they suspect him of talking to Josie."

Sanchez took her coffee cup to the kitchen and put on her utility belt holding her holstered Glock. She was in her usual uniform today: blue shirt, black pants, and tactical boots. She walked over to Alvera and gave her a goodbye hug. "I've got about a dozen phone calls to make and have to find another place for Lo to stay to be secure. I can't leave her home alone."

"And I have to get in to work also. Remember the video too, please." She looked worried. "I know it's a lot to ask. But I'll owe you a big one."

"No problem." Sanchez hesitated, "You might be in danger too, you know. Suppose the gang finds out you knew Josie? They had your photo right in front of them. They must have found your phone number on her cell phone. You two would have made a lot of calls back and forth, right? Maybe they'll decide you know something."

"I hadn't thought about that."

"Well, be careful, will you?" Sanchez turned to go. "How secure is this building anyway?"

"We have a doorman downstairs, and each apartment has its own individual security system. I need a remote to get in and out of the garage."

"Sounds pretty basic. I don't want to scare you, but these guys would get past that pretty easily."

"Great, Lori. You just made my day. Now I'll lie awake all

night too."

***

Sanchez spent the rest of the day making phone calls and talking to people about the case. She called the guys at vice and walked over to their shop to see how far they had proceeded in viewing the videos Nick Carter had recorded. Fortunately for Alvera, they had not gotten very far due to a bust they had made on Thursday night. That had all the staff tied up interviewing witnesses and logging their own evidence into the record. She thanked them and said she had someone else available to view the files, so she would log them back into her custody. She wasn't sure how she would get them processed, but she would figure that out later. She took the thumb drives with her and placed them in the locking compartment of her car's trunk for now. She couldn't leave them in the department.

She called Deputy Littlehorse in Gila County and asked him if his investigators could give the cabin a more intensive search. She said there might be drugs hidden in it somewhere and explained her reasoning. He agreed to take another look. He reported that all the fingerprints had been identified and the three prominent men's prints belonged to the victim and the two men who had been at the gymnasium crime scene. She filled him in on the new information discovered on her end that might tie into the murder in his county. He promised to search the cabin that afternoon if nothing bizarre happened. She asked if he expected something bizarre to happen, and he replied he expected it every day and was rarely disappointed.

She called Natasha Stillwater at Maraxx Pharma and arranged a meeting at 3:00 p.m. to share her news. Stillwater said she had uncovered new information also.

Montero called and asked if she was OK because he hadn't heard more from her since late last night. She had talked to him after she and Bordou had busted Hernandez but hadn't followed up this morning. He said he was going out to the VA to check on their warehouse and hoped to have more news that evening. She told him about how Grosse's signature appeared prominently on Maraxx Pharma bills of lading and that he might want to look into invoices and shipping documents out there while he was visiting.

Next she called Lolita's cell phone to see how she was doing and caught her between classes at school. She told the teenager that she was concerned about her security and wanted to meet her after school to talk to the security people who were protecting her.

"What security people?" Lolita asked. "Dad said we didn't need any bodyguards because we have a state-of-the-art security system at the house. He told me to always lock it up when I was home. He said that would be all I needed."

Sanchez's heart felt like it would fall from her chest. She winced and bit her tongue as she let her anger subside. She asked, "How about when you're at school or out driving? Suppose someone follows you from home to school, or the other way around? They could wait by your car to grab you."

"Well, now you're making me nervous, Lori. Geez Louise. Are you trying to scare me?" Lolita sounded upset. "Well, that's what Dad said. He thinks you're exaggerating the threat. Anyway, he'll be back on Wednesday and will work from home the rest of the week, so don't worry."

Sanchez was frustrated. She didn't have any direct evidence about a threat to Lolita, but she had a gut feeling that she was in danger. And she cared for the girl. She was bright and independent, and Sanchez liked that about her. She saw a little of herself in Lolita looking back to when she herself had been young and rebellious. She made up her mind to do something about the situation.

"Listen, Lo. I need to talk to you right after school. Can I pick you up at school so we can talk?"

"Yeah, I guess so, why?"

"Well, we learned some new facts about the case, and I wanted to ask you about them. You're at Arcadia High School, aren't you?"

"Yeah, I guess that would be OK. I get out at two thirty today. I could meet you in front at the bus loading area if you know where that is. That's where I usually pick up my Uber ride."

"Yeah, I do. I'll see you at two thirty p.m. Thanks, Lo."

She reviewed her options. She couldn't force the girl to do what she wanted, but she was worried about her. And she wanted to talk to her father and ask why he thought there was no risk. She decided to simply reason with Lolita and see where that got her. She still needed to find a place for her to stay if she could spirit her out of the family house.

Sanchez then dealt with the scourge of paperwork that seemed to preoccupy a major part of her time at the office. That was one reason she avoided the office whenever she could get away with it. She checked the log listing the contents of Hernandez's apartment and noted that he had a cell phone she hadn't seen. The record said he had several text messages and voice mails that an officer had transcribed that morning.

She scanned the list of texts. One caught her eye. It had been sent the evening of his arrest to someone named Paco, also called El Burro. The text said: *Two women at gym Mon night. Megan is trainer and Lolita is Ns bitch. May see you w N. Might no 2 much?*

"What?" Sanchez said out loud. "You've got to be kidding me."

Bordou, who sat in the cubicle just in front of her desk, stood up to look over the partition. "What's so funny?"

"It's not funny at all," she said. "I just read a text that prick Hernandez sent to someone named Paco. He said there were two women at the gym on Monday night. He knew about Lolita and Megan being there and says they may have seen something."

"Really? So who's Paco?"

"I don't know for sure, but I think he's the Sinaloa hit man who's doing some of these killings. This tells me the gang might know more than I thought about what happened that night. It also means that Megan and Lo might be in real danger if Hernandez told others that there may be witnesses."

"Yeah, it sounds like they could be targets. What should we do?"

"Listen, I've got to pick Lo up at school. Can you call Megan Faux and warn her that there may be a threat? I've got to go."

She left to meet Lolita at her school on East Indian School Road. She figured she had time to pick her up and then make the meeting at Maraxx Pharma too if everything went well. It rarely did.

Sanchez turned the Charger onto Indianola Avenue in front of the high school about twenty minutes after she had left the station. The school was a widely spread horseshoe-shaped building. She was expecting to see a string of buses lined up alongside the main school entrance. But in this day of Uber and nervous parents who drove their kids everywhere, instead she found a string of cars backed up in that area. There were only two school buses waiting for passengers. She thought she would have to wait for at least ten minutes to allow cars picking kids up to crawl through the narrow street that was jammed with traffic.

Then she looked over to her left and saw Lolita standing about a hundred feet away on the curb along the adjacent street. She was dressed in her usual shorts and tank top with her small blue backpack slung over her shoulder, the one with the Olympic logo sewn onto it. She must have realized how crowded it was and shifted away from the traffic to make it easier for Sanchez to pull up.

She stood right at the corner of Indianola and East Indian School where there was a slight widening in the road. Sanchez saw a gap in traffic creeping out of the school and exiting onto the major road. She swung her Charger out into the opposing traffic and began to make a Y-turn much to the outrage of all the nervous parents who had waited in line for innumerable minutes. A car she cut off honked at her, and someone gave her the finger. She quickly rocked back to make the tail of the Y and then burned rubber as she completed the turn in the reverse direction, quite pleased with her driving skills.

She looked over to see if Lolita had watched her moves and was surprised to see a black panel van pull right up next to the girl and slam on the brakes. Lolita jumped back from the van as two men climbed out of its side door and approached her. They ran forward and grabbed her by the arms. She struggled and kicked one man in the groin. He let go of her while she tried to get away from the other man. It all seemed to happen in slow motion. Two teenagers standing nearby did nothing but watch and cringe. Another videoed the whole event and didn't help either.

Sanchez was shocked into action. Her car was blocked in by traffic, so she couldn't respond by driving along the road to block the van from moving. The street was not an option, but the sidewalk was clear next to her and she decided to go for it. She cranked the wheel to the right and pressed on the gas to climb onto the curb. Once one wheel was up, she gunned it, and the vehicle lunged over the curb and down the sidewalk. She honked the horn in warning, and kids ran for cover as she rocketed along the walkway and onto the grass next to it.

Up ahead, she saw that both men now had Lolita by the arms and were dragging her kicking and screaming toward the van. She was only seconds away and began to honk the horn even more, partly in rage and partly as warning. Then she threw the switch for the siren, and that stopped the men in their tracks. They looked at each other, and one broke away to run to the van. The other hesitated enough for Lolita to kick him in the privates again, and she broke free.

Sanchez rolled up next to the man Lolita had just kicked, opening her door as she passed him and slamming him to the ground. Then she took aim at the van and rammed its sliding door with the Charger, causing a massive collision that resonated across the school grounds. The car squealed to a stop, and she jumped out. The man on the ground regained his feet and ran to the van as it peeled away, leaping through the open sliding side door.

Sanchez ran after the van as it rounded the corner and saw that it had no license plate. She stopped at the road and tried to catch her breath. The adrenaline was overwhelming, and she had to stop and bend over for a second. She turned around just as Lolita ran to her and threw her arms around her, tears streaming down her face.

Thank God! She's OK, Sanchez thought. She held her tightly, and they both sighed loudly. She felt on the verge of tears herself. She pulled back to look at Lolita's wet face, and they both half shrieked and half laughed at their near miss.

"Are you OK? My God, I thought they had you," Sanchez said in a thick voice. "Did they hurt you?"

"No. I'm OK," Lolita murmured between sobs. "I'm so sorry, Lori. I'm sorry."

"Why sorry? I'm just glad you're all right."

"Because I didn't believe you. Because I thought you were being overly protective." She hugged Sanchez again. "Oh I'm scared. I can't help it." She was shaking in Sanchez's embrace. They held each other for a while.

Then people began to run up to them to see if they were unharmed. Most of them were supportive when they understood that they had just witnessed an attempted kidnapping. One man came up, grabbed Sanchez by the arm, and yelled at her for being a reckless driver. He threatened to call the police until she produced her badge and two women bystanders told him to go away.

Sanchez called in the incident, and a patrol car soon appeared. She provided the description of the van and the direction it had fled: a black Chevy with a bashed right side.

Many people came up to talk to them—some of them kids Lolita knew—wanting to know if she was all right. The police report took a half hour, and Sanchez remembered to call Natasha Stillwater to postpone their meeting.

When everything had been documented, Sanchez climbed into the Charger with its left front fender caved in and started the car. She and Lolita drove slowly to a local Dairy Queen and had milkshakes to calm their nerves.

As they sat in the car slurping their drinks, Sanchez said, "After this meeting, we're going to your place and then mine to get our overnight things and then to a friend's apartment for the night. You'll like her and you'll be safe. OK?"

"Yeah, I'm going to call my dad and say I'm staying with you. That way he won't worry if I don't answer the home phone. He still calls there first, then my cell." Lolita gave Sanchez a sad look. "I won't tell him about this tonight. He'll panic and then feel awful."

"OK. Let's go."

The Charger limped away with a wheezing sound and a steaming radiator, but it was still drivable.

Chapter 21

Monday afternoon, April 8, 2019

Phoenix, Arizona

At Maraxx, Sanchez asked Lolita to wait in the outer office while she met with Natasha Stillwater. She was pleased to see that the VP had done a great deal of research since their last meeting the week before. She had investigated the leads that Sanchez had given her and compiled a small summary table of her results.

"I followed some of these lots of product through our shipping department. You were right: some of our shipments have irregularities. It seems that about one out of five shipments is either diverted or contains Randman Labs products in place of our own brand. This shouldn't be happening. We don't ordinarily transship someone else's products through our plant."

"Are you sure that all the shipments of Maraxx products are really yours and that they haven't been substituted into your packaging?"

Stillwater looked worried. "That is a possibility we also have to look at. We need to know if someone is not only switching bottles but may be counterfeiting our packaging too." She gasped. "That would be devastating."

"No kidding. Will you check for that?" Sanchez hoped they would or she might have to get involved. "We have people that could work with you on this because it's a public safety issue. I suppose your larger clients also will need to be involved."

"But that's just the thing. This will damage our reputation. We have to change our procedures to provide an extra level of certification guaranteeing that our products are really ours. That will take a few days to put in place. In the meantime, we may have to recall and test a lot of our shipments to ensure quality. It's a daunting project."

Sanchez empathized with the woman. She was ensnared in a huge packaging and shipping debacle that could unleash a scandal for the company. Unfortunately, her friend Elon Grosse seemed to be one of the ringleaders of the criminal enterprise.

"Our board is meeting today with all of us managers to decide how to handle the situation, both practically and from the PR standpoint. We will notify all the customers first—I've already begun such action through our contracting people, but we must discuss how to secure the product line."

Sanchez wanted to address another part of the pharmaceutical scam. "Who else can sign off on these shipments? Isn't that handled through contracts? Who else besides Grosse could be involved? I mean, outside the shipping department?"

"Technically, any of our senior managers can authorize a shipment if necessary. But I will have to see about that and find out if anyone else outside of the usual channels has been doing this. I have signed in a pinch, but Grosse normally never signed for these orders. It would have been out of the normal chain of operations."

"I need to talk to George Martin, if you could arrange that for me. He may be involved in actually making the shipments."

"That will be difficult, Detective." Stillwater looked angry. "He disappeared from the shipping office right after I announced we were beginning an investigation this morning. I don't know where he is."

"Oh great. Maybe he's on the run. Can you give me his address? We can try to locate him." She waited while Stillwater brought up his address on her computer. "Do you suspect him of being in on this scam?"

"I have a feeling he has been involved from the very start. He was mixed up in a number of the problems we had already identified. We were about to remove him from his position as head of shipping."

"I'll send a car to this address to look for him. He's a person of interest now." Sanchez stood up and shook Stillwater's hand. "It looks like your friend Grosse was entangled in some mischief. Working with a gang in this scheme could explain where his sudden wealth came from. Good luck, and keep in touch as you make progress. And be careful—the gang involved may take revenge."

She walked out the door and found Lolita talking to a young woman, presumably from the office. Just as Sanchez was ready to signal her friend to join her, her phone rang. It was Deputy Littlehorse from Gila County.

"You were right," he said. "We did a more thorough search of the cabin and found a cellar under the main room. The iron stove in the living room was sitting on a metal plate that could be moved to one side. It hid a trapdoor that led us to the staircase and room below."

"What did you find?"

"Carter had a stockpile of pharmaceuticals down there and a lockbox full of cash," he said. "The bottles all read *Maraxx Pharma Inc.* We counted twenty-five of those five-hundred-pill bottles of oxycodone with forty-milligram doses. Those would sell on the street at maybe twenty bucks per pill, so each bottle had a street value of ten thousand dollars or more. There were other prescription drugs too, but we're still taking an inventory. I'll send it to you when it's final."

"You said there was cash too?"

"Yeah, just over sixteen thousand bucks in mostly twenties. This guy was in business in a big way. The men who killed him may have been looking for his stash."

"That sounds likely. We think they were trying to make him divulge who he shared information with as well. We believe they're the same men who killed a VP from Maraxx Pharma. Nick Carter worked for Maraxx as a trainer in their gym and had some drugs like oxy and steroids that he was dealing out of that venue. Maybe he stole them from the company. That would explain the hoard of drugs."

"Maybe. Well, I'd better go and finish up here. Thanks for the tip, Sanchez." He hung up.

She noticed a text come in from Bordou: *Can't locate Megan Faux at home or office. No response to phone.*

That could mean anything, not necessarily anything to worry about yet, she thought.

A second text from Bordou arrived as she considered what to do next.

P.S: Van located five miles away. Empty. Stolen this AM.

Well, that was inevitable too, she thought. *It's not my day.*

Sanchez realized that she had been so caught up in her work that she had neglected to worry about how the kidnapping had affected Lolita. She had calmed down by the time they had arrived at Maraxx Pharma, but then Sanchez had gotten preoccupied with the meeting. She looked at Lolita, who seemed to be OK, but looks could be deceiving. The girl might need more support to help her handle the trauma she had experienced.

It wasn't every day that someone tried to grab you and throw you into a van. Sanchez felt sorry. She should have thought about this more carefully. Maybe she was screwing this up. Lolita looked like a fully grown woman, but she was only sixteen, which was still very young and impressionable. Sanchez thought, *I would make a lousy parent.*

"Hey, Lo!" she called out. "Ready to get out of here?"

Lolita looked up and smiled, but Sanchez thought she detected another emotion just below the surface. "Yeah, I'm ready to go."

It was after five o'clock by the time they got rolling to fight rush hour traffic. Lolita seemed fine but maybe sad. Sanchez glanced at her a few times to make sure she was OK. The kid was tough, but Sanchez couldn't take anything for granted.

They drove to the Thompson house so the girl could pack a few clothes and other school essentials. Then they swung by Sanchez's apartment, and she packed a duffle with clothes and grabbed her go bag. After an hour and a half, they arrived at Alvera's place, Sanchez parked the car in the guest slot, and they made their way upstairs.

Sanchez made the introductions. "Lo, this is my friend Clara. She works for the DA's office downtown."

"Pleased to meet you, Lo. I understand you experienced an ordeal today." Alvera shook Lolita's hand. "Welcome to my home. I have a guest bedroom you can use as long as you need to. Lori tells me that we have something in common—we both need protection for a few days."

"What?" Lolita asked, surprised. "You need protection too?"

Sanchez looked at them both and nodded her head. "We think the same guys who tried to grab you today may want to harm Clara. You see, you both were at the gym the night of the murder."

"I was the one who found the body," Alvera said to Lolita as she glared at Sanchez. "It was awful."

"I didn't even know what happened until afterward when Lori came to look in the back." Lolita seemed to still be in shock after all that had happened. "Now someone wants to kidnap me—or worse." Her face began to turn pink and her lip trembled, like she was feeling miserable.

Sanchez saw what was about to happen and stepped over to Lolita and threw her arms around her in a bear hug. "We're not going to let anything happen to you, sweetie. You're safe here with us."

Alvera took the cue and put her arms around Lolita from the side, hugging both her and Sanchez. "She's right, Lo. You'll be safe and snug right here. And you and I are going to look after each other and get to know each other. OK?"

"Sure, thank you. You have a nice place here," Lolita said as she looked around. "Thanks for putting me up."

They made small talk for a few minutes, and the girl told Alvera about the kidnapping attempt and how scared she had been. They decided to order in Chinese food for dinner and have it delivered. While they waited for the food to arrive, Alvera showed Lolita to the guest bedroom. She showed her where she could unpack her things and offered her a nightgown. Then Alvera joined Sanchez in the living room.

"You know, Clara, I'll stay too. I wasn't sure I made that clear over the phone."

"Oh yes, I assumed you would. You feel like you have to keep us safe. I get it." Clara smiled. "Lo is very impressive. But she is also very young to have to bear all that has happened to her alone. Where's her father, anyway? Why isn't he here for her now?"

"There are some issues," Sanchez said. "She has him convinced that she's an adult and can take care of herself. He believes her, so she has to play the brave soldier role. It's an arrangement they've made, but I think he has forgotten that she is still a child in many ways."

"Well, I only have two beds. Do you plan to sleep with me in my bed or with her? She may need you to comfort her during the night. I think this brave façade may break down at some point."

"I don't know about that. We shared a bed for three nights at my place, and it was fine. But we didn't have a choice on that." Sanchez looked toward the guest room where they could hear the shower running. "She's a great kid. I think I assume she's an adult too. Maybe I should crawl in with her and give her a shoulder to cry on."

"Yeah, it's been rough for all of us." She paused. "I miss Josie. It hurts to think about her."

"Maybe you need a shoulder to cry on too. I'm sorry I haven't been around to support you more, Clara. I'm not used to thinking about other people's emotions in these situations. I'm always tied up with casework and forget about the toll it takes on people, especially friends."

"I know, Lori. You have so much to do, and now, on top of that, you have to keep us safe. It's too much for one person."

"Look," Sanchez said earnestly. "How are you going to handle these investigations at the DA's office? Are you going to recuse yourself from Josie's murder case? I need to know."

"Yes, I talked to DA Davis and told him I knew the victim, so I couldn't be involved in the gym murder and the break-in at her place. But I will handle the drug-related cases at Maraxx Pharma and the VA, and whatever else comes out of them."

"Good. That sounds like a good division of work. It gives you a reason to keep your name out of it. And that way you and I can work together on the pharmaceutical side of things. Montero is very concerned about what has happened at the VA and his comrades in arms."

"Yes. It's quite concerning that those people have been getting substandard drugs," Alvera said. "I have a meeting with someone from the VA's Office of Investigations out there tomorrow to talk about what they have been doing about it. The man I talked to sounded very noncommittal about sharing information."

"They seem afraid to admit their shortcomings. Look at how long it took them to admit they had problems with scheduling and treatment." Sanchez looked at her watch. It was nearly 7:00 p.m. "Where's that food? I've got one more thing to do before I can relax tonight. I'm going with Montero to stake out a warehouse."

"You're kidding. Why tonight?"

"It's the other warehouse where the Randman shipments seem to come from. I wanted to see what they do there. He volunteered for a short stakeout of the place."

"OK. But when will you get back here?"

"By ten or eleven. You still have your silver pistol, don't you?" Sanchez grinned. Alvera had a nickel-plated .38-caliber pistol for concealed carry. "When I leave, I want you to lock up tight and keep that thing handy until I get back."

"No problem, Lori. But I hope you're overestimating the threat."

The Chinese food arrived then, and Sanchez stood by with her handgun as Alvera opened the door. There was no trouble with the delivery, and Lolita joined them to eat right after that.

Sanchez got up to leave. "Don't take any chances, you two.

I'll be back as soon as I can. And Lo, don't worry about me."

Sanchez left the apartment as the sun began to fall in the western desert.

Chapter 22

Monday evening, April 8, 2019
Chandler, Arizona

Sanchez waited outside on the street in front of Alvera's apartment house. She scanned the street and landscaping surrounding the building looking for any suspicious activity that could signal it was being surveilled. She didn't see anyone watching from a parked car or loitering by the garage, the most likely place to gain entry past the guard's cameras. She had stopped on the way out to advise the guard to keep on his toes because there was a threat. He seemed to take the warning seriously, because he pulled his sidearm out of the holster to show her he was armed and ready.

She wondered if she should have put in a request for a patrol car to be stationed in front of the building. Maybe she would have to do that in the morning. But Captain Teller would protest that it wasn't in his budget and that she should ask the DA's office to cover the cost. What a guy.

She cast an eye toward the setting sun and wondered where Montero was. He wasn't usually late. She checked her watch. He was ten minutes behind schedule.

Clouds were moving in from the north off the Mogollon Rim, a possible sign of unsettled weather. That happened sometimes in the spring but rarely brought a shower, just wind. It also meant that the moon would be hidden from sight, which was good when she was on a stakeout. An unmarked vehicle was harder to notice in the dark of night.

Montero rounded the corner in his white truck, and Sanchez considered its color. White was not a desirable shade for a stakeout vehicle, but at least the moon wouldn't light them up like a spotlight tonight. They would have to make do. She was grateful that he had volunteered his truck for the mission since she had a damaged vehicle. Thank God she would get her Interceptor back in the morning and she could unload the half-wrecked Charger. She imagined she would get the usual lecture about treating department vehicles like carnival bumper cars.

"Good evening, ma'am," Montero said as she slid into the passenger seat. "I'll be your Uber driver for the evening."

"Very funny, but don't call me 'ma'am' again," she responded with a grin. "Thanks for coming out with me on a stakeout. We haven't done one of these for a while."

"Yes, well, it seems the only way we can spend quality time together lately." He chuckled as he pulled away from the curb. "How's Lo doing? She must have been terrified."

"She's holding it in pretty much right now. But I can't stay out too long. I think she'll need some support before she can sleep."

"Well, at least she's with Clara. How's *she* holding up?"

"As well as can be expected." Sanchez consulted the map on her cell phone. "Head right out on I-10 toward the Santan Freeway intersection. The warehouse is in that mess of industrial buildings out there. We'll need to exit east on Chandler Boulevard."

"OK. Great."

"Clara's fine, I think, but I need to pay more attention to her too. I'm going to stay at her apartment with the two of them until this shit gets resolved. The kidnap attempt came out of left field. I'm worried the thugs might try to harm Clara as well."

"Why's that? Because she might have seen them?"

"That and because she was Josie's girlfriend, so they may think she knows about Josie's investigation and newspaper story."

"You can't protect them and do your job too. Have you asked the department to assign a protective detail to them? It seems that they would qualify under these circumstances."

"In a logical world, yes, but I'm afraid to ask Teller about it. I'm hoping the DA can do something. I'll talk to Clara. She seems to think it would be overkill, but then, there was what happened today."

"The kidnap attempt? Yeah, a pretty persuasive argument, I would think."

"Hey, how busy are you the next couple of days, Guillermo?" She gave him her seriously-needing-a-favor look.

"Oh no. Not me," he said defensively. "Besides, I'm in enough hot water already for just knowing you."

"What is that supposed to mean?"

"My superior wants me to shepherd a small congregation out in Parker by Lake Havasu for a couple of months while they locate a replacement priest for the church. I think they want to separate me from you now that you're in the news again. Afraid I'll get sucked into one of your situations."

"What? That's crazy. Why me and why now?"

Montero gave her a surprised look. "Are you kidding? Haven't you been watching the news lately? You're all over the papers and TV: 'Police detective saves girl from kidnapping in violent confrontation.' You and Lolita were all over the news tonight. And they got a photo of Lo doing gymnastics at some competition. They're building the story up big and showing her photo everywhere."

"Oh no. I didn't know any of that. I've been on the go for days."

"They've even shown Clara's photo as the woman who discovered the murder at the gym. By the way, I thought she was being kept out of this?"

"She should be. I don't know how they found that out. Is Lo mentioned in any of the news accounts of the gym murder?"

"Not that I've seen. But it may be a matter of time before someone connects the attempted kidnapping with the gym case."

Sanchez indicated where to drive once they had left the freeway and eased onto Chandler Boulevard. They cruised south on North 56th and turned onto Frye Road. "Stop here a minute. It's right up there where the floodlights are. Let's sit and observe before we approach, OK?"

"Sure." Montero doused his headlights. He pulled out a pair of binoculars and looked the warehouse over—at least, the part he could see. "So this is the Randman warehouse?"

"I don't know for sure. It's where the shipments to Maraxx come from."

It was a medium-size steel building with two drive-in doors on rollers and three loading bays on an outdoor dock. No trucks were currently backed up to the docking area. There were lights on in the building, but they couldn't see any activity from their viewpoint. No vehicles arrived or left, but three people came out of a smaller manway located next to one of the drive-in doors. They each walked to a vehicle and soon departed the premises via a large gate in the chain-link fencing. It was apparently the conclusion of a shift.

"I don't see anyone else entering the place, so maybe it's the end of the day," Montero commented. "Do you want to wait to see what happens next or move closer and maybe sneak up to one of the windows?"

"Let's see if we can pick out any night watchmen first." Sanchez picked up the binoculars and scanned the warehouse and the fence surrounding the property. "Pull up so we can get a closer look. Maybe see the back end of the building."

Montero started the truck and crept forward along the road without turning on the headlights. When they were within a hundred yards of the front gate, they stopped and waited. From that vantage point, they could see that there was a trailer parked next to the warehouse just past the loading docks. It looked like it could be a guard shack with lights streaming through the windows. A man emerged from the warehouse through the manway, locked the door behind him, and walked to the trailer. He entered, and they saw him sit down at a desk.

"It's eight p.m. He must have locked up for the night. I wonder if he stays here all night," Sanchez said.

It was completely dark now. As they watched in the quiet of the night, they saw one of the large vehicle doors open slowly. A five-ton box truck with a sixteen-foot-long enclosure pulled out of the warehouse and stopped. A man exited the cab and ran back to close the door while the driver sat in his seat. When the door was closed, the driver honked his horn and the guard stepped out of the trailer to wave at the driver. The passenger climbed into the cab, and the truck slowly crawled through the front gate. The guard walked out after them, closed the gate, and locked it with a chain and padlock. The truck turned left and drove past Montero and Sanchez as the two observers ducked down to hide from the headlights.

"That's odd," Montero said. "Who delivers pharmaceuticals at eight p.m.?"

Sanchez scanned the warehouse again. "I think they're closed up for the night, so there isn't much going on here." She shifted around in her seat and watched the box truck swing north on North 56th Street. "Maybe we should follow them and see where they're going."

"I'm up for a drive," Montero said. "Let's see where they go."

He turned the truck around and turned on his headlights once they had moved away from the warehouse. He loosely followed, staying back far enough to not be noticeable to the other driver. He had experience in tailing suspicious vehicles from back in his day at the El Paso Police Department.

The box truck merged onto I-10 southbound. Montero followed at a half-mile interval as the vehicle exited onto Highway 347 and headed south. They drove for miles, passing agricultural lands and crossing the Gila River. They followed the truck south through Maricopa, where it merged onto I-8 and went westward for more than a half hour. At Gila Bend, they exited the freeway and drove south on State Route 85. The road headed straight south as they continued through vacant land.

"Is this a reservation of some kind? I don't know what's out here," Sanchez asked as they passed through miles of desert with little to distinguish one mile from another.

"I don't know either. Maybe it's an Indian reservation or just a federal reserve of some kind."

The truck barreled on past Childs and then slowed down. It eased onto a gravel road that crossed the highway and drove east into the desert. Montero hesitated to pursue the truck until it was nearly out of sight in the dismal landscape, then he followed cautiously. Soon it became clear that they were following a drainage system up an outwash plain that flowed out of the small mountain range to the east, just barely visible in the scattered moonlight. They crossed small dirt roads that had been beaten into the desert pavement about every mile. The road they traveled turned here and there to follow the terrain and crossed a dry streambed twice. The truck turned once at a crossing with another gravel road and then climbed up into a low pass in the mountain range they had seen from afar.

"I can't get too close, or he'll know I'm following him. But I guess by now he knows we're here," Montero said. "Where the hell is he going?"

Driving slowly, he switched his truck's headlights off as they crossed the pass, guiding the Toyota by sporadic moonbeams. Then he stopped.

There was no box truck in sight. No taillights or movement in the desert landscape before them. They sat in the Toyota and watched for any hint of a vehicle ahead. Nothing.

"Where in blazes did they go?" Montero asked loudly. "I can't see anything out there."

"Shit!" Sanchez said. "We lost them."

Chapter 23

Tuesday morning, April 9, 2019

Phoenix, Arizona

Lolita and Alvera had waited up for Sanchez, who had returned around midnight the night before. After listening to her explain what she and Montero had been up to, they all had gone to sleep. Sanchez had crawled into bed with Alvera on her king-size mattress. It was roomy enough that they could enjoy a comfortable night's rest. But before Sanchez could fall asleep, Lolita crawled in beside her and put her head on her shoulder. Then she released an ocean of tears and concerns as her new friend tried to comfort her. They eventually fell asleep amid their worries and had a restless night.

Alvera was the first up and made coffee in her sturdy Braun MultiServe apparatus, letting the others sleep in. Soon Sanchez slipped out of bed, leaving her young friend to blissfully slumber.

"That kid can really sleep up a storm," Sanchez said as she shuffled into the kitchen in her T-shirt and boxers, yawning and rubbing her eyes. "She cried herself to sleep after confessing how scared she was. I think she kept her head on my shoulder all night." She held her arm out at her side and rotated it around in circles for a few seconds to loosen it up.

"You two were cute sleeping like that. I didn't want to wake you." Alvera smiled warmly at her friend. "You know, I think you'll be a great mother someday just from watching you with

Lo."

"Who, me? No, I'm too busy to be a mom, and I wouldn't know what to do." She seemed both pleased at Alvera's comment and embarrassed by it. "But she is a darling, isn't she?"

They both shared a wistful smile, and then Sanchez looked at the clock. "Holy shit! It's eight o'clock. I'd better get moving." She gulped her coffee and searched the countertop for something sweet to eat.

Alvera laughed at her antics. "Sorry, no doughnuts. I'll have to bring some pastries in for breakfast if you're both going to be here all week."

Sanchez smirked at the comment. "I'll get my caffeine and sugar at the office. I have a lot to do today." She looked through the open door into Alvera's bedroom and grinned. "I plan to get you safely in your car to work and then drop her off at school. I'd better get in the shower."

"Me too. I have a case to prepare. You can take the guest shower if you like, and I'll use mine. But we'll need to wake sleepyhead soon."

They set about the business of getting ready for work.

***

Sanchez drove the Charger to drop off Lolita at school with the strict understanding that she was to stay in the building all day. Sanchez would pick her up at the end of the school day at about 3:00 p.m. Lolita would not step outside until she saw Sanchez's car, which was going to be the Interceptor. She would call Sanchez at midday to make contact.

Next Sanchez drove to the motor pool, where she exchanged the damaged Charger for the repaired Interceptor. She had to sign for the car and was given a lecture about proper use of department property. Sanchez stood there and listened with stoic fortitude. In the end, she asked if the manager would have let the kidnapper get away or if he would have used the car to save the girl. He swore at her, and she left feeling she had won her argument.

She drove to the department and conferred with Bordou on progress made in the cases they were working on. Lab results confirmed their suspicions about the drugs they had found in Nick Carter's locker. The Maraxx Pharma drugs were of high quality, and the Randman Labs drugs were inferior to the point of having less than half the potency of the brand-name ones. The generics also contained enough impurities that should have prevented them from being sold on the market in the first place. The quality-control problems seemed to span the range of drugs manufactured by Randman Labs.

"I wouldn't take any of those drugs," Bordou said. "And the results from Montero's VA pill samples are the same. He was right. The smooth pills were the brand-name ones, and those with the rough finish were the low-quality ones. The vets have been fed bad medicine. It's outrageous."

"I'll let him know the results," she said. "Some are even worse than that. Almost like they were just fake pills altogether. One of the oxy pills was talc, as in talcum powder. Not a painkiller at all. No wonder people are upset. You'd think someone would have discovered this problem earlier."

"Well, we may have other problems too," he said. "I've tried to locate Megan Faux but haven't been able to get ahold of her. I hope she's all right."

"It might be worth going by her apartment to see if you can find anything useful. Maybe she just went out of town for a few days."

"I'll try to swing by later. By the way, we've released the entire gym from crime scene status. I can check to see if anyone there knows her schedule."

"It's pretty much shut down now, isn't it? They don't have other staff, do they?"

"I don't know that. I can check."

"Say, last night, Montero and I staked out that warehouse in Chandler and followed a truck that left there after eight p.m. It drove way out in the desert, and we lost it in the middle of nowhere."

"Why were you following it?"

"We thought it was pretty odd to be delivering pharmaceuticals at that time of night. And I don't know what they were doing out in the desert. There wasn't even a town nearby." Sanchez looked puzzled for a minute. "I've got to look up satellite images of that area and see what lies out there. That part of the desert looks very desolate, but there may have been some mining activity in the old days. I'm meeting Montero again at ten to go back out and look at the scene in daylight. Maybe we can figure out what happened."

"OK, I have a meeting too. Good luck with the mystery." Bordou gathered his papers and walked toward the elevator.

Sanchez sat down at her computer and called up Google Earth to locate the area in question. She found the roads they had driven and followed their route up to the mountain pass. She saw that on the other side of the mountain—the side they did not travel—there were many small dirt roads and trails that sprawled out from the main gravel road. There was nothing remarkable about the landscape except that there were a number of arroyos that crossed it and drained down the mountain slope to the east.

She spotted a dark object showing on the aerial view. When she zoomed in, she saw what appeared to be an abandoned quarry. She continued to scan the area and found a small building about a mile away from the quarry on the far side of the valley. One of the smaller roads ran across the valley connecting the two sites. When she zoomed in on the building, it disappeared in the pixels of the photo. She made prints of the area so she could find the two features later in the field.

By that time, it was nearly ten o'clock, so she packed her bag and walked out the back door of the station to her parking spot. The Interceptor was still partly in the shade of the building and therefore not as hot as a sauna when she climbed inside.

She picked up Montero at his house, and they headed west on I-10 at high speed. She hit ninety miles an hour on the nearly empty freeway. They cut south on State Route 85 and made good time along the road to Childs. They had to slow down considerably on the gravel and dirt roads they followed after that.

"I think you set a new speed record from Phoenix to Childs," Montero said. He had enjoyed the ride but apparently felt he needed to remind Sanchez she drove too fast. "Now we just follow that gravel road east toward the pass. This ground looks easier to cross in the daylight. Last night, I couldn't see the bumps and arroyos so well."

"It was easier in your truck though with the higher clearance, but we can make it across here if I can crab-walk across some of these drainages."

She drove confidently along, and they reached the pass in seventeen minutes with a few scrapes and bumps along the way. "OK. We're here," Sanchez said.

She stopped just after they had summited the pass. They looked out across a broad sloping valley that was maybe ten miles wide and shaped by an alluvial outwash plain. Ruts in the desert surface marked where four-wheel enthusiasts had come through on the old mining roads, exploring the vacant land. The desolate landscape had a reddish-brown hue where oxidized volcanic rocks highlighted the tan and gray of the desert pavement. Only a few low shrubs along dry washes added a hint of green. The heat of the day caused a shimmering, mirrorlike quality as the reflection of light formed mirages of lakes and pools hovering above the overheated land.

The gravel road continued through the pass and arced around the side of the valley before turning back toward the center of the plain. Sanchez and Montero followed it and carefully checked each turnoff onto the side mining roads. After two miles, they noted there was an intersection where a smaller road turned off to the left and down into a quarry—the same one Sanchez had seen in the aerial view on Google Earth.

The quarry was currently abandoned, but showed evidence that there had been some recent earthwork activity. A gently sloping road led down the quarry wall to the relatively flat bottom that encompassed about an acre of hard rock. The far side of the quarry had been excavated into a sheer rock wall, and the other sides were steep with exposed rocks. Huge mounds of loose rock and debris piled around the periphery of the pit. The rock on the vertical side of the pit was comprised of limestone, and broken lime and volcanic rocks were found everywhere else.

"Geez, it's hot," Sanchez said as she stepped out of the car. "I hope the guys at the motor pool topped off the radiator before they gave me this monster. I'm going to need the air-conditioning today."

"The dashboard thermometer says it's a hundred and twelve degrees already, and it's only noon," Montero said as he stood next to the car and looked around. He did a 360-degree scan of the landscape and pointed at a dark object in the distance. "What's that?"

She turned to follow where he pointed and said, "That might be the small building I saw on the aerial photo." She consulted the printout she had with her. "Yeah, I think that's it. Let's check out this pit, and we'll drive over there next."

They climbed back into the car, and she drove slowly down the gravel ramp into the pit. She directed the vehicle over to the fifty-foot-tall rock wall and parked, leaving the motor running while they disembarked. Sanchez left one window open about three inches so she could reach inside in case the doors locked themselves while they were outside the vehicle.

"I got locked out of a car once when I walked away for some reason. I'm always afraid it will happen again." She grinned at the memory. "This looks like good-quality limestone."

"Yeah, I wonder why they stopped mining it." Montero walked up to the rock face and examined it. "It's solid rock. No major fractures in it."

Sanchez bent down and studied the gravel that formed the ground they were standing on. "This is crushed rock like regular road base. And there are tracks like cars and trucks have been driving around down here. Maybe the truck was parked in here when we lost it last night. Maybe the two men in the cab were waiting for someone."

"It's a remote location if they were meeting someone to transfer loads to another vehicle. But why come all the way out here to do that?" He stooped down to examine the tracks in the gravel. "Looks like a dual-wheel truck like the one we were tailing."

"You could park a dozen trucks in this pit if you were hiding from someone. But why here? It doesn't make sense."

After a few minutes, they got into the car and enjoyed the cool air. Sanchez drove out of the quarry and headed for the building they had seen in the distance. Montero used the air photo to direct her through the maze of dirt roads. In five minutes, they could clearly see the building ahead.

"There it is," he said. "It looks like a gas station . . . Wait. Stop here a moment."

She hit the brakes, and they stopped to look ahead. A white shuttle bus had pulled up to the building and stopped next to it. As they watched, they could just catch a glimpse of people leaving the bus and walking into the building. Then the bus made a U-turn and drove away along the road.

"What the hell was that?" she whispered. "Bus service out here?"

She drove up to the building and stopped. They got out of the car and walked to what looked like the front door. No one seemed to be around. She knocked, but there was no response. She peered through the dirty glass pane of the door but could only see partway into a small empty room. The door was locked. She turned around and noticed that the twin gas pumps in front of the building looked like they had recently been used.

As they stood there wondering what was going on, a tall, thin man with a mustache suddenly appeared from around the corner of the building.

"Can I help you?" he asked. "Did you need some gas?"

"Where'd you come from?" Montero asked.

"I hang out in the back. I drive in from Childs for the day," he said.

"What is a gas station doing out here in the middle of nowhere?" Sanchez asked.

"You'd be surprised how many four-wheeler types come out here on the weekend. They all need gas after tooling around the desert all day. And water. They forget to bring enough water."

"Oh," she said. "I guess I never thought of it, but I can see a lot of folks not thinking ahead for desert conditions. Especially the newer people moving in here from California. They seem unprepared a lot of the time."

"Well, do you need gas?" he asked again.

"No, not now," Montero said. "Did a bus just pull up here and drop people off?"

"Oh, it stops here to get gas or water sometimes, but then continues on the tour. It belongs to a tour company that shuttles people around to see things in the desert. Sometimes the tourists stop here to eat lunch inside to get out of the sun." He looked as though he wanted to go. "If that's all, I'll go back to my radio show."

"OK, thanks," Montero said.

He and Sanchez walked back to the car and entered the cool interior. They watched the man walk around the building again and disappear. They looked at each other with slack jaws.

"Do you believe there are desert tours out here?" she asked.

"Not really."

"Why a gas station, do you suppose?"

He shrugged his shoulders. "Well, if there are people driving around out here—maybe a mining company—then they would need gas."

Sanchez looked at her cell phone and noted the time. She tried to make a call, but there was no service in the middle of nowhere. "Hell, it's almost one o'clock. We've got to head back so I can pick up Lolita."

They loaded up, and she cranked the car into a U-turn. She

drove back toward the pass at a fast pace, bouncing along over the bumps. Montero hung on and protested when they hit the really big bumps.

"Should we come back to watch for trucks again tonight, Lori?" He looked at her determined face as she sped along. "It seems that there's something funny happening here at night."

"I'd like to. I wish it wasn't so far from the city, though. It's a bit of a drive."

"No kidding."

They were back on State Route 85 northbound by 1:30 p.m. Sanchez hammered the gas, and they shot north. As soon as her phone picked up a signal, it beeped and emitted a variety of sounds as it caught up on the day's missed communications. There was a text message from Lolita that all was well and she would see Sanchez after school. Sanchez replied and left a message indicating that she might be a little late but to stay inside until she was in sight.

"Makes you realize how many messages you can get in a day. It was nice to not have this thing beeping all the time when we were in the desert," she commented.

"I don't have as many apps and contacts as you, so I don't get nervous when my phone isn't chirping and beeping like yours."

Sanchez snickered at his comment. "Well, hang on. We're on the open road. We can really cruise now."

Montero hung onto the armrest on his door.

Chapter 24

Tuesday evening, April 9, 2019
Chandler, Arizona

That night at 7:00 p.m., Sanchez and Montero waited in his pickup truck on Frye Road. They were going to observe the warehouse again and see what activities might take place. If another truck came out of the building late in the evening, they would follow it and hope it went to the same desert location as the evening before.

This time, they came better prepared for an excursion into the desert at night. They had brought night-vision goggles with them, one pair for each of them, so they could follow the truck without turning on their headlights. At least, that was the plan. The sky was clear tonight, which favored using the goggles. Moonlight would provide plenty of light for Montero to see the road clearly so they could follow the truck more closely with no lights. Under those conditions they were less likely to lose the vehicle as it crossed the pass. They felt confident that their reconnaissance of the terrain that morning would also help them in their pursuit.

Just after they arrived, a truck approached from the opposite direction and turned into the warehouse. The guard they had seen the night before came out to open the front gate and let it into the compound. He then walked to the warehouse and opened the vehicle doorway so the truck could enter. As it drove through the door, they could see another box truck inside the building. Then the door closed.

At ten minutes after eight, the large vehicle door reopened, and the truck that had driven in rolled out and pulled up to the gate. A second truck that looked just like the one they had followed the night before also drove out the door and pulled up behind the first vehicle. The guard closed the door of the warehouse and then opened the gate to let both trucks leave. They drove onto Frye Road past Montero's pickup truck, which was hidden behind a roadside stand.

Sanchez watched the guard close the gate and walk inside his trailer. Meanwhile, Montero kept track of the trucks as they drove up North 56th Street. He pulled out from behind the stand and followed at a distance.

The trucks continued along the same route as last night, to Gila Bend and south on State Route 85 past Childs. Two hours after they had left the warehouse, the trucks eased off the highway and proceeded east across the desert like before.

When he turned his truck off the highway, Montero put on his night-vision goggles and killed his headlights. He could see perfectly well and kept up with the trucks ahead as they jostled along the bumpy gravel road with its many dry washes and ruts. Montero drove along steadily, keeping within two hundred yards of the second truck.

Sanchez donned her goggles as well to see how effective they were and was immediately impressed by how clearly she could see in the night. She took them off so she could scan the surrounding area from a wider perspective. The goggles limited her peripheral vision a great deal, and she felt that she was in a culvert. It was a little claustrophobic for her liking.

It took about thirty minutes to reach the crest of the pass where they had lost track of the truck last night. This time,

Montero closed the gap between himself and the last truck to less than a hundred yards. The trucks crossed the pass, and he continued right behind them.

They dropped inot a deep gully that crossed the road, causing them all to slow down. Montero had to back off a little to avoid getting too close and being spotted in the moonlight. He let the vehicles run ahead about three hundred yards as they lumbered down onto the outwash plain.

Sanchez put her goggles back on. "They're turning into the quarry," she whispered. "We can approach and watch what they do down there."

"I'll back off a little more. Maybe I can stop just above the rim of the pit and we can walk over to see what's happening."

He watched the second truck enter the pit and pulled up, being careful not to let his vehicle show above the rim. He shut the engine down. They exited the vehicle and walked twenty yards to the edge of the quarry to spy down below.

"Where are they?" Sanchez asked as she swiveled her head all around looking for the trucks. "I don't see them." She unfastened her goggles.

"What the devil is going on? They were just there." Montero removed his goggles too. "They drove into the pit, and there's only one road out of there. We saw that this morning."

They looked at each other. The trucks had vanished into thin air!

"That's simply not possible," she said. "They must be here somewhere."

"Let's walk down there. But I don't like it. It feels like a trap," he said.

"We'd better gun up," she said in a deliberate manner. "I don't want to be caught out in the open down there."

She moved over to the right side of the pickup and grabbed her go bag from behind the seat. She pulled out an M4 automatic rifle, the standard issue from her unmarked car. She checked the magazine and charged the weapon. "I have a handgun for you, Guillermo. I hope I'm just being paranoid. But you know how it goes sometimes. Better safe than sorry."

"I have my Glock 22. I hoped we wouldn't need it but came prepared." He looked down into the pit. He took out the night-vision goggles and carefully scanned the walls of the pit. "I think there may be a secret panel somewhere or an optical illusion to make us think the walls are solid. I don't see any cracks or door or anything like that. But logic tells me it has to be true."

"I trust you on that. You've see more weird shit than I have, so I'll take your word for it." She held the rifle in her hands and was wearing her belt and holster. "We need a plan. Should we sneak down on foot or just drive down there and see what happens?"

Montero gave her a neutral look. "Suppose we do both? If I had a secret door somewhere, I'd have cameras around to warn me if anyone came close."

"And the cameras might track movement outside your lair, right?"

"Yes."

Sanchez walked carefully along the road behind the truck as Montero drove slowly down the ramp. Nothing seemed different than it had earlier in the day. He let the truck roll down the slope, and she watched the pit for any signs of activity but saw nothing out of the ordinary. Not movement, no lights, no anything.

Montero drove to the bottom of the pit and swung the truck around so it was facing the ramp in case they needed to make a quick exit. He stepped out of the cab as Sanchez tiptoed up to examine the sheer rock wall in the moonlight. She placed her head against the face of the wall to listen for any sounds emanating from it.

"I don't see or hear anything. But look at this, Guillermo. Tracks from the trucks run right up to the wall here. It's like they drove right through it."

He squatted down and examined the tracks. "You're right. They drove in here." He pointed to a portion of the wall. "But there's no obvious opening or even a crack where a door should be."

She pounded on the rock face with her fist. There was no hollow sound at all. "These walls seem to be solid rock. If there's a door, they did a hell of a good job concealing it."

"What should we do now, Lori?" he asked.

"We could wait around and see when the trucks come back out of there."

He turned her way and shrugged his shoulders. "If they were delivering something or picking it up, they would need an hour or two to change loads and drive out again. Maybe we can see if they emerge from the wall."

"That sounds like a reasonable thing to do since we're out here already." She walked to the truck and slid into the passenger seat. "Let's move up out of the quarry and find a good observation spot. We'll wait them out."

They drove up the ramp to the rim of the pit and took up a position where they had a good view of the pit wall but could remain unseen by anyone driving out of the quarry. They waited in the truck at first with the engine off, but then decided they could hear activity better if they were outside the vehicle.

It was springtime in the Arizona desert. The high temperatures of the day had given way to a chilly night. Sanchez and Montero shivered. Even though the heat had reached into the nineties during the day, the nighttime temperature had fallen to about sixty degrees. That was cool by any standards, but was especially so for Arizonans who were used to warmth during the daytime. Luckily, Montero kept an extra jacket in the truck for such occasions. Sanchez wrapped herself in the blanket he also carried for picnics and emergency use.

"Look over there, Guillermo," she whispered. "There are lights on at that gas station we visited. Do you think they're doing desert tours tonight?"

"Well, I'll be . . . ," he said quietly. "What are they up to?"

Time moves slowly when on a stakeout, and tonight was no different. They were cold and tired by the time two hours had passed. They were about to call it a night when there was a low rumbling sound that they could feel through the ground as much as hear. As they carefully watched the mine pit, a vertical crack formed in the wall on the far side of the pit. The crack was only visible because of a faint light emanating from within the wall itself. The crack grew wider until they saw a huge slab of rock measuring nearly twenty feet wide and twelve feet tall swing back to create a doorway much like when a vault door opened. It slowly pivoted backward until the slab was at a ninety-degree angle to the wall, when it stopped moving. They could see a giant room inside the rock face and a truck poised to drive through the door. They also saw a loading dock with a few men standing next to it. One of them held a rifle in his hands.

The truck drove out of the wall and proceeded directly up the ramp. A second truck followed. The vehicles labored up the slope under a full load of cargo. Then the doorway began to close, and within seconds, they could not see any sign of it. They stayed perfectly still until the trucks left the pit and drove away along the gravel road and into the night, heading for the mountain pass they had crossed before.

"I'll be damned," Sanchez said. "Someone has a secret warehouse or factory out here. They're loading up drugs to take back to the warehouse in Chandler."

"Why in the world would they do that? It's in the middle of nowhere."

They sat in silence for a minute. By then, the clear night was only dimly illuminated by the moon, which was setting in the west. A vast array of stars sparkled overhead, and the Milky Way looked so close that Sanchez felt like she could reach out and touch it.

"Let's drive over to that gas station again and see what's up there," she said.

They climbed into the cab of Montero's truck and rode across the valley on dirt roads, arriving in ten minutes. There were no lights in the building or any signs of activity at all.

They parked next to the gas station and disembarked. They walked around the premises and found a door at the rear of the building. Sanchez tried the doorknob but found it locked. She shined her flashlight on the ground in front of the door and called to Montero, "Hey, look at this."

When he came over, she pointed to the numerous footprints that led up to the doorway. "It looks like a lot of people use this door, Guillermo. And I don't buy the desert tours story."

"We saw a bus here this afternoon. If it was a panel truck or van instead, I'd suspect someone of smuggling illegals here to hide them. But there's no place for them to go." He shined his flashlight through a window. "There isn't anyone here."

"I could pick the lock, and we could look around inside."

Montero glanced at her and shook his head. "Look over there." He pointed at an inner doorway. "I think I see a security keypad inside. You could set off an alarm." He backed away from the building and looked around for cameras. "This whole place may be under surveillance. We'd better get out of here."

Sanchez looked at her phone. "It's getting late. Maybe we should call it a night. I've got a ton of stuff to do tomorrow."

"I agree. We need to think about what we've just seen— decide what it means and what to do next. Could someone really have an underground manufacturing plant out here in the desert?" He looked pensive. "Why here?"

"If you have to keep a secret, this is the place to hide," she said. "No one would look out here, not only in the desert but under it." She pondered the new information. "This could be the missing piece of the puzzle. I bet this is the source for all those drugs. And it wouldn't surprise me if our old friends the Southside Crips aren't involved somehow."

They loaded up, and Montero drove west across the valley to the mountain pass. From there, it was a bumpy but steady ride until they reached State Route 85. Sanchez fell asleep as he shepherded the truck back to Phoenix.

Chapter 25

Wednesday morning, April 10, 2019
Phoenix, Arizona

The next morning, Sanchez wished she could sleep in for an extra hour, but duty called. She had to drive Lolita to school, and that required her to rise early. She luxuriated in a warm shower to drive the cold out of her bones from the midnight escapade of the night before. Then she caught up with her roommates over Danish pastries and coffee that Alvera thoughtfully had provided. The assistant DA departed early for a trial that started at 9:00 a.m.

At 7:45 a.m., Sanchez rushed Lolita to the high school and just made it in time for the first bell. She reminded the girl that she would pick her up at the end of the school day and wished her good luck on her English test.

Sanchez arrived at work about 8:20 a.m. and was greeted by Captain Teller, who wanted an update on the Grosse case. Apparently, he was under some pressure from a friend of the mayor who worked at Maraxx Pharma and wanted to know if it was or wasn't a suicide. Luckily, the coroner's preliminary report had been released, and her earlier gut instinct was confirmed. Teller was not impressed and instructed her to make that case her highest priority. He admonished her for getting her photo in the news again; it looked like grandstanding to him. He also told her she might have to pay for the repairs to the Charger. "I may take that damned Interceptor away from you if you don't stop damaging department property," he said maliciously.

Sometimes she just couldn't win.

She walked to her desk and read through her emails. A friend at the Arizona Secretary of State's office had come through with information about Novarios, S.A., the company that had bought Randman Labs. She had wondered what Novarios, S.A. was and why they would want to buy a bankrupt drugmaker. It didn't make sense unless Randman had valuable patents or some other hidden value. The information she received had nothing to do with that but it did turn up an interesting fact: Novarios, S.A. was owned by a Mexican holding company called Quintantas Investments, which was wholly owned by Bross Ambros Logistics.

Checking out company histories and affiliations was useful when investigating certain types of crimes. Quite often, gangs had oblique interactions with otherwise legitimate companies, and sometimes they were customers of banks or insurance companies just like thousands of other small businesses. It usually took pints of strong coffee for Sanchez to dig through such complicated interactions, and the effort made her eyes glaze over. Today, she was practically falling asleep when she read the mission statement of the Bross Ambrose Logistics company.

But something caught her attention. She scrolled back up the screen and saw a list of the people on the board of directors. She stopped and reread it. John Parlance. She knew that name. He was the attorney for José Battelle, one of the enforcers for the Sinaloa Cartel. He had defended Battelle in a case involving murder and kidnapping. Parlance was not a stellar member of the bar and no friend of hers.

"What the hell is Parlance doing on the board of a logistics company?" she whispered to herself, immediately becoming suspicious.

Next she looked into the filings Randman Labs had made when Novarios, S.A. had purchased them. She did a document search for Parlance in the company's papers, but his name did not appear. But he did witness the signing of the merger documents. She decided that his name appearing twice was no coincidence.

She called Alvera and left a message because her court case was still in session. Maybe Alvera could have someone dig into the relationship between these companies. Then she remembered someone at the Drug Enforcement Administration named Todd Smeckler she had met while working another case. He was a good-looking guy she might have taken an interest in at one time. While his cell phone was ringing, she tried to recall if she owed him any favors. She was a little worried about how many quid pro quos she had outstanding and would eventually have to make good on.

He answered right away. "Todd Smeckler here. Can I help you?"

After hearing his voice, Sanchez immediately remembered that they had been out on a date and it had not gone well. She should have thought of that before she had dialed his number.

"Hi, Todd. This is Lori Sanchez calling. How have you been? Long time no see." She couldn't be more original than that while she tried to recall what had gone wrong with the date. She decided to play it straight and stick to police work.

"Oh yeah. Hi Lori, how have you been? I haven't heard from you for a while . . ." He paused for a long time, perhaps trying to remember her and the not so memorable date.

"Just calling about a case I'm working." She decided to just go for it and forget the other issue. "I ran across a company called Bross Ambros Logistics and wondered if you knew anything about them and their relations with any of the Mexican gangs, especially Sinaloa. I noticed the name of a lawyer on their board who had some dealings with the cartel."

"Oh, that name sounds familiar. Give me a sec . . ." He must have been looking something up because the line was quiet except for the sounds of paper shuffling in the background. "Yeah, I thought so. That company paid a fine last year to the government for money laundering. Apparently, we couldn't prove anything, but the executives agreed to settle to make it go away. They do business with a lot of border companies, including the cartels. Often it's nothing significant, but they're so intertwined you would need an army of lawyers to sort out all of their dealings."

"Oh, that's interesting. I'm investigating a pharmaceutical firm that merged with a Spanish company, and they were purchased by one of their subsidiaries. It's pretty confusing." She thought she had better be more definitive. "I wondered if Bross Ambrose could be financed by cartel money in some way."

"It's possible. If you want to send me an email, I can see what I can find out for you."

"Really?" She was surprised. "Yeah, that would be great. I'll send it over as soon as I can get it together."

"Hey, no problem." He sounded like he was in a hurry. "Look, I'd like to chat, but I have a meeting starting right now. Good to talk to you, Lori." He hung up.

That was helpful, she thought. *Now what's his email address?* She began to dig through her business card index and swear under her breath.

Bordou stepped up to her desk. "What are you looking for? And you know you're swearing out loud, don't you?"

"I am?" She raised her head and looked all around her at her coworkers, most of whom had heard this mumbling before. "Sorry, everyone," she said. Then turning to Bordou, she whispered, "I can't get away with anything anymore." She grinned.

"Say, we still can't contact Megan Faux," he reported. "Her car is parked in its usual space at the gym, but no one has seen her for two days. Her mail hasn't been picked up at her apartment, and we found her phone on her desk at the office."

"Her phone was left behind? That's a big deal." She held up a business card. "Do you think she's been grabbed by someone? There seems to be a lot of that going around lately." She gave Bordou an inquisitive look. "Someone may be cleaning up all the witnesses to this whole drug business."

"I'm beginning to think that's exactly what happened. Josie Vale must have run into a major operation for them to go to this amount of trouble. But why Faux? She wasn't in the night that Vale was killed, was she?"

"No. I don't think so." She thought to herself for a minute. "Did you look through the security tapes again?"

"The security guard is doing that and said he'd call me as soon as he had something. I was about to drive over there if you want to ride along."

"Yeah, let me do one thing here first—about fifteen minutes, OK? I want to ask that guard how so many names have been released to the media. I think he might be our leaker."

"OK."

"Oh, and Jeff, I'll fill you in on what Montero and I have been up to for the last couple of nights while we drive."

***

Sanchez and Bordou sat in the security office at the Maraxx Pharma gym going through the surveillance footage. The guard had isolated the video feed showing the hallway that led to a side door of the gym and had copied it onto a thumb drive. At 7:22 p.m. two nights before, two men could be seen carrying a woman out the side door. The woman appeared to be Megan Faux, and she was either unconscious or dead, although they could not see any blood in the video.

"Shit! They got her," Sanchez mumbled. "That must have been right after dark, right?"

"Yes, and just about when I was doing my rounds in the main building," the guard said. "They must have timed it for then."

"Why was she here so late that night? Any ideas?" Bordou asked.

"She kept really irregular hours. She hosted one of her special sessions that evening and so may have stuck around for one of her clients."

"How could these two thugs get in here at that time?" Sanchez asked. "Aren't the doors locked after five?"

"Yes, but Nick and Megan blocked the door open if they were expecting someone after hours," the guard said. "People were always coming and going."

Sanchez fixed a stern eye on the guard. "Megan wasn't here the night of the murder, was she? No one said she was, and she didn't show up on the videos we reviewed. But one newspaper said she was here."

The guard became very nervous. He looked at the wall and didn't respond until Sanchez grabbed his arm.

"Well, she wasn't inside really," he blurted. "She met some of her clients here, and then they drove over . . . well, to her place." He looked caught in a trap. "So she was here long enough to meet one of her men and then drove off. That was about midnight, I think."

"Why didn't you tell us that before? You know that's obstruction of justice?" Bordou asked loudly. "And why wasn't it on the videos?"

"At first, Megan said she'd pay me to keep her name out of it. And there's a blind spot in one of the cameras by the main entrance." He huffed as he tried to defend his actions. "But then she welched on the deal, so I told the guy from the *Tribune* she was here."

"You realize you may be the reason she was kidnapped, don't you?" Sanchez shouted at the man as she brought her face up next to his. "I should charge you with obstruction of justice right now!"

She looked at her watch. It was 1:15 p.m. It was getting late, and Lolita hadn't called her at noon like she was supposed to. She began to worry.

"Look, we're taking this thumb drive with us," she said. "I'm not going to arrest you now because I'm in a hurry. But you had better come clean right now, or I'll come back to hook you and perp walk you out of here after I call your boss and the press. You got that?"

She marched out of the security office and waited for Bordou to catch up. "We have to swing by Lolita's high school and pick her up early. I'll walk in and find her. I can't have her out of my sight until we get these murders solved. That idiot in there must have given her name to the paper too."

"OK. Let's go."

They jogged to the car, and Bordou sped out of the parking lot. Sanchez dialed Lolita's cell phone. It rang through to her voice mail.

It took ten minutes to drive to the school even with light traffic. When they turned off East Indian School Road onto Indianola Avenue, it was clear that something was wrong. Only a few students were standing outside on the sidewalk waiting for their rides, and there were fewer cars than usual parked alongside the curb.

"What's going on? Where is everyone?" Sanchez asked. "Pull up over here. I'll ask those kids what's happening."

Bordou edged up to the curb, and she rolled down her window. "Hey, you guys. Where is everyone?"

A teenage girl wearing shorts that probably didn't pass the dress code called back, "Oh, we were let out early today. Some last-minute teachers' conference or something."

Sanchez waved thank you and had Bordou drive right up front to the main entrance. "I'll go in and look for her."

As soon as he stopped the car, she jumped out and ran into the school. She was inside for fifteen minutes and then came running back to the car. She was angry when she climbed in.

"They let the students go at noon today. I found one teacher who said she saw Lo get into a black car—possibly a Nissan—with an Uber sign in the window. Maybe she thought she'd save me some trouble and ride directly home."

"Then maybe she's already at Clara's place. We can drive over and see."

Bordou turned the car around to leave. As he pulled into traffic, she called Lolita's cell again. No answer.

"OK, Jeff. Step on it. We have to find her."

Jeff slapped his red flashing bubble light on top of the car and began to drive like he meant it. He raced across town toward Alvera's apartment building.

"Maybe you can call Uber and confirm that she took a ride from the school," he said. "She might also have decided to go back to her house for more clothes or something."

"I sure hope you're right. But I'm getting a bad feeling about this."

She called the station to ask if the department had a contact number for Uber that would cut through the privacy red tape and get her someone who could help her. After talking to a few people, she got the number for Uber's police liaison.

By that time, Bordou had raced up to the front of Alvera's place, and Sanchez ran into the building. She rode the elevator up to Alvera's floor and opened the door to her apartment. No Lolita.

She pulled out her cell phone, punched in Alvera's number, and got a response immediately. "Hey, Lori. I just finished up. I won my case."

"Great, Clara. I'm looking for Lo, and she's not at school or at your place. Have you heard from her today?"

"Oh no," Alvera said. "I thought you were picking her up from school."

"I was supposed to, but it let out early today, and she took an Uber from there. No one has seen her since then—about noon."

"Gee, Lori. What can I do?"

Sanchez felt defeated. Worse, she felt that she had let Lolita down. She should have kept her with her all day. No more of this school stuff. She felt her face tighten up, and tears began to flow down her cheeks. She began to sob quietly.

"Lori, are you OK? You sound like you're crying."

"I am. I lost her. I don't know what else to do. Maybe call Uber."

"Hey," Alvera said. "Stay there. I'll be home in a few minutes, and we'll figure this out." She hung up the phone.

Sanchez dialed the Uber contact number.

Chapter 26

Wednesday afternoon, April 10, 2019
Phoenix, Arizona

Sanchez was on the phone with a representative of Uber Technologies, Inc. trying to convince her that she really was a police officer who needed to know if one of their drivers had picked up a fare at Arcadia High School. The agent refused to answer without a court order. Sanchez told the woman in no uncertain terms that she would never ride Uber if the company didn't provide for the safety of their passengers and hung up.

By then, Bordou had parked on the street and walked up to the apartment. Alvera arrived a few minutes later and, after trying to calm Sanchez down, attempted to contact Uber herself. Sanchez and Bordou were both on the phone with members of the police force's gang unit trying to find out what they knew about the Southside Crips' involvement in retail pill sales on the street. Bordou inquired whether Devon Jones was affiliated with the gang and whether his posse had a favorite hangout.

After twenty minutes of jabbering, Alvera ended her call and waved her hands to get everyone's attention. When Bordou asked his party to hold a second and Sanchez ended her call, she gave them an update.

"We may have good luck with Uber. The woman agreed to help us but needs assistance from her technical people to track which cars were in the area. She'll call back in a few minutes unless her legal counsel shuts her down."

"That's great. I just learned that Jones hung around with a cartel heavy named Paco something, a.k.a. El Burro," Bordou said and then went back to his conversation.

"How'd you get them to cooperate, Clara?" Sanchez asked. "That bitch gave me the party line about client privacy."

"Well, I was polite, for one thing." Alvera grinned at her friend. "And I told her that as assistant DA, I would be instrumental in the review of their license to operate in Phoenix next year."

"You sneaky rascal." Sanchez laughed. "I thought you couldn't do that sort of thing—lean on people."

"I didn't lean on anyone. I just told her I would be involved in the review process, which is true."

"Well, whatever. It seemed to work. Let's hope she can give us something useful." She paced back and forth across the carpet wearing her tactical boots under Alvera's watchful eye. "I learned that the Southside Crips have been pushing opioids on the street. It's odd because they have moved into a niche the other gangs haven't exploited in a big way yet—prescription drugs."

"So what? The Crips are distributers of prescription drugs? Who is their source, then?" Bordou asked. "I thought they were minor players in coke and meth."

"So who's their source?" Alvera repeated in a distracted manner. "All these drug-related issues we have been hearing about seem to come from a new source of generic prescription drugs. How are they all related?"

Sanchez's phone pinged that she had received a new voice mail. It was Montero, asking how she was. "It's Guillermo. I should call him back and see if he's heard from Lo." As she prepared to hit the speed dial key for his number, she noticed she had two new emails. She logged into her mailbox and saw that one was from Todd Smeckler. She opened it to read the content and passed on the message to the others: "'Bross Ambros Logistics has three board members who've been linked to the Sinaloa Cartel in the past. Bross Ambros does its banking through a Mexican bank in Guadalajara that is being watched for money laundering. The company buys and sells a lot of properties in Mexico and the US as a way to launder cash. It seems that the cartel is backing the organization and its subsidiaries. Be careful. These are serious dudes. Todd.'"

"Sounds ominous. Is that the company that bought Randman Labs?" Alvera asked.

"It's the parent of the one that bought them. It has cartel written all over it," Sanchez said. "I wonder if they own property here in Arizona."

"I can check that out easily enough. Lori, give me the names of these companies, and I'll check a database we have," Alvera said. "Then you should call Guillermo and see if he's heard from Lo."

Bordou added, "I have an address for Devon Jones's crib. It's down near South 24th and East Roeser. He shares a house with some guys, maybe other gang types."

Sanchez made her call and Alvera worked the database while Bordou checked on Jones's associates.

"Hello, Guillermo. It's Lori," she said with urgency in her voice. "Have you heard from Lolita today? We're trying to find her."

"What? No. I haven't talked to her today." He sounded concerned right away.

"I was to pick her up at school today, but it let out early. She apparently took an Uber from there and we haven't heard from her since."

"That doesn't sound like her. She would have called if she was going somewhere else." He paused and then added, "What can I do to help?"

"I'm not sure. Clara is waiting for a call from Uber to let us know where she rode to." She stopped speaking for a moment. "I don't know what to do either."

"You're all at Clara's?"

"Yeah, but we need to get moving soon. Well, as soon as we have a plan."

"I'll be right over." He hung up.

Sanchez asked Alvera, "Did you find anything we can use?"

"Well, I don't know if this helps us with Lo or not, but I have a list of properties purchased in the metro area that Bross Ambros has an interest in. That includes subsidiaries." She took a sheet of paper off her printer. "They are all over town."

Sanchez looked at the list and said, "This one is the warehouse we were at last night. It's the address that ships the Randman Labs product to Maraxx Pharma. Montero and I staked it out to see what they do there."

Alvera's phone rang, and she jumped up from her desk to reach it. She waved at the others in excitement. "It's Uber!" she cried.

They all stopped what they were doing to listen to her side of the conversation.

"So what can you give me then? . . . No names . . . OK, but how about where they went? . . . But that's not helpful. I need to know if they picked up Lolita Thompson . . . I don't care about your damn policies! We're talking about a possible kidnapping here. She was last seen entering one of your vehicles and hasn't been seen or heard from since . . . I am not threatening you . . . Maybe I should talk to your attorney right now . . . Well, find him. Yes, we'll take it to the next level. Yes, I'll hold." She glanced at the others and then said very loudly, "Yes, Lori, tell the news people that she was abducted by a car with an Uber sign in the window. Uber drivers may be involved." She smiled at them, then spoke back into the telephone. "Well, yes . . . Maybe we don't have to tell the news media every detail of the kidnapping, but I'm sure that thousands of parents would want to know if Uber was involved." She held her hand over the mic on her phone. "Lori, don't really call the news media." She smiled again. "At least not yet."

Her conversation with the Uber person continued for a few minutes. Finally, she gave the woman her email address and stood by to see if a list of rides came in. "Yes, I have it now. Thank you for your help on this. I'll call back to let you know if you can be of further assistance in this case." She ended the call and brought up the list on her computer.

"Here's what she could give us. There were eleven hails for rides at the high school. Eleven drivers responded to the request. One of them showed up for a rider but didn't find anyone waiting there. He thought he'd been stiffed, so he put in a claim. Apparently, a driver can do that if someone hails—makes an appointment—for a ride but then cancels after he has already responded to the call. He needs to get paid something for his effort. The woman at Uber couldn't tell me the name of the owner of the account that stiffed the driver, but she said the last name on the account was the same as Lolita's. That gave her legal cover to not mention Lolita's name."

"But that doesn't help us. We assume Lo called for a ride, but now you say she never took it?" Bordou shook his head. "That doesn't make any sense."

"Well," Alvera continued, "Uber sent us the locations of

twelve of their vehicles that were in the immediate vicinity of the school and where they drove to after responding to the hail. All locations except one matched the billing addresses of the accounts used. In other words, the riders were probably kids who rode Uber home to those addresses."

"What about the last car, number twelve?" Sanchez asked expectantly.

"All the cars that work for Uber have GPS trackers on them. So even the car that didn't register to take the ride from Lo was being tracked. The driver went to the school and then traveled south afterward. He drove to the last coordinates on the list."

Alvera read the coordinates while Sanchez keyed them into her Google Maps app and shouted, "That's Frye Road, right by the warehouse!"

Just then, the buzzer rang at the door. Alvera checked who was in the lobby. It was Montero, so she buzzed him up and unlatched the front door. He entered as they were discussing what to do next.

"Hi," he said. "Any news yet?"

"We're pretty sure we know where she went," Sanchez said. "She stepped into a car that had an Uber sign on its window. That car is now at the warehouse that you and I shadowed the last two nights. We were just deciding how to proceed."

"Let's go down and pound on the front door," Bordou said loudly. "Let's see if the car is still there. Do we have a license plate for it, Clara?"

"No, the Uber rep didn't give me that. But if you see a black Nissan with an Uber sign in the window, I can call her back and see if she can tell me more," Alvera responded.

"OK, fine," Sanchez said. "Bordou and I can drive down there and look for the car. If we see it, we'll call you with the tag number, Clara. You can call the Uber person and ask for confirmation. Once we have that, we can knock on the door. Hopefully, the security guard will let us look around."

"And, if not? Then what?"

"Then we get a warrant?" She looked at Alvera. "Do we have enough for a warrant?"

"I don't know, Lori. It's pretty thin evidence, even if the car is still there. If it isn't there, I would have a hard time convincing any judge to issue a warrant."

"Damn it! We're talking about Lolita here!" Sanchez shouted. "We have to do *something.*"

"Suppose I go there and ask for a donation to charity?" Montero suggested. "Maybe they'll let me in and I can spot something to determine if she's there or not. If I see something, I'll let you know right away. If not, you can knock on the door and be more aggressive."

Alvera looked stricken. She knew what that meant. "All right. I'll wait here in case Lolita shows up, incredible as that may seem. I'll wait for your call about the license plate and will call Uber afterward. I don't want to know what you decide to do then, especially if it doesn't involve a warrant."

"OK, let's load up and go find Lolita." Sanchez looked everyone in the eye in turn and then headed for the door.

"Do you want to pick up your car and get your vest?" Bordou asked.

"There isn't time. She's been missing for three hours now. Every minute counts."

Sanchez, Bordou, and Montero strode out of the apartment, ready for action.

Chapter 27

Wednesday afternoon, April 10, 2019

Chandler, Arizona

Bordou and Sanchez waited in his Durango across the street from the Frye Road warehouse. The black Nissan sedan with an Uber sign in its front window was parked right in front of the building. Bordou typed the license plate—BDE3844—into the department database. Montero, who was watching from his own truck, let Alvera know that they had located the Uber car that Lolita had likely ridden in. She said she would call Uber right away for confirmation of the tag number.

Montero rang Sanchez on his phone. "I'm ready to try my luck. Be ready in case things go sideways."

Montero started his truck and drove through the open gate onto the warehouse grounds. He slowly pulled his vehicle up next to the Nissan and got out of the car. He took a few minutes to gether some papers out of the back seat of his car and used the time to scan the contents of the Nissan while doing so. He noted what looked like a rag you might use to smother a victim. He noticed that one window of the car was open a crack, so he walked around the vehicle for a closer look. As soon as he approached the window, he caught the clear and strong odor of ether. This was clearly the car the kidnappers had used. He knew they had probable cause to search the car but not the building yet.

He walked up to the manway next to the main vehicle door

and knocked loudly. There was no response, so he pounded on the door again with more gusto. He tried the doorknob and was about to step inside when the door was suddenly yanked open. A tall, dark man with long dreadlocks and a scruffy goatee confronted him—Devon Jones, based on the photo that he had seen before. Jones had a revolver tucked in the front of his pants.

"What you want?" Jones demanded. "We don't let people in here."

Montero winged it. "I'm a priest collecting for the Blind Charities. We're asking businesses in the area to contribute to our annual fund. Would you like to contribute?"

"Hell no. I ain't blind," Jones said mockingly. "You get on out of here. This is private property."

Montero peered around the corner of the doorsill. He saw what looked like an office area and asked more forcefully, "Are you sure your boss won't want to contribute? I could just ask him really quick." He spoke loudly enough for the burly man sitting at a table nearby to hear him.

"No means no, Priest. Now get out." He looked past Montero to the parking lot outside. "Hey, that gate's supposed to be closed. You open it?"

"No. It was open, so I drove in." Montero smiled at the man at the table, who stood up. He took the opportunity to push past Jones and stepped toward the other man. "Sir, would you like to contribute to the Blind Charites? We do good works for the blind in this state."

Jones grabbed him by the arm and held him, exclaiming angrily, "Stop, Priest, or I'll throw you out."

The man at the desk shouted at Jones, "Let him go, you idiot! He's just a priest."

Montero shook Jones's hands off of him and walked to the

table with his hand out.

"Thank you, brother. As I was saying, I'm with the Blind Charities, and we're collecting for our annual drive. Do you have a family member or friend who suffers from blindness?" He studied the man, who looked like he had suffered from hard work and abuse in his life. "If so, there are many services that our stricken brothers need to help them in their daily lives."

"I know someone who's blind. I'll give you something. How about twenty bucks?" he asked.

Montero accepted the cash and nodded his head. He then added, "Maybe some of your employees would like to contribute too." He looked hopeful and glanced around the interior of the warehouse. That was when he noticed a small blue backpack with an Olympic logo on it—one he had seen before.

The man seemed to have lost his patience. "No, no one else . . . I must work now. You can leave now."

He nodded at Jones, who now hustled Montero toward the manway and thrust him through it in an indignant manner. Jones followed him closely as he stepped outside and slammed the door shut after him.

"Get in your truck, Priest, and drive out of here. I'll shut that gate after you." He glared at Montero. "And don't come back."

Montero didn't object. In fact, he wanted to get out of there. He climbed into his truck and started the engine as Jones took long strides past him toward the front gate. Montero punched in Sanchez's number in his phone. When she answered, he simply said, "He has a gun, and Lo's backpack is inside the warehouse."

He backed out of his parking space and slowly started to drive toward the gate, but stopped halfway there. Jones motioned for him to move on and he began to shout. Montero waited a little longer, then inched forward carefully as Jones started to walk in his direction. He was almost at the gate.

***

Bordou started his car and turned on his red and blue flashing lights built into the car's grill. He revved the engine and quickly pulled out onto the street. Both he and Sanchez kept their eyes on Montero's truck and knew he was creating a diversion to prevent Jones from guarding the gate. Bordou rolled down the road at twenty miles per hour and entered the gate just as Jones pulled the pistol out of his belt. He drove right through and honked his horn to attract Jones's attention.

He pulled up behind Jones and shouted, "Devon Jones, possessing a handgun is a violation of your parole! You're under arrest!"

Jones saw the flashing lights and the obvious unmarked police car, and took off for the warehouse. He ran inside and slammed the door as Sanchez and Bordou leapt out of the car.

"I'd call that probable cause, wouldn't you?" she asked. "And hot pursuit?"

"Looks like it," Bordou chuckled. "But now we have an armed suspect holed up with who knows how many other gang members in a warehouse."

"But we know from Guillermo that Lo is here. We have to go in."

"We have to call in backup right now, then," he said. "We're in Chandler, so we'll have a jurisdictional issue."

"Just call it in," she said as she ran forward, knees bent, body arched to present a smaller target. "I'll try to get the big door open."

Bordou slid into the front car seat and radioed for support—all units in the area. Then he got out and sprinted toward the manway, just as Montero, Glock in hand, approached the side of the vehicle door close to where Sanchez stood peeking into the warehouse through a small glass window. Bordou ran up behind her.

"Guillermo, what's the layout inside?" she asked.

"One large room," he said. "The door swings in to the left. Table inside to the right, about twenty feet in. Racks of shelves behind that as far as you can see. Left is the loading area with a forklift and two trucks parked near the big door. Lo's backpack was behind the table. That's all I saw. Oh, and Jones and one other man was all I could make out."

"OK, got it. Jeff, you go low and right; I'll go high and left. Guillermo, can you push the door open for us with one arm and then stay back?"

"Right," Montero said.

"On three—one, two, three," she said quietly.

Montero heaved the door open and stepped back around the doorframe to relative safety as the other two rushed into the warehouse. Bordou shouted, "Police!" as loudly as he could.

Sanchez entered at the same time and swung the muzzle of her gun left as the door opened. She saw a man directly ahead of them and one near a truck to the left. The one closest to them had his gun out and fired at her. She had to stand steady as the shots struck the wall around her. She squeezed off a three-shot burst, wounding the shooter, who retreated behind a pallet of boxes.

Bordou spotted another man by the table. It was Jones. He had raised his pistol and shot twice, the bullets tearing into the wall by Bordou's head. Bordou returned fire and hit his target in the torso, knocking him backward over a chair.

They stepped forward, and Bordou shifted right while Sanchez went left. He saw yet another man come out of the shelf racks behind the table, shooting with a handgun. Bordou fired again but missed, sending the man hiding behind the racks. He advanced to the table and noticed Lolita's backpack on a shelf behind it. He had visual confirmation that she had been there.

Meanwhile, Sanchez had moved left and slapped a big red button that opened the truck door. Then she traded shots with the man behind the truck. He had cover but she didn't, so she kept up fire until she could advance to the same pallet the other shooter was hiding behind. He popped up and shot at her from close range, nearly hitting her.

Great, she thought. *Now I've got people shooting at me from both sides.*

Montero edged around the corner of the truck door when it opened and could see her dilemma. He opened fire on the man behind the truck, who immediately backed off and ran deeper into the warehouse. Montero rushed to the truck to cover Sanchez's flank.

Sanchez fired two rounds through the tops of the boxes and managed to hit the guy behind the pallet. He fell to one side, dead. She reloaded and watched Bordou as he moved up to the first rack to trade shots with someone hiding behind the third row.

Bordou heard sirens in the distance and was relieved that they would get some backup. He caught Montero's attention and motioned for him to go outside. Better that only police were inside when the cavalry arrived. "Guillermo, get out there and put down your weapon. Tell them what's up."

Montero ran outside and stowed his gun in his truck before the police arrived.

Bordou finally hit the man shooting at him and heard the sound of footsteps retreating toward the back of the warehouse.

He yelled, "Lori, I think they're making a run for it!"

"Yeah, I'm moving left to get a better look."

Bordou heard her run to the second truck. He reached for his shoulder mic and told the arriving officers that the perpetrator might be exiting the warehouse via the south end and someone should cover the doors down there. He heard the first patrol unit arrive and head to the other end of the building. Then two Chandler police officers burst through the truck door, weapons drawn.

He held up his badge for them to see. "I'm Bordou of Phoenix PD. That's Sanchez over there. We're here in hot pursuit of a man involved in a kidnapping in Phoenix. There are four or five more gangbangers in here. Thanks for the quick response. It was getting hairy."

Sanchez shouted, "The priest is with us! Don't shoot him!"

"OK, coming in on your left," one of the new officers announced. "Any friendlies in here too? We heard there was a kidnapping victim."

"Possible, but we haven't found her yet. Stay aware," she responded.

***

Within fifteen minutes, six more officers arrived, and they all cleared the warehouse. Two gang members were killed, two were wounded, and two were captured. Jones was one of the dead ones. Only one officer was injured in the fray.

Still, Sanchez was very disappointed in the raid's results. There was no Lolita, even though they had clear evidence that she had been brought here. She set about interrogating the surviving gang members. She had them all brought into the small office space within the warehouse. Handcuffed and shackled, they were standing or sitting, depending on their injuries. Bordou stood beside her as she spoke. The Chandler police stepped out of the warehouse to give them some privacy out of professional courtesy.

"In a kidnapping case like this, you will all be charged on a federal level. If you drove the car or just stood around in the same room, it's all the same thing. You're all equally guilty in the eyes of the law." She let that sink in a few moments. "If the girl dies, you're all equally guilty of murder. You know what that means? You all get the death sentence."

One of the gang members mumbled, "No. They don't do death sentences anymore, right?"

"Wrong!" she shouted. "This is Arizona. We have the death sentence for kidnapping and murder at the state level. It overrides federal law since you're within state lines. I just want you to think about that while I interrogate you one by one. Whoever helps me will duck the kidnap charge. Your buddies might cop a plea too, but whoever talks to me first gets the deal." She wasn't really in any position to offer anyone a deal, but these guys didn't know that.

The men squirmed, silently looking at each other. They were playing it tough and seeing if they were all going to stay tight lipped. But maybe they were wondering if one of the others would break down and give her what she wanted. Or maybe they didn't speak English. It didn't really matter. They knew the score.

"Let's start with you, buddy." She stared at an uninjured suspect who seemed to be the youngest one there. He looked like he was just a teenager compared with the others. "Come with me," she said, taking him by the arm and practically dragging him out of the office. Bordou stayed with the other three detainees and looked as menacing as possible, holding his gun on them.

She dragged the man around the corner and down four rows of storage racks, where she stood him up against the side of a pallet of boxes. He didn't say anything and had his face made up as if he would never cooperate.

She brought her face next to his and whispered, "You'll talk if you know what's good for you. The girl is a friend of mine, and I'll do anything to get her back. So make up your mind to help me, and you're the one with a pass on the kidnap. Or don't, and I'll stick you with extra charges. You understand me?"

He just glared at her.

She smiled and pulled out a bandana that she tied across his mouth as a gag. Then she took the Black Jack stun gun, a benign-looking object, from her belt. It was set for thirty thousand volts. She held it in front of his face to show him the current that arced between the two prongs. Controlled blue lightning flashed before his eyes.

She held it up to his crotch and hit the switch. He screamed, but the gag muffled his cry. His eyes were wild with pain. He fell to the floor.

"You see, that was the low setting. You're not supposed to use it that way. The area is too sensitive, and it does a lot of damage." She looked at the man. "Do you want to talk, or should we try the next setting? They say that after three of these, you'll never get it up again and your balls atrophy. You know what that means? Atrophy? They shrink."

She reset the stun gun, pushed it into his crotch, and fired the trigger again. He twitched and moaned, and an acrid smoke odor filled the air. He wet himself.

"Wait," he mumbled weakly. "I'll talk. No want to die."

"Oh, I wouldn't kill you. But talk now or we try again." She sounded as deadpan as she could. "Where's the girl?"

"The mine; the factory," he whispered as he tried to catch his breath. "In the truck."

"They took her to the mine? When?"

"As soon as she came here. Into truck." He could hardly speak.

"OK. I hope you told me the truth. Let's try a third time to see if you lied." She held up the stun gun and let it arc in front of his face again.

"No! Is truth. No lie."

"The gas station is the entry to a tunnel? And it leads to the mine where the cartel men are?"

"Si. How you know?"

"You just told me."

"Oh shit. I'm a dead man," he mumbled.

"OK. Can you stand up? Don't bother. I'll drag you. And remember—you tripped."

She took off the bandana and got a firm grip on his shirt collar. She dragged him along the concrete floor back to the others, letting him drop in front of them.

"He got the deal. You others will fry for this." She walked away dramatically and went outside to talk to the other police. Bordou stared at the man on the floor and looked worried.

In a few minutes, two Chandler police officers took the detainees off Bordou's hands. Sanchez came in with evidence bags and bagged Lolita's backpack after going through it for any personal effects that could be used to locate her. Her cell phone wasn't in the backpack, but it was disassembled on the table nearby. Someone had pulled out the battery and SIM card so it couldn't be traced. She bagged the components separately.

Sanchez stepped over to Bordou and asked him to follow

her outside. He did, and she pointed to his car, where Montero was waiting.

"What did you do to that man?" he asked under his breath as they walked side by side to the car. "He looks like you nearly killed him."

"I just scared him a little, that's all." She chuckled. "He believed that my stun gun could melt his balls."

The look on Bordou's face was priceless.

When they reached the car, she told both of her companions, "I know where they took Lolita. We need to pick up my car and some gear. I have a plan, but you two may not like it. It may be messy."

Montero rolled his eyes. "You always have messy plans, Lori. You can tell me what I'm in for on the way to your armored chariot."

Chapter 28

Wednesday evening, April 10, 2019

Childs, Arizona

Sanchez drove the Interceptor in first gear with Bordou right behind in his unmarked Durango. They drove at about twenty-five miles per hour in the dark of the night—it was 10:02 p.m.—bouncing across the now familiar bumps and arroyos of the unpaved road that led into the quarry. Montero was in her passenger seat looking grim faced. He wore a spare bulletproof vest and held his Glock 22 in his hand. He had extra magazines and a Maglite tucked into pockets on his vest.

"I don't like your plan, Lori. You'll get killed." He had repeated this mantra to her for nearly two hours as they drove southwest from Phoenix. "We should wait for backup—for the SWAT team."

"We can't wait that long," she said earnestly. "You know how they work. They make these elaborate plans and take forever to take action. This way we can surprise the gang and hopefully find Lo before anyone is the wiser. Then SWAT can take down the mine in a frontal assault. That's what they like to do. It justifies all that hardware they have."

"I don't think Pima County can get a SWAT team over here before dawn. They have to come all the way from Tucson." He wasn't sure what they would do if Sanchez's plan stirred up the gang members and ensnarled them in a desperate battle. After all, the quarry site seemed to be the exclusive domain of the Sinaloa

Cartel.

"All the more reason to go in now," she said, a serious tone to her voice.

"So you hope to get in and out before the cartel realizes that no trucks are coming to pick up a load. How'd you figure that out?" He was still skeptical about her reasoning. Then it became clear to him. "Because the warehouse was raided before the evening trucks could leave."

She stopped the car fifty feet from the gas station and got out to stretch her tired muscles. It had been a long drive from Phoenix, and she was exhausted. Only adrenaline and a vast quantity of caffeine kept her alert. "By midnight, gangbangers will realize the trucks are late and suspect there's a problem," she explained. "They might tighten up their security after that."

She looked west to the area where Bordou waited for any signs of activity from the quarry. She spoke into her handheld radio mic and asked quietly, "Any movement?"

Bordou responded, "Nothing yet. Just a coyote howling in the distance. Are you in position?"

"We just got here. We'll begin in about fifteen minutes. Out." She clipped the radio onto her belt again.

She and Montero shuffled over to the back of the car, and she opened the trunk. She pulled out an AP-9 automatic machine pistol she had borrowed from the property room at the station. It was left over from a former gangbanger case. She hefted it in her hand and liked the feel of it. It was a compact, largely inaccurate, nine-millimeter weapon with a huge magazine capacity—forty rounds. She had picked it up with four extra magazines with the idea that she would be prowling through a dark tunnel underground with no backup. Firepower seemed like a good idea. The department's usual weapon of choice for assaults was the M4 carbine. A great rifle, but it may not handle well in the tight confines of tunnel operations.

She added six flashbang grenades to her vest and carried her usual Glock .45 on her belt and her .45 XD-S in its ankle holster. She was loaded for bear. She wondered if it was overkill. Her mission relied more on stealth than anything else. But if she was discovered, she might have to shoot her way out of there. *Better safe than sorry*, she thought.

She wore her hair up in a ponytail and had a black ball cap pulled down tight on top of that. A Black Diamond LED headlamp was strapped to her forehead. She was still dressed in her black trousers and black tactical boots with the blue short-sleeve shirt covered by the black bullet-proof vest.

Montero was outfitted with his vest, his .40-caliber semiautomatic handgun and Sanchez's M4 carbine and flashbangs just in case. According to their plan, he probably wouldn't see any real combat but would act as the backstop for the tunnel so no one could creep up behind Sanchez once she was in it. He would let people out of the tunnel who she sent to him for rescue. Hopefully, they would only be Lolita and Sanchez, but there could be other captives in there whom they could liberate. Their experience with the cartel was that the gangbangers held hostages for a variety of reasons, and who knew what Sanchez would encounter under the desert.

"OK. Let's see if we can get a response at the door." She walked over to the gas station and pounded on the back door.

No response, so she tried it again. Still no response.

"I'll try to pick the lock and see if there are any sensors inside," Sanchez said. She knelt down and went to work with her lockpick set. It took three minutes to manipulate the tumblers and unlock the doorknob. But there was apparently a deadbolt on the inside, so she broke the glass and reached through to open the door.

She stuck her head inside and looked for sensors or booby traps. All clear so far. She stepped in and moved across the room to the inner door. This presented a serious barrier, made of steel with no windows and no exposed hinges. There was a numeric keypad mounted on the doorframe.

Sanchez pounded on the door with her fist. She hoped there was a guard inside who would come to investigate why someone was beating on the door at this hour. No one came to answer.

The next step was to damage the keypad and see if that woke anyone up. She examined it and pulled out a small screwdriver to remove the face of the pad. Then she undid the screws holding the pad to the doorframe so she could expose the wires that ran to the electric power. She cut the power wire with a small wire cutter and then removed the battery. In most security systems, that would send a signal to a monitor or the main keypad warning that a breach had occurred. A verbal alert would follow announcing that a sensor had malfunctioned or a battery was low. She hoped that no one was around to notice.

She signaled Montero that she was ready to force the door. She had a hammer and a crowbar with her. She chose the crowbar, inserted it in the crack between the edge of the door and the doorframe, and began to pry. The steel frame was sturdy. She worked it for a minute or two and created a half-inch opening. That let her see where the deadbolt was located. She thought that the easiest thing to do was to pry the hell out of the doorframe until the frame moved out beyond the length of the bolt. Then the door would swing open. She signaled for Montero to join her, and they both put their backs into it. The crack widened, and finally, the bolt slipped out of the frame.

They opened the door. They both smiled, partly because it was open but also because no one with a gun was waiting on the other side.

There was a ten-foot-long landing behind the door and a steel staircase behind that, which descended into gloom underground. They listened carefully for any signs of danger but heard nothing threatening.

"I'm going in. Remember the word is *Jupiter*," she said, tucking the crowbar in her belt.

"Be careful in there," he said, realizing she needed no reminder on that count.

Sanchez clicked on her headlamp and carefully descended the staircase. At the bottom, she gave him a thumbs-up and called back, "It's a tunnel like I expected." Then she pulled out the AP-9 and proceeded down the darkened corridor into the desert underworld.

She was in a well-dug tunnel that was nearly straight and about six feet wide and seven feet tall with dim sconce lights every hundred feet and electrical and other cables running on steel hooks along one side. The floor appeared to be concrete, and the walls were carved out of the bedrock of the desert, mostly caliche in this portion of the tunnel. It reminded her of one of the first tunnels she had been in at the border, where smugglers had transported their cargo in small cars running on iron rails set in the floor, like in a mine. She could see tire tracks in the dust. In this tunnel, it appeared they were using rubber-tired vehicles like ATVs to drive back and forth.

She proceeded with caution until she came to a wide spot where a doorway opened into the wall on the left. The wooden door had a small diamond-shaped window set into it at eye level. A dim light emanated from within. She peered in and saw no one. The door had a simple latch instead of a doorknob, so she lifted it. She held her breath and opened the door a crack to look inside.

She listened first for movement but heard nothing. She entered the darkened room, swiveling her head in sync with her handgun to see what lay around her. The room was empty except for a pair of cots, a table, and two chairs facing a computer monitor. The monitor was flashing a message that read: *Warning. Keypad Failure.*

She breathed a sigh of relief as she stood there gawking at the monitor.

Suddenly she heard a subdued whirring noise that sounded like an electric motor coming from the tunnel, and a light flashed across the window in the door. Then she heard footsteps outside the door. She switched off her headlamp and backed into a corner at the back of the room by the cots. She steadied the AP-9, aimed at the doorway, and waited as the door opened.

A short, swarthy man with a mustache and Latin features who didn't notice her in the shadows entered the room and headed for the desk. He set a food container down on the table and prepared to sit. That was when she hit him over the head with the butt of her gun. He fell to the floor like a sack of groceries. He was unconscious for only a few seconds, but that was long enough for her to check him for weapons and stick his handkerchief into his mouth as a gag. She flipped him onto his belly, sat on him, and handcuffed him before he could put up a struggle.

"Be quiet and don't move. If you attempt to call out, I'll hit you with my crowbar. You got it?" she said in a low voice. "*¿Habla inglés?*"

He nodded his head. "OK, don't move." She considered her

situation. Maybe he could tell her something useful. "Are you the guard for the back door?"

He nodded again.

"Are you the only one back here at this end of the tunnel? Any other guards?" She wondered if he would give her an honest answer.

He nodded his head and mumbled something. She removed the gag so he could talk. She pressed the muzzle of her weapon against his eye socket so he could see what would happen if he screamed. "Only me here. No one else," he said.

She stuffed the gag back in his mouth. Then she saw a box holding several extension cords nearby and reached for it. He tried to roll over, but she sat down hard on him to stop any attempt at getting up. She used an extension cord to tie his ankles together and then did the same for his knees. Then she lifted him into a kneeling position and asked, "Is there a map of the tunnel on this computer?"

She watched him closely. He began to nod but stopped partway through and turned his head to shake it, indicating no.

"I guess you aren't going to be of any use to me. I might as well shoot you now." She pushed the Glock's muzzle into his face again, and he began to nod vigorously.

"Oh—now it's yes. Show me."

She lifted him up and sat him in the chair. "I'm going to undo the cuffs for a moment. I want you to bring both hands out in front of you and relock them." She lowered her voice to sound more menacing. "If you try anything, I'll club you so hard you're never going to see straight again. You understand?"

He nodded his head, and she undid one cuff. He slowly brought his hands around in front of him and recuffed himself.

"OK, turn this warning off. Don't try to be cute and warn

someone else."

He reached up to the keyboard and clicked a few keys. He waited for her to read each keystroke, and then he voided the warning. Next he opened a file with the tunnel map on it.

"OK. Good work."

She studied the map. It showed a nearly straight tunnel extending from the gas station to the quarry. The room they were in was the only one along this portion of the tunnel. But near the quarry the tunnel contained several large rooms and a series of smaller rooms scattered along its lengthy axis. These may have been the rooms where the drugs were manufactured. In the center of the map there was a large side room that showed equipment stored in it.

"What is this here?" she asked, pointing to the machinery.

He mumbled, "Generator room."

Of course, she thought. *They need a generator to run all this equipment and whatever they have in their factory.*

"Now zoom in on the rooms over here." She pointed to the factory area.

He clicked a few keys, and she could see more detail of the rooms near the factory.

"Where is the girl being kept? In one of these rooms?"

He nodded and pointed to one of the smaller rooms to the left, about a half mile away and just on the edge of the many rooms along the tunnel. "Room ten, I think," he mumbled and tried to smile.

"OK," she said and stopped to think. She wasn't sure she could trust this guard in any way. But at least he had showed her a map that she already had memorized in general terms. She made up her mind and hit him hard on the back of the neck. He passed out.

She dragged him to the first cot and threw him on it facedown. She uncuffed his hands and tied them behind his back with an extension cord. Then she tied another cord to the one already tied to his ankles and cinched it up to his hands behind his back. He was hogtied. She checked that his gag was secure and he couldn't spit it out somehow.

She left the room and was surprised to find an electric utility cart, resembling an elongated golf cart, parked in front of the door in the wide portion of the tunnel. The keys were in it. *So that is how they drive around underground without polluting the already stuffy air down here*, she thought. A yellow hard hat and a pair of clear safety glasses were lying on the driver's seat. She quickly put them on and climbed into the seat, setting the AP-9 next to her within easy reach. She vaguely remembered how to operate a gulf cart, having used one a few years ago. This was similar.

She turned the cart around and began to drive toward the factory end of the underground complex. She drove at about five miles per hour, but it felt like she was flying. She noticed that there was better airflow as she drew closer to the quarry, like some giant fans were circulating the air from unseen vents.

The tunnel was comprised of a series of nearly straight segments that zigzagged slightly. After a few hundred yards, the sconce lights were more closely spaced and the tunnel became wide enough for carts to pass one another in two-lane traffic. The color of the walls changed as she passed through bands of different rock types. She was seeing more frequent bands of tan limestone the farther along she drove.

She came to an intersection where a large side tunnel joined the main axis of the system. She heard a loud motor in the distance and saw a sign that read *Generador*.

So that's where the generator is located. It must have a place where the generator exhaust vents to the surface. It meant she was halfway along the tunnel system. She felt the air being sucked inward as if there was a great exhaust fan farther up the side branch of the tunnel.

She encountered the first of several wide areas that opened on to wooden doors. Most of them were numbered with large digits. She saw fourteen first, and then they descended in sequence.

Sanchez found number ten and pulled the cart up to the door. She turned the motor off and stepped out to listen by the door. She heard men's voices speaking in Spanish inside the room. The guard had lied to her.

She backed away and started up the cart again. She had little reason to believe anything the gangbanger had told her. She stopped at the next door and listened. This time, she heard a man's voice, loudly telling someone about a fish he had caught.

She drove on. Farther down the tunnel she came to a room with a dim light shining through the window. She tested the door latch and found it unlocked. She peered in at several cots where a number of women were sleeping. Some were snoring quietly.

A single lamp focused a small circle of light on one cot where a young woman was reading. She looked up and saw Sanchez in the doorway. Her face reflected surprise and concern. Before she could say anything, Sanchez raised her finger to her lips and beckoned her to come forward. The woman nodded and came to the door.

"Where is the girl they brought in today?" she asked. Then she realized that she didn't speak English. "*¿Dónde está la chica que trajeron hoy?*"

The woman smiled and answered in Spanish, "The prisoners are in room seven next door. Are you here to help them?"

"*Sí,*" she answered, speaking Spanish. "Are you OK? Are

you prisoners too?"

"No, but we must work for the bosses, or our families will suffer."

"Do they treat you well?"

"Sometimes."

"*Gracias.* I will send help for you soon. Tonight, I can only help the girl."

"And the others?"

"What others?"

"They have several women for pleasure. Maybe help them too?" Her eyes were hopeful.

"I'll see. Good night."

"I will pray for you." The woman lowered her head as if her fate were sealed.

Sanchez carefully closed the door and stood outside. *This is a bigger operation than I thought possible.* She looked down the tunnel and saw no activity. She drove quietly to the next door marked with the number seven and turned her cart around, facing the way she had come in case she had to make a hasty exit.

She listened at the door. She heard a woman's voice moaning and a man's grunting. Then she heard the sound of a hand slapping flesh. She knew the sound well. She lifted the latch and spied through the crack in the doorway. A man was on his knees next to a cot where he was plunging into a woman whom he was choking with one hand while he took his pleasure.

There were six cots in the room. Four of the others were occupied by half-dressed women who were pretending to be asleep. A small figure was sitting hunched over in the fifth cot, watching the rape taking place. She was sobbing and cringing with each move the man made. She turned when Sanchez stepped quietly into the room and closed the door. It was Lolita.

The man did not hear Sanchez creep up behind him and raise her crowbar in the air. But the woman he was choking looked up, and her eyes followed the tool as it came down on his head with a dense thud. The man's body slumped to the floor as blood issued from the great wound he had suffered.

"Lori! Is it you?" Lolita asked in a startled voice. "Oh my God."

Sanchez rushed over and threw her arms around her as Lolita tried to stand up next to the cot she was on. They hugged and kissed each other with joy.

"Are you all right, Lo? Did they hurt you?" She pulled back to look at the girl, who was dressed only in her panties. "Oh Lo, I'm so sorry."

Lolita hugged her again and sobbed softly, "They're very cruel men, Lori. You have to be careful."

"Where are your clothes? You need to get dressed." Sanchez noticed that her friend was chained to the bed by her ankle. "Oh shit."

"We're all chained like this," Lolita said. Then she said to the other women, "This is my friend, Lori . . . She'll save us."

Sanchez inspected the half-inch chains and examined how they were attached to the cots. Lolita's ankle was held in a steel band that was fastened to one end of the chain by a bolt. Her ankle was chafed where the band had cut into her flesh. The other end of the chain was attached to the side rail on the cot frame by a similar steel band. The cots themselves were not very sturdy, being made from light-weight angle iron with wire spring mesh between the rails, but the shackle didn't look easy to break out of.

Sanchez decided that the chain might be something she could attack with her crowbar. She examined the links and saw that they were bent in ovals like all chains were, but the ends of each link were not welded together. With enough force, a single link could be opened up a couple of tenths of an inch and the link could be slipped out to undo the chain.

"We can bend the links if we pull hard enough," Sanchez said. She got down on the floor on her back with her feet up against the rail. Then she grabbed Lolita's chain and pulled on it, using her legs as the muscle to stretch the chain. "It moved a little. Lo, get down here with me, and we'll both pull."

Lolita lay on her back and placed her bare feet up against the rail. She grabbed the chain with Sanchez, and they both heaved against the steel links. The chain gave a little.

Sanchez sat up and used her fingers to separate two links where a gap had opened. The chain now dangled from Lolita's ankle, and half of it remained affixed to the cot rail.

"I'm free!" Lolita cried. "Let's do the others now."

They moved from bed to bed, tugging on the chains to open up single links that could be unfastened. Soon all the women were set free. Everyone was able to stand up and slip into some clothes except the woman who had been paped. She couldn't rise from her cot. It was only when she walked over to lift her up that Sanchez realized she was Megan Faux, the Maraxx Pharma gym trainer. She was far from the tall, sexy woman she had seen only a few days before. Now she was covered with bruises from the beatings she had taken. Sanchez was shocked by the sight.

Sanchez and Lolita pulled her to the side of the cot and held her in a sitting position. "Where are your clothes, Megan? Can you walk at all?" Sanchez asked.

Faux just stared at her and murmured something unintelligible. She was barely conscious. One of the other women brought over what Sanchez guessed was left of her clothes. They managed to put a shirt on her that they could button up, but otherwise she was unclothed.

"OK. Listen up, everyone. We're getting out of here. I have an electric utility cart outside the door. We all have to ride in it, so squeeze on board." She turned to Lolita. "Hey, Lo, can you drive a golf cart? This is just like one."

"Sure, I used to go to the golf course with my dad all the time."

"If anyone sees us, I'll need you to drive it as fast as you can up the tunnel to the staircase at the end. Montero is waiting at the top of the stairs. The password is *Jupiter*. Yell it out before you climb up, OK?"

"Where will you be?"

"I'll be holding up the rear."

"Oh, I see."

Sanchez cracked the door open and looked into the tunnel. She saw no one, so she waved for the others to hurry through and step onto the cart. She and Lolita carried Megan out and hoisted her into the front seat. Another woman sat with her to hold her in place. When they were all on board, Sanchez climbed in the back and took up position with the AP-9 to shoot at any gang members who came in pursuit.

Lolita jumped into the driver's seat and started driving slowly along the tunnel. The dim headlights showed her the way ahead.

All went well at first. They edged past the numbered doors until they passed number ten, where two drunken men had just stepped out to urinate in the tunnel. Lolita could do nothing other than race past them and she stepped on the accelerator, driving as fast as the cart would go. Unfortunately, the cart was not designed for a heavy load and struggled to increase speed.

The men were startled at first but began to shout in excited

Spanish that the women were getting away. There was great commotion in room number ten, and several more men ran out to witness the women escaping. They argued among themselves with a great deal of very ugly swearing. None of them seemed to be in charge, but they all were upset. Finally, two men with handguns started after the sluggish vehicle, and one raised his gun for a shot.

Sanchez felt that they were going to be caught at this speed, so she shot a few rounds to keep the pursuers at bay. The quick burst of automatic fire sent the men back into their lair and left one on the ground bleeding. Soon more guns appeared, and a volley of poorly aimed shots ricocheted off the tunnel walls.

"Hey, ladies, this isn't working!" Sanchez said as she stepped off the cart to lighten its load. "Anyone who feels she can run should get off and run ahead of us. Otherwise, we're going to be overtaken by a mob."

Two women jumped off. The cart immediately doubled its speed, racing up to seven or eight miles an hour. They passed the generator junction and continued onward as the two women jogged easily ahead of the cart while Sanchez brought up the rear on foot. She quickly calculated that at the present rate it would take them nearly eight minutes to travel the last half mile to the stairs. That seemed like an eternity.

Shortly after, they heard a clamor behind them as two utility carts, one behind the other, appeared in the tunnel, both apparently operating with fully charged batteries. When they were only two hundred yards away, the men on board began to fire automatic weapons up the tunnel. Most of the bullets dug into the walls, but some ricocheted and came close to hitting the escapees, who cowered for safety. Apparently, the gangbangers wanted them back even if they were shot up.

Sanchez fired short bursts of 9mm death back at them and nailed two of the men traveling in the first cart. The cart bounced into the wall and created a traffic jam for about a minute while its riders jostled into different seats. Then the carts quickly closed in.

Sanchez dropped her first magazine and slapped in a second just in time to fire about twenty rounds at her pursuers. That slowed them down again, but they persisted and she had to finish the magazine to hold them at a distance. She dropped the empty magazine and inserted a third.

One of the women running ahead was hit by a ricocheting bullet, forcing her to limp on with help from the other runner. This was clearly not working well, so Sanchez dropped back at one of the zigzags in the tunnel and waited for the carts following them to draw closer. Then she pumped about twenty rounds into the first cart when it was only a few yards away. Both carts stopped and men shouted at her as they hid behind their carts for protection. The problem was the ricochets were getting too close for comfort. But the halt in shooting bought the retreating women a couple of minutes to work their way up the tunnel.

The gangbangers were closing in. Sanchez fired the rest of the magazine to make them hit the deck. Then she tossed a flashbang grenade and sprinted away up the tunnel to the next zigzag. She barely ducked around the turn before a hail of bullets zipped past her and hammered the wall across from her position. She inserted the last magazine in the AP-9 and fired again at the approaching men. They were getting used to her tactics and fired ahead as they drove into her onslaught and two more grenades she pitched at them. She fired at them again and sprinted ahead as they took cover.

At this time she realized that the distance to the next zigzag was longer than before. She would be exposed for too long if she tried to run for it. Instead, she ducked into an alcove in the wall and flattened herself against the wall in a shadow, holding her breath. The first cart was practically on top of her before its occupants realized she was standing next to them as they drove by. They swung their guns in her direction to no avail. She unloaded the rest of the final magazine into the cart, mercilessly killing all three men on board.

Sanchez realized she could barely hear now because of the roar and echo of the gunshots unleashed in the fusillade of death all around her. It was eerily quiet, the whole scene surreal with the dim lights, lack of sound, and dead bodies splayed out over the seats of the cart.

As she stared at this mayhem, the second utility cart rammed into the first one, and she dropped the AP-9 on the ground to draw her trusty Glock. She shot every man on the second cart as they fired at her. It happened in slow motion. She saw each man aim, fire, and react when her bullets hit him in the chest or shoulder or belly or head. Somehow she was not hit . . . until the very end.

Something struck her in the chest, and she buckled from the impact. She dropped her Glock, and it skidded away from her. She went down on one knee. Pain racked her body in this surreal world.

Suddenly, a huge man appeared silently in front of her with an ugly face stained purple from tattoos. He apparently had been running behind the carts on foot. Now he laughed as he walked up to her with his gun pointed at her head. He looked familiar. She had seen him in photos and videos, and had witnessed the results of his vengeance before. He was Paco—or El Burro—the

Sinaloa hit man.

"Now I have you, bitch!" he bellowed in Spanish that she could barely make out. "You little whore, I will have some fun with you in my bed. I will make you cry for your mother, and then I will make you moan like a wounded dog."

He smiled with rotting teeth and made motions with his hips like he was raping her. He used all the degrading words that Mexican men used when they thought they owned a woman. She could barely hear him but knew what he meant. He stared down at her lustfully and raised his weapon to strike her on the head.

It was the end.

But no. Her vest had saved her and the bullet only knocked the wind out of her. She finally caught her breath. *Thank God for the vest*, she thought. She reached for her backup gun—her faithful XDS—and raised it for a shot at the same moment his hand came down. She cringed, anticipating the blow, and fired. Her heavy .45 slug tore a hole in his face and exited with an even larger hole out the back of his head, his blood and brains splattering against the tunnel wall. His misguided fist scraped the rock next to Sanchez's head as he fell.

She had survived to fight another day.

She ran up the tunnel, holding the side of her chest where it felt as if she had been kicked by a mule, as the old-timers at the PD used to say. It was hard to breathe, and her mind was in turmoil.

She arrived just as the cart full of women rammed into the staircase. They all ran up the stairs shouting at the top of their lungs, "Jupiter! Jupiter! Jupiter!"

Sanchez struggled up the stairs and helped drag Faux up to freedom. Then she threw herself into the arms of her good friend Guillermo Montero. She marveled at the clarity of the night sky and the myriad of bright stars in the Milky Way as the women around her murmured among themselves.

Chapter 29

Early Thursday morning, April 11, 2019

Childs, Arizona

Sanchez hugged Montero with all her might and let him hold her for a full minute.

"You were in there for nearly two hours. Are you OK? Your eyes look weird, like you're freaked out or something."

"Really?" she asked while her head rested against his shoulder. "What time is it?"

"After midnight. What happened? Was it bad?"

"Yes. I thought I'd die at the end. I'll tell you about it later, OK?"

"Sure. Were you hit?" He turned her around so he could search for blood.

"No. But it was close."

Then she saw Lolita walk up to them, and she reached out and pulled her in for a group hug as well. They squeezed each other, overcome by emotion.

"Are you all right, Lolita? Did they hurt you?" she asked.

"I was terrified. I woke up with my clothes torn off, and this big ugly man was staring down at me and fondling my tits. He told the others to save this one for him like I was some piece of candy or something. But the other men left me alone. Instead, they took turns raping Megan. She was the new piece of meat, and she has big tits. That really turned them on."

"Thank God I found you. I was so worried," Sanchez said as she kissed Lolita's forehead. She pulled away to look at her friend shivering in the cool night air. "We've got to get you covered up. It's cold out here. Come to the car. I have a spare uniform in the trunk."

Sanchez escorted Lolita over to the Interceptor and opened the trunk. They dug out black pants, a blue shirt, and a pair of Keds sneakers. While the girl got dressed, Sanchez walked over to where the other women were huddled next to the gas station. She saw Faux lying on the ground, still barely conscious. She took her pulse and looked into her eyes with her headlamp. Faux flinched away from the bright light, which was a good sign. Sanchez lifted her clothing to look for gunshot wounds. There was blood, but not enough to indicate she had been wounded by a ricochet.

"Can you talk? Are you OK?" she asked.

"I hurt all over. And inside. Where are we?" Faux looked extremely disoriented and her breathing was irregular.

"Let me see your neck where that asshole was choking you." Sanchez gently moved the woman's head from side to side while she felt her neck for injuries. "I think he crushed part of your larynx. Can you breathe well enough?"

Faux suffered a coughing fit that brought up blood.

"I think we may want to get you in the back seat of the car and cover you up. I have a blanket in the trunk." She asked Lolita and another woman who seemed strong enough for the task to help move Faux. They struggled to lift her inside, helped her get comfortable, and then covered her with a blanket.

Next Sanchez walked over to the other women she had rescued. "Are you OK? Who was shot? Let me see the wound." She sat down next to the one who had been shot in the calf.

Someone had tied it up with a piece of cloth, but that had bled through already.

Sanchez untied the bandage and examined the wound. It didn't look too bad; the bullet had entered through one side and exited out the other without doing a lot of damage to the bone. But it was bleeding freely. She got up and retrieved her first aid kit from the car. She applied disinfectant and a powder used to help blood clot faster. Then she placed a sterile pad on both sides of the wound, and Lolita helped hold the pads in place while Sanchez wrapped the injury with gauze tape.

She slowly walked back to the door at the top of the staircase where Montero was standing guard in case anyone came running out with a gun. He seemed exhausted from the constant need to remain vigilant.

"We have to get these women out of here. I'm really worried about Megan. She's not breathing right, and if something moves around in her throat, she could suffocate. The gunshot wound needs attention too."

"We can't call from here. Cells are dead." He looked thoughtful for a moment. "We could drive into Ajo on State Route 85 and look for help there. I'm surprised we haven't heard from the Pima County sheriff yet. I thought they would have sent a car out here looking for us by now."

"I think there must be miscommunication on that end." She scrunched up her face as she thought. "We need to drive to Ajo with them. I think there's a medical care facility there that can at least do the basics. If needed, the paramedics can summon a Flight for Life helicopter from Phoenix."

"You're right. The old hospital closed when the mine closed several years ago, but there must be a clinic of some kind."

"Here's the thing: I need you to drive our victims in. I have to stay here and watch for any bad guys. And you need a break from this monotony." She smiled at him because she was asking another favor on top of all the ones she owed him already.

"No, I can stick it out. I'm OK."

"The other reason I need to stay is I can arrest these assholes whereas you can only shoot them." They both laughed at that. "Bring back coffee. Lots of it, and doughnuts, if you can find them in that godforsaken little town." She laughed again and punched him in the shoulder.

Sanchez removed a few items from her arsenal and took the M4 that Montero had been using, plus his extra magazines. She directed where the women should sit so they could keep Faux from falling to the floor along the bumpy road. Once they all had piled in, Montero revved the engine and turned on the heat as he drove slowly away.

She radioed Bordou to let him know the rescue had been successful and to thank him for standing guard so long. She explained why the Interceptor was rolling away and that he was not alone out here. Then she had to concentrate on the job at hand.

She sat in the dark inside the gas station so that she could cover the top of the staircase in case someone emerged. She got just comfortable enough to rest but not to fall asleep.

She listened to the coyotes call back and forth across the valley, howling about their successful hunts or whatever else they did at night. *It's a whole other world out here at night*, she thought. *And hell in the underworld below.*

***

Montero returned two hours later. He brought bags of doughnuts and other snacks along with two big thermoses of hot coffee. Sanchez set about wolfing down the tasty morsels and gulping caffeine while Montero told her what he had learned.

"I banged on the door of the clinic that's in town. The paramedics took the women in and are going to take good care of them. They did call for a helo to carry Megan and the one with the gunshot wound out to Phoenix. Then I stopped at the sheriff's office." He rolled his eyes.

"What's the story?"

"The deputy said they were told to sit tight until the SWAT convoy arrived from Tucson. They didn't even know we were out here all night." Montero took a sugar doughnut. "They'll be here in a half hour or so. It takes a while to get ahold of everyone in the dead of night."

"Well, at least we won't be overrun just yet."

"We'll have to see. A deputy named Collier was very apologetic and said he would have come right out if he had known we were already here and in contact. He called it 'contact with the enemy.' I think he's in the National Guard, so that's good."

"Sounds groovy," she chuckled, a little punchy.

"Has anyone tried to come out?" he asked.

"I had one guy stick his head up an hour ago. He pointed a gun at me, so I shot his ear off. I was aiming for his forehead, but he surprised me." She snickered. "I think he and the others went back underground and are planning something. We'll need reinforcements soon."

Montero had concern inscribed on his features. "How are you holding up? You want to talk about what happened earlier?"

"You're worried about me again, aren't you, Guillermo?" She knew where he was going with this. He was worried about PTSD, afraid that what had happened might trigger a strong and terrifying reaction.

"I saw something in your face I haven't seen in a while, that's all." He tried not to look directly at her. She was a proud woman, and she had to maintain her view of herself. He didn't press.

"Well, I understand your concern," she said as she stared through the window at the stars. "I've been sitting here listening to coyotes and thinking about the fact that I killed several men tonight. It's on my mind."

"It's a terrible thing to kill a man."

She chuckled. "Now you're quoting old movie dialogue to me?"

"Even bad men."

"Yes, but men nonetheless." She turned toward him with a wistful look. "It was them or me. And I'm glad I made it and they didn't, but still . . . And the big one at the end had me dead to rights. . . . El Burro."

"You killed El Burro?"

"Yes. In a split second, it could have been me."

"I'm sorry, Lori. It's too much. We should go home and let SWAT handle the rest. You've done enough."

"But I had to save Lolita, didn't I?" she mused. "Funny— I've only known her for a week, and I love her like my own daughter or a little sister I never had."

Montero considered what she had said. This was not like her. She was the bravest person he knew, and now she was having second thoughts. Not good right now.

They saw a sheriff's vehicle approach along the road from the west. It drove straight through to their location and stopped behind the Interceptor. Two tall, lean men dressed in khaki shirts and olive trousers stepped out wearing tactical vests, the usual assortment of gear strapped to their belts. They waved at Montero and walked over.

"I'm Bob Lambert, and this is Carlos Santana—no, not that one. He can't sing." They all laughed at that. "We understand you two and your fellow officer Bordou have been out here all night keepin' a lid on things. We appreciate your work and dedication. It seems that our fellow officers back in Tucson didn't get their story straight."

"It's not the first time," Santana said with a knowing shake of his head.

"Why don't you two tell us what happened here and what we can do to help out?" Lambert asked as he grabbed a doughnut. "We've got all night."

Sanchez told them the whole tale, from the kidnapping to the warehouse fight, to the quarry and gas station events, and finally to her mission underground that wound up including rescuing the women prisoners. It took an hour including all the questions and comments. She sketched out a map of the tunnel system as best as she could remember it. When she was finished, Sanchez felt exhausted. She helped herself to some more coffee and another doughnut while the deputies called in for two more backups to help secure the two ends of the mine and tunnel system. They replaced Bordou at 3:00 a.m. so he could come over to the gas station for much needed refreshments.

When they were assembled around the last of the coffee, Lambert returned from a long radio conversation. "I just got off the horn with the sheriff, William Sneath. He's taken direct charge of this operation from the Pima County point of view, saying it is within his jurisdiction." Lambert raised his eyebrows. "I told him what you've done and that as far as I'm concerned, it's your case." He looked from Sanchez to Montero to Bordou for understanding. "I hope you realize this is an election year."

Everyone shook their heads and scowled at the all too common refrain. They were obliged to suffer political shenanigans every four years. They all stared at the ground.

"He talked to your Captain Teller in Phoenix and said he had the highest regard for your work and intends to give you full credit for the investigation . . . I guess your captain made him formalize that in an email last night. Anyway, they agreed that you would return to Phoenix, write your reports, and coordinate from there during the siege."

"Siege?" Bordou and Sanchez shouted it at the same time.

"What the hell?" she asked.

"It seems that, hearing about the impregnable nature of the quarry and the dangers of invading an elaborate underground tunnel system, Sheriff Sneath has opted to contain the situation and negotiate with the gang members rather than engage in a large-scale battle." Lambert spit on the ground and stared at his shoes.

"That's the dumbest thing I've ever heard!" Sanchez shouted and threw her coffee cup on the ground. "That son of a bitch Sneath hasn't even been down here to see for himself. What the frick is he thinking?"

Montero looked equally glum. "He's thinking he doesn't want to screw up with a big operation that may kill a lot of his deputies in an election year. That's the kind of thing that can give his opponent an edge." He shook his head and continued. "And as long as these criminals are contained, maybe they'll eventually negotiate or surrender. Some deputies' lives could be saved."

The others stared at him in disbelief. He had hit the nail on the head. It was all politics as usual.

"Some things never change." Sanchez spit on the ground.

"Damned politicians."

Santana made his position clear. "I guess if you look at it that way, maybe we can wait awhile and see what happens. But it goes against my grain to let these bastards get away with what they've done."

"I'm sure glad I got the women out when I did. Otherwise they would have been brutalized for days while some politician talked on TV." Sanchez was becoming despondent. She lowered her head and muttered, "What a shitty deal."

"I guess that's it for us. It was nice meeting you guys," Bordou said and stepped forward to shake hands with the deputies. "Keep us informed of what happens, will ya?" Then he turned to Sanchez and placed a hand on her shoulder. "Come on, Lori. You can't win this kind of fight. We'd better go before the shit hits the fan."

They shook hands all around, and Sanchez grudgingly turned toward the car with her gear. Being as tired as they were, they moved slowly.

Lambert came over to say one last thing. "Detective Sanchez, I just wanted to say I'll write your story up in my report so it won't get lost or misappropriated somehow. And I'm glad I finally met you. You're a living legend in some law enforcement circles, you know."

"What? You're kidding, aren't you?"

"No, ma'am. You should check out this site online. You're on there." He handed her a business card, tipped his hat, and walked to his car.

She read the card he had given her: *www.modernheroesofthelaw210.org.*

She showed it to Montero as she climbed into her car.

"I'll be damned," he said.

Chapter 30

Saturday, April 20, 2019
Phoenix, Arizona

Ten days later, Sanchez stood at the bar counter in Alvera's apartment pouring sangria into stemless wine goblets and listening to the conversation around her. Her boyfriend, Tom Smith, was attempting to slice a key lime pie into ten precisely equal pieces while Lolita's father, Eric Thompson, speculated on whether it could be done. It was taking way too long as far as Sanchez was concerned. She just wanted to savor her favorite dessert.

Lolita, standing next to Sanchez, was telling Sanchez's friend from the department, Sandoval, and her boyfriend, Carlos, about the new gym where she would be training under the guidance of her father and a new coach they had interviewed. She bumped hips with Sanchez. "And Lori has agreed to let me stay with her and Tom whenever my dad is out of town. Isn't that right, Lori?"

"Yes. It seems you've become the daughter I never had. Or something like that." Sanchez smiled at Smith. "We're still working on that." She put her arm around Lolita's shoulders. "I love having you in my life."

Bordou and his wife, Kathy, were talking to Alvera in the living room. Bordou said, "I understand that Josie Vale's article came out under her byline after all at the *Phoenix Tribune*. She certainly uncovered a big story."

"And it's gone national," Alvera said. "All the media outlets are covering it and giving her credit. It's what she always wanted—that recognition."

"It's just too bad she can't be here to enjoy it," Kathy said.

"I know. I miss her so much." Alvera suppressed a tear.

Bordou changed the topic. "And the case is proceeding well, I understand."

"Yes, it is. We have the full cooperation of the VA administration here in Phoenix and in Washington. It took some prompting, but our DA has influence in the right circles in DC."

"Just so I understand," Kathy said, "the Sinaloa Cartel spun off a company to buy up Randman Labs so they would gain a foothold in the legal pharmaceutical business? And that was so they could substitute their drugs for ones in existing contracts that Randman already had?"

"Well, it's more complicated than that. They wanted to buy Randman's reputation and their pipeline into the legitimate markets. That way Randman could replace shipments from other manufacturers with fakes, and at the same time sell the legitimate drugs on the black market for a huge profit. They made out both ways," Alvera explained.

"We don't know the details of the quarry operation yet, but will someday," Bordou said. "We know that the cartel must have made their own drugs from scratch or by importing from China. And they pressed and packaged their own pills under a variety of labels. The underground operation in the desert was huge. A whole factory was built under our noses and operating with impunity. A complete desert underworld."

"It's scary that they could get away with so much and for so long," Alvera said.

"I'll never look at a pill in the same way. Who knows what's in it?" Kathy shook her head.

Sanchez called Alvera aside and whispered to her, "I just wanted you to know that I erased all the remaining sex videos. I figured we didn't need them as evidence after all, and why wreck the lives of so many unsuspecting victims of Nick Carter? So you have no worries there, OK?"

Alvera looked her friend in the eye and gave her a wan smile. "Thanks, my dearest friend. I'll never forget your friendship and loyalty and will love you forever." She hugged Sanchez a long time. "We are friends to the end."

"To the end," Sanchez said, nodding.

By this time, the key lime pie had been served up on plates, and Smith called out for them all to come to the kitchen and take a piece. Soon everyone was standing around the center island and selecting their exactly equal pieces of pie. Forks stabbed into the dessert as they laughed and conversed.

"Say, everyone, could I have your attention for a minute?" Montero called out while tapping his wineglass with a fork. It did not ring properly without the stem. "I've just learned that Lori has been named hero of the month on the Modern Heroes of the Law website. We have a celebrity in our midst."

Everyone cheered and clapped their hands. Sanchez was embarrassed but pleased at the same time. "Well, we officers live to serve and protect, after all."

Everyone laughed.

"It's just a blog, right?" Thompson asked.

"Well, I guess so," Sanchez chuckled.

"I don't know about that," Montero chipped in. "I did some research on the site. It has a regular following among police across the country. The blog has a following of over ninety thousand fans."

"Wow! Lori, you're famous," Lolita said cheerfully. "I guess we all knew you were a hero already. At least, you always will be to me."

Bordou added, "The captain said we're up for another commendation too. He even seems to like you now that you helped uncover a major conspiracy to undermine our pharmaceutical industry."

"*With* the help of my fellow officers who deserve equal credit," Sanchez added jovially. She glanced over at Alvera. "And let's salute the help and work of our favorite assistant DA." She raised her glass in Alvera's direction. "She has real influence. She got one of the largest corporations in America to help locate our dear friend Lolita when it mattered most. Here's to Clara."

All glasses were raised in Alvera's direction. Then they all cheered as Lolita ran over to hug her.

"The prettiest and best DA ever," she called out.

Alvera blushed at the compliment but hugged the teenager and laughed.

It's good to see her laugh, Sanchez thought.

"How is the standoff going down in Pima County?" Kathy asked.

The room fell silent for a moment. Sanchez chose to answer.

"You've all heard about the hostages who were killed, right? Today, the gang members threw out another woman who was tortured and killed. She's the fourth one so far." She looked around at her friends to assess their reaction. "The cartel is making a new demand today. They want to be guaranteed safe passage from the quarry to the Mexican border with all their hostages. They'll kill one hostage a day until the sheriff agrees, and now the governor must comply."

"Where did they get the hostages in the first place?" Thompson asked.

"They were laborers whom they pressed into working at the factory. The sheriff never figured the cartel would kill its own workforce in a situation like this." Sanchez looked grim. "We should have gone back to rescue them right then. I even told one of the workers that we would be back for them."

"You assumed the sheriff would do the right thing," Montero said. "You only said what you thought would happen. You can't blame yourself for *his* folly."

"I know," she said, "but we could have tried. Now we may still have to go back in the hard way, but with fewer people to save."

They were all silent for a few moments, and several people spoke up to change the subject. Soon the mood of the party regained its cheer.

"Oh, I have an announcement," Thompson said. "Megan Faux has been released from the hospital to a rehab facility. She's expected to make a full recovery in time. Of course, she'll have multiple psychological scars to deal with. I lobbied our board of directors to keep her on in her job and cover all her medical costs. When she's ready, she can come back and take over the management of the gym."

"And I have an announcement too," Lolita said loudly. "My dad is going to do almost all of his marketing from home so he doesn't have to travel as much. I'll have my dad back." She broke into a fabulous smile.

Everyone raised their glasses to that.

Sanchez refilled all their glasses and then called for another toast. She looked around the room, and her eyes rested on Montero first, then Alvera, then Smith, then Lolita. She walked over to put an arm around Montero and raised her glass high. She smiled broadly and proclaimed in a cheery voice, "To all of us—the best of friends!"

They all laughed and repeated, "To the best of friends!"

Coming Soon!

Desert Mischief

By Fred G. Baker

Detective Lori Sanchez killed the son of a Cartel kingpin during a police raid near Phoenix. Now the kingpin wants retribution against her. A world-class assassin is sent to find her and carryout a sinister plan.

Guillermo Montero accepts a job to organize a conference in a remote desert location. The conference is a cover for secret meetings between four high tech companies that have discovered a new computing technology. He convinces Sanchez to provide security for the meetings to protect the principals involved and to prevent theft of top secret information.

Then everything goes wrong. Industrial spies abound at the conference and assassins try to kill one company CEO. Killers stalk the night and Japanese ninjas are involved.

About the Author

Fred G. Baker is a hydrologist, historian, and writer living in Colorado. He is the author of *An Imperfect Crime, Desert Sanctuary, Einstein's Raven, Zona: The Forbidden Land, The Black Freighter,* and the *Modern Pirate Series* of short and long stories. He is also the author of nonfiction works such as *Growing Up Wisconsin, The Life and Times of Con James Baker of Des Moines, Chicago, and Wisconsin, The Light from a Thousand Campfires* (with Hannah Pavlik), and others.

***

Request for Reviews.

Thank you for reading my book. If you enjoyed it, please write a review on Amazon.com. Reviews are important to help authors get the word out on their books. I would appreciate your time to write one.

Please look for my other books on Amazon and Kindle Books. Just type in my name to see other titles that may be of interest to you. You can also check out my website at www.othervoicespress.com.